# THE
# WITNESS

BOOKS BY JOHN RYDER

# THE WITNESS

## JOHN RYDER

bookouture

Published by Bookouture in 2021

An imprint of Storyfire Ltd.
Carmelite House
50 Victoria Embankment
London EC4Y 0DZ

www.bookouture.com

ISBN: 978-1-80019-290-4
eBook ISBN: 978-1-80019-289-8

*To my son, from a father who grows prouder with each passing day.*

# PROLOGUE

All Savannah Nicoll can see around her are threats to her life. The heavy guy backing his truck from a parking bay could slam the gear selector into drive and crush her against the trunk of her car. The gangly youths in baseball shirts might drag her into an alley and slit her throat. A panel van coming her way might slide its side door open so that strong hands could haul her inside and transport her somewhere she could be buried in a woodland grave.

This is life for Savannah now. The constant assessments, the living in fear. The ever-present alertness needed to function on a day-to-day basis without going into a complete meltdown. This is the life of someone in the United States Federal Witness Protection Program.

An hour after she'd appeared in the witness box, a US marshal had stood at her side as she said a tearful goodbye to her mother, her two closest friends and her former life. That was eight days and two hours ago. Not that she's counting.

The sleepy Colorado town of Pagosa Springs is a world away from the metropolis that had been her former home. Granted, Houston isn't a glamorous city like New York, LA or Miami, but it's still a place with a city's level of entertainment options. Pagosa Springs may possess a few bars, and its local hangouts would, individually, actually be considered kitsch in Houston, but they are lame when clustered together as the only options.

Enjoying an active social life is a long way ahead in Savannah's future, but she needs to have a hope for better days, a life vest of normality to get her through the days of dread she's experiencing.

The truck drives off without incident. The youths bounce their baseball back and forth among their group and toss uninterested looks Savannah's way as the panel van pulls to a stop and disgorges a geriatric man who's more gnarled that any tree stump she's ever seen.

This is what Savannah now has to live with. Imagined threats. Heart-stopping anxiety. And overwhelming relief when imagined perils turn out to be nothing more than people going about their day. This is the life of someone in witness protection. She's toyed with the idea of adopting a puppy or kitten, something her mother always forbade when she lived in the family home, but it's not something she's gotten around to doing yet. At this moment in her life, she can only think about herself, her needs and, as much as the aching loneliness she's living with might be alleviated by a pet, she knows she isn't ready to allow another person or creature into her life, much less depend on her.

As much as she clings to the knowledge she's done the right thing, the honorable thing, by standing up in court and giving her version of events, Savannah also knows that someone wants her dead. It's this piece of knowledge that has Savannah fearing for her life every waking moment, that has her double- and triple-locking every door and window of her new home. It's what haunts her dreams and has her waking in a cold sweat several times each night.

# CHAPTER ONE

Ursula Parker-Nicoll scans the room with a practiced eye. The grand ballroom of the Marriott Marquis is a familiar haunt of hers. The great and good of the city are all in attendance. The mayor, the DA, a scattering of blue bloods and a few of the nouveau riche who use events such as this to attain a social status beyond their ancestry. Tonight's function is a fundraiser for underprivileged children, and as one of Houston's blue bloods, she's supporting the charity both with her presence and financially by buying a table. Back before she married Savannah's father, Ursula worked as a paralegal for the man who rose through the ranks to become DA.

No one she sees gives her the slightest cause for concern, until she feels the presence of someone behind her. There's a momentary warmth at the back of her neck, then she hears a whisper that turns her blood so cold it's a wonder it can still move through her veins and arteries.

"Your daughter will be dead by noon on Monday."

Nine words of heart-stopping threat. Nine words no parent ever wants to hear. Nine words spoken with the surety of death and taxes.

Ursula knows there's a threat to Savannah's life. That's why her daughter is in the Witness Protection Program. That's why she's had to reconcile herself to never seeing Savannah again.

She whirls round to see who's delivered the message and sees the back of a man with all the wrong connections. Ignacio Perez's son had been killed by Savannah's boyfriend, and he blamed Savannah for leading his son and thus instigating the fight in which he died. No matter their family's standing in Houston society, Perez hadn't just pointed a grieving finger, he'd made threats. Dire threats that due to his underworld connections were taken seriously by all concerned. Perez lost his son, and thanks to the threats he'd made at the trial, she's as good as lost her daughter.

There had been no other option but for Savannah to go into the Witness Protection Program. Ursula hated the idea of saying goodbye to her daughter, but surely it was better to say goodbye to a living child than goodbye to a dead one. She's already buried one child and there's no way she can survive burying another.

Her mouth tightens as she scowls at Perez's back and sets off in search of the mayor and the DA. There's no point in having a social status if you don't use it.

"Gentlemen, may I have a moment of your time?"

"Of course, what is your query?" As worried as she is, Ursula doesn't miss that neither man asks how they can help. No matter the champagne flutes they hold, they are political animals first and foremost and will never allow anyone to put them on the spot by issuing a careless word.

"You both know about Savannah being in WITSEC?" Two nods confirm the question. "Ignacio Perez has just whispered in my ear that she'll be dead by noon on Monday. That's just thirty-nine hours. You have to help her. Have to get him arrested and have him undo whatever he's done."

The mayor's hand rests on her arm. "My dear Ursula, I'm sure that Mr. Perez is only screwing with you, trying to rattle you, and if you'll forgive my frankness, he very much looks to have achieved his aim. Please do not worry, the WITSEC program is locked down on many levels and I'm sure your daughter will be as safe as if she was in the vaults at Fort Knox."

"With respect, Mr. Mayor, I don't think you're quite grasping the seriousness of the situation."

"I am, I assure you, grasping it, but I also know how hard the US Marshals work to keep it secure."

Before Ursula can say anything else, an aide approaches and leads the mayor away.

The DA leans over and whispers in her ear. "Contact the US Marshals. If you get nowhere with them, try getting in touch with a guy called Kyle Roche. If anyone can help you, it's him."

Kyle Roche isn't a name she's heard before, but the DA is someone she's known for more than thirty years and she trusts him.

# CHAPTER TWO

Kyle Roche arrives home to see his clothes fluttering from the upstairs window of his home. It's not the first time he's seen this and he doesn't think it'll be the last. Leigh had been karaoke drunk last night and the arguments had started with their usual predictability. Accusations of infidelity were leveled at him and, while all were groundless, Leigh's ears had been deaf to his protestations of innocence.

Roche gathers up his clothes and bundles them into the back of the Buick he's driving this week. The suit he'd worn to his son's graduation has landed in dog crap, so he scrapes as much of it off as he can and puts the suit into a bag he stows in the Buick's trunk. His clothes need to be aired as much as Leigh needs time to cool down and sober up, but the dog crap on his best suit has left him more pissed than usual. He vows to himself that this time it's going to have to be Leigh who is first to offer an olive branch.

With the option of a change of suit now robbed from him, Roche guns the Buick's engine and sets off towards the bar where he'd arranged his meeting.

All of Roche's client meets happen in bars until he gets a measure of his client. Based on the customer's initial inquiry, he'll choose a bar suitable to the occasion. Sometimes the bars will be low-end with more chance of a fight than a decent wine list, and sometimes they'll be so classy Roche can't pronounce their names with any degree of confidence.

This is Roche's life. Always moving with, against and across the tide.

*

Today's meeting is in a bar with a name more pretentious than someone who refers to themselves in the third person. It's above twelve bucks for a draught beer and is so modern and stylish it makes Roche feel twice his age. Even at noon it's filled with patrons who are selecting fancy dishes from an unpriced menu.

A woman approaches him. She's slender, well dressed and has an air about her that Roche can't quite pin down. The woman looks around the bar in a way that makes it impossible to gauge whether or not she's showing approval of their surroundings. The best Roche can figure is that she's so blue-blooded she thinks a place like this is her taking a walk on the wild side.

He raises a hand to draw her eye his way, and she walks over, all cool poise and repressed emotions. Roche is used to such demeanors. Nobody ever sought his help when things were good in their lives.

"Mr. Roche?"

"That's me." Roche stands and offers a hand that isn't taken. He could blame the crumpled suit or the graying stubble on his chin that are a result of Leigh's incessant jealousy, but he doesn't care. She is here because she needs him, and he can see from her clothes that she'll be a profitable client. For profitable clients, he is prepared to tolerate rude behavior. "Mrs. Parker-Nicoll?"

"I am."

"I understand you want my help."

A hesitation to moisten her lips. A glance around as if afraid of being overheard. A final swallow before she opens her mouth to speak again. "I have been told you're a man of rather considerable and unique talents. That you have contacts in lots of unusual locations, and that you're half private investigator, half fixer."

Roche nods at her evaluation of him. He knows his reputation. It's how he gets new clients and retains old ones. "Whatever you tell me will be confidential. I presume you got my name and number from someone who you trust. Whoever that someone is, they trust me to help solve your problem, and you can too. So, how can I help you?"

She gives another look around before continuing. "To cut a very long story short, my daughter, Savannah, was in a bar with her boyfriend. When they went to leave, this guy was making unwelcome advances towards her. The boyfriend and the guy got into a fight that ended up with the boyfriend pulling a knife and stabbing the guy in the chest. The guy died and his family blamed Savannah for his death, as they claimed he must have been led on. My daughter's not like that. She's loyal. The family of the guy is connected to unsavory elements and a lot of threats were made against Savannah. She did the right thing and testified. She was the sole witness. More threats were made and the authorities took them seriously. Savannah went into the Witness Protection Program just over a week ago. But I was at a function last night, where I was informed that my daughter would be dead by noon on Monday. I want you to find her, keep her safe and find out how her safety is being compromised."

Roche tries his best to remain professional, but doesn't react quick enough to prevent the low whistle escaping his lips. There's nothing he can do except own the indiscretion and move on to get answers to the multitude of questions that are buffeting his brain from every angle.

"Okay, that's a new one for me. Witness protection is handled by the US Marshals. I take it that you contacted them."

"Of course. They stonewalled me and told me not to worry. That she had a new identity and there was no way that she could be found. Please, Mr. Roche, while I'm sure you'll think I have a typical parental bias, believe me when I say my daughter is a good woman. Since college she's worked for charity after charity. All her life she's helped others and been a force for good in this world. She's in witness protection because she stood up and did the noble thing. The right thing. Surely that means something; surely she ought not be targeted because she's honorable."

Roche keeps his tone gentle so as not to offend his new client. "The US Marshals may have a point. It's noon now, so that's twenty-four hours until the deadline. Your daughter could have been relocated to anywhere in the country. The Marshals may have already moved her to a more secure location after you contacted them. As for your daughter's character, I think the fact she had the courage to testify regardless of the personal risk tells me everything I need to know. What makes you think that I can find out where she is, get there in time to save her, actually save her and then find out who's leaked her new location or arranged the hit on her?"

Mrs. Parker-Nicoll's mouth puckers into a tight ring her words have to squeeze through. "Three reasons. Number one, as I mentioned earlier, I'm told you are a man of considerable and unique talents. In short, you get things done. Number two, I'll pay you $150,000 to find and save my daughter and another $100,000 to bring to justice the lowlife who's giving up her new identity and location." A hand moves in a whatever gesture. "Naturally, I'll cover any expenses you incur. Number three, since I told you what I need from you, you haven't once said it's impossible or that you can't do it. That tells me I'm asking the right man to save my daughter's life."

"And if I fail to find her in time? What do I get then?"

"Your expenses. I'm gambling on you saving Savannah and I want you to be fully incentivized."

Roche doesn't have to think about the deal that's on offer. It promises a good payday if he's successful, and if Savannah's details have been compromised, it stands to reason other members of the program will be at threat as well. Stemming the leak is an appealing thought. It'll save lives and he's always keen to redress the imbalance in the karmic columns of his life.

"You've got yourself a deal. Now, considering we've less than twenty-four hours, I need answers from you, and I need them fast. No hesitation, no obfuscation."

She licks her lips and fixes him with a questioning look. "Why is this happening so soon? She's only been in the program just over a week."

"My guess is that it's because time heals. Right now the people who want her dead are grieving. They'll want to lash out. To spread the hurt around, or just get themselves the vengeance they believe will fill the void in their hearts. As time passes, that anger, that need for revenge lessens. The way I figure it, if they don't set the wheels in motion in the first month after their son's death, they'll never do it." Roche rises from his chair. "Now if you'll excuse me, I need to get started."

# CHAPTER THREE

Roche draws up beside the unmarked car and looks across. Detective Zimmerman is picking his teeth with a cocktail stick, something he does whenever his hands are free.

"Hey, Zimm. Thanks for coming." Roche knew Zimm would come. The detective is one of his best sources, and he is one of the Zimm's most regular benefactors.

"What you after this time?" Zimm isn't ever slow in getting to the point and, with the time constraints pressing against Roche the way they are, his bluntness is something he appreciates for once.

"I'm looking for someone in witness protection. A local girl who gave evidence and then entered the program." Roche displays a photo he'd gotten from the mother. "Savannah Nicoll. Twenty-five and been in the program a week past Friday after appearing as a star witness in a homicide trial. She's from a moneyed family, but they're not crazy rich, just very well off. The mother received a whispered threat against the daughter in her ear at a cocktail party from a member of the victim's family—"

"Stop right there." Zimm's tone drips enough sarcasm to soak his shirt front. "Your case is some rich broad has heard a threat. You don't have a case because threats like that are made all the time. No way can someone in WP be found. All you're doing is lining your pockets on the back of a rich broad's fears."

"That was my first thought. It's an impossible case, right? The US Marshals have the program sewn up. Once someone goes in, unless the witness is dumb enough to make direct contact with their family, they're never heard of again." Roche aims a finger at his own chest. "I've never taken money for a case that hasn't been real and you know it. Sure, things have been tight for me lately, but I'm a long way from living on the street again. The mother is in the kind of position where she has the local DA, mayor and congresswoman on speed dial. She went to all of them and was told the same thing: There is no threat provided her daughter follows the instructions the Marshals will have given her."

"Then why are we even talking?"

"Because it was the DA who gave her mom my number. He's heard whispers. The kind of whispers that suggest a monumental cover-up to me. The real clincher though: the victim's father is Ignacio Perez."

Roche falls silent and lets Zimm digest the significance of the name. Perez: the CEO of one of Houston's largest accountancy firms. Their clients deal in large numbers and so do they. The DA's office and the IRS have had a running battle with Bay Associates for years due to them managing the books for the so-called legit businesses owned by Houston's largest crime syndicate. Nothing has ever been proven, but there's no doubt Perez has the right kind of connections to avenge his son's death should there be a chink in the armor of the program.

"That makes it different." Zimm flicks something he's dislodged from the cocktail stick onto the ground. "If you're wanting me to tap into the system and look her up, you gotta know that I can't do that. It's all sealed, and all we know about people in the program is that it's a waste of time asking questions about them."

Roche picks his words with care and keeps his face as neutral as he can. "I thought that would be the case."

"So why we even talking?"

"I'd never be so insulting as to call you a dirty cop, but let's not jerk around here. I pay you for answers. Do you know anyone in the US Marshals I could have a similar arrangement with, so I can find Savannah?"

"Nope. I told you, man, the Marshals are buttoned down tight. Real tight. You want an introduction to someone in vice or narcos, I can do that, no problem. Not the Marshals though. Ain't no way through their door unless you get an invite."

"Not even for ten big ones?"

"Not for a hundred."

Roche nods at the bad news Zimm is delivering. He's got other ideas on how to find Savannah; they're just more illegal than handing a cop a bundle of used notes in exchange for information.

# CHAPTER FOUR

The common misconception about computer hackers is that they're overweight geeks with their own unique place on the spectrum. They're pictured as lonely loser types who inhabit basements or converted lofts. They can be dirt poor or mega rich from their hacking, but they're always thought of as nerds, losers, the person you'd not miss if they didn't attend your party or left early.

Xandra Bastion is, or has been, all of those things and none of them. She came into Roche's orbit a few years back when her girlfriend at the time had been kidnapped in order to force Xandra to hack into a bank and steal money. Instead of doing the kidnapper's bidding, Xandra had used her skills to track down the kidnapper's location and hired Roche to extract her girlfriend.

The girlfriend was saved within three hours and dumped in four. Xandra doesn't do vulnerable. She does control. Against all sensible notions, she and Roche struck up a friendship and something of a business arrangement. He does work for her on a pro bono basis, and she looks for secrets in forbidden places for him.

Xandra's home is in Houston's Bellaire neighborhood. Technically a city in its own right, Bellaire is close enough to downtown to enjoy the city's finest offerings and attracts lots of moneyed people who've outgrown an apartment but aren't yet wealthy enough to buy their way into a gated community.

Roche swings the Buick onto Xandra's drive and then backs onto the street when he remembers the oil leak that is one of the Buick's less-endearing foibles. Like Xandra herself, the house is preened within an inch of its life, and he doesn't want her pissed at his old clunker leaving a stain on the drive.

As always, Xandra is dressed as if she's about to go on a date. Compliments about her hacking skills or business achievements get humble disclaimers, but it's her appearance that holds all her vanities and insecurities. Even when working out, Xandra has to look her absolute best.

Roche tosses a greeting at her and gives her the bare bones of his case.

"You want me to hack into where?"

"The US Marshals office. Specifically, the files or database they have on people within the Witness Protection Program."

A manicured eyebrow lifts as far as the latest Botox injection will allow. "That's not a quick hit. First off, I don't even know what the software is called, let alone how to access it."

"Are you saying you can't do it?"

"Go fluff yourself, Roche. Your amateur psychology bounces off me like cheesy pickup lines."

"Yeah right. You've never gone short of company from what you've told me. Who was it last night? A dude, a dame?"

"Both actually." Xandra doesn't break stride as she leads Roche to her home office. "Young couple I met online. She was fun, but he was no Don Juan."

Roche takes his usual seat in the office and watches the multitude of screens as they come into life and start the tasks commanded them by Xandra's dancing fingers. He knows better than to speak when Xandra is working. Her concentration must be absolute for her to operate at her best, and she never gives even a fraction of a percent less than her best.

There's nowhere that has defeated Xandra in terms of hacking. She's accessed Pentagon files for the heck of it, checked out the security tapes in Fort Knox and once, after a late-night drinking session with Roche, tapped into the *Washington Post*'s server and altered the headlines of the sport's stories to innuendo-laden quips.

"There's a pot of coffee in the kitchen. Be a sweetheart and go fetch it."

When Roche returns he finds Xandra drumming her fingers and scowling at the array of monitors.

"Problem?"

"Yeah. It's secure. Real secure." A frustrated flap of her hand gestures at her central monitor. "I'm not saying I can't get into it. It's more that I'm unlikely to get in anywhere near to your deadline."

"How far off will you be?"

"Wednesday." There's anger in Xandra's tone and Roche knows her well enough to recognize that it's the sting of defeat. Wednesday might as well be the moon for all the use it is. Savannah is scheduled to be dead by noon tomorrow, Monday, at the latest. Common sense suggests the hit will take place at night, sometime between two and five in the morning when there is a lull between revelers returning home and early birds setting off for work. It's also when there is the greatest chance of the victim being asleep. In short, he has less that twelve hours to find Savannah and get to her before any potential hitman does.

Roche points at the screen. "So box number one is closed. Time to look inside box number two."

# CHAPTER FIVE

"What do you mean, box number two?" Xandra can't pull her mouth into a tight line due to the collagen she's had injected into her lips, but that doesn't mean she isn't trying.

"The witness protection stuff is a bust, so we have to find something easier, more accessible in the time frame allowed." Roche sees Xandra's reaction to his words and speaks with care. "I'm guessing that facial recognition software is something you can get into in no time at all."

"You're not wrong. I may or may not have used it to stalk a former lover and check out who they cheated on me with."

"Here." Roche passes over the picture of Savannah as he shakes his head at her casual attitude towards breaking the law. "I'm guessing that people in the program don't get facial reconstruction surgery, so this is pretty much what she'll look like."

Xandra takes the picture, glances at it then feeds it into a scanner. "You're a moron. She has shoulder-length blonde hair that can be restyled in several ways and that's before you factor in coloring it."

"Surely that won't matter. Doesn't the software pick up on fixed points around the face? Jawline, mouth, eyes, nose and lots of other things?"

"Of course it does but look again at the picture. What do you see about Savannah that makes her memorable? What facial features has she got that would make her stand out in a crowd? What about her looks is special, or even partway unique?"

Roche looks at the photo again. So far he's only glanced at it. Finding a general location for her is the first step on his road to solving the case. He's had no need to know Savannah's features to do that.

Now he's taking a proper look at her, he sees what Xandra is getting at. Savannah is neither film-star pretty nor gargoyle-ugly. She's got girl-next-door looks, provided you live in an average street, in an average town, in an average state. Nothing about Savannah's appearance gives her a distinctive look. Not one thing about her face would make you notice her across a room for good or bad reason. She does have a tattoo of a unicorn below her left ear though. That's a good identifier, even if it does look like a stock design.

"I get what you mean. But still, surely the facial recognition software is designed to get round that kind of issue. To see past all the similarities and identify the differences."

"Of course it is. But look at the photo again. She's smiling big for the camera. She's glammed up and is obviously having a good time."

"Yeah, so?"

"You're such a man. Such a macho asshole at times you can't tell shit from sugar without dipping a finger in and tasting which is which." Xandra lifts her coffee and uses the mug as a pointer. "Think about how she's feeling now. She's going to be a whole other person than the one smiling in that picture. Her hair is up so you can see that nice identifying unicorn tattoo on her neck; however, she has long hair in an updo. If she's trying to stay hidden, then she's surely going to have her hair down so the unicorn goes back to mythical status."

Roche ignores the insults Xandra tosses at him with such casual abandon. He's ribbed her plenty about her sex life to brush off any minor insults that come his way. Instead, he focuses on what she's really saying. In the picture Savannah is carefree and happy, her life is good and it shows on her face. Now though, now she's been uprooted from her life and placed elsewhere, she's bound to have a different outlook. She'll no doubt be missing her family, her friends and everything about her former life. The fact that she's in witness protection means there's a credible threat to her life. She'll be scared and will probably have feelings of abandonment and acute loneliness, but most of all she'll be scared. Her life will be one of constant fear until enough time passes that she realizes she's safe in her new life.

In Roche's mind Savannah will try to assuage that fear any way she can. She'll restyle or color her hair. Baseball caps and oversized sunglasses will be used to hide her features from casual observation, and she'll do all she can to keep herself anonymous until she's got confidence in her new life.

"Look at this, Roche." Xandra aims a painted nail at her screens. "I'm running her photo through the software and only looking at the past two days. So her appearance is as current as possible."

Roche looks and sees a whirling series of images on one screen and a list of names and locations on another. A counter at the bottom of the list shows two hundred and fifty-seven entries at first look, but soon jumps to two seventy. There are way too many possible hits to run down in the specified time frame.

"Is there a way to narrow things down? We know her height and approximate weight. Can they be factored in?"

"Yes and no. Heights only work if there's a control measure in the same shot. For example, a New York trash can whose height we can learn and then use to calculate hers. Without seeing full-length images, it's impossible to gauge someone's true height. What if she's wearing boots or heels of some kind? The same applies to weight. Bulky sweaters hide a multitude of sins and I'm sure those puffer jackets do the same."

"So you're saying it's hopeless."

"No. I'm not saying that. Computers always yield answers. What I'm saying is there may be more answers than you have time to deal with. There's another issue. The big cities have cameras equipped for the software. Rural towns might not have any cameras at all."

"Dammit, Xandra, can't you say anything positive?"

"Well, maybe I can." Xandra's smile flashes perfect teeth at Roche. "While I can't get into the Marshals files as quick as you need me to, I think I may have worked out who created the software."

"Who? How?"

"It's a guy called Tomas Gilmoure. Twenty years ago he was a virtual tsunami compared to the Millennia Wave, as a bunch of hackers were known. I surfed into town on the back of some of the stuff he did. Legend has it that he secured a whole bunch of government security contracts by accessing the systems and leaving his own proposals as screensavers on the monitors of all the biggest hitters, the president included. I know you think I'm good, but Gilmoure is the best by a considerable distance. Or at least he was until he defected from the poacher's side and became a gamekeeper. I've heard he gives his staff a hundred thousand bonus for every piece of software they create that he can't get in to."

"Okay. So this guy's good. If it is him, how do you know it's him and, more importantly, do you have an in with him?"

"See this line of coding here?" Xandra's finger traces one line of many on the monitor to her left. "It's the trigger for a User Bomb."

"Which is?"

"It's a line of software that is designed to kill the computer of anyone who tries to interfere with the coding to gain access. I'm not talking about just shutting down the computer. I'm talking about removing every trace of everything you've ever done via that computer. If you buy through a website like Amazon and then trigger a User Bomb, your Amazon account gets wiped. Same for bank accounts, tax returns, everything. User Bombs are designed to put bedroom-bound troublemakers out of commission. Some versions will even list all porn sites visited on any social media feeds they find. This one has Gilmoure's signature all over it. He likes to add screenshots from the computer and email them to all the user's contacts. Rumor has it, he's got packets of screenshots attached to some of his User Bombs that feature some real kinky tastes."

"Wow." Roche wipes a hand over his face. This isn't a world he knows or even understands, but he gets how much damage a User Bomb can do and would hate for one to hit his laptop. "So what does telling me this achieve?"

"The likes of Gilmoure or myself can get round them but it takes time. If I asked Gilmoure for information on how to get into the database he'd laugh in my face and rightly so. None of us ever admit to another that we're stumped. For a hacker that's like announcing you're impotent or barren." The mug gets pointed at Roche again. "You, on the other hand, you have your own ways of asking questions and I'm sure you could persuade Gilmoure to give you what you need."

# CHAPTER SIX

A Sunday afternoon is when Savannah judges the grocery store will be quietest. Maybe the produce might not be as fresh as other times of the week, but that's a small price to pay for not having to encounter many strangers.

Everywhere around are scenes and interactions she both feels are normal and fears are precursors to her death.

The guy leafing through a magazine about trucks could be waiting for his chance to follow her home and then do the bidding of the Perez family. Likewise, the huge biker dude carrying a stack of six-packs could be her intended nemesis.

The more she looks around her, the more Savannah is shaking. Her fingers are rattling the basket against her knee, and it's all she can do not to drop it at her feet and dash headlong out of the grocery store and back to the house that has been her prison for the last week.

It's the words of her US marshal handler that Savannah hears in her ears. Introduced only as Janie, the handler gave her a thorough picture of what her new life would be like. The pitfalls, the psychological stresses and the best way to combat the ever-present fears with which she would start her new life.

Janie preached calmness. Taught her to recognize which fears were real and which were imagined. An example of Janie's logic was the question "Would you walk down a dark alley swinging your purse and wearing a dress that barely covered your interesting parts?" Janie had asked after Savannah's vehement denial that

Savannah already knew some basic common-sense procedures that would keep her safe. She'd reminded Savannah that as a woman she would be used to certain men looking at her in a way she wasn't always comfortable with. What she had to try to do was not imagine any man who found her attractive was going to try and kill her.

As the days passed, Janie explained how Savannah would be introduced into her new life. With few transferable job skills she could put to use in a place like Pagosa Springs, Savannah would have to find work in a bar or restaurant until she found her vocation. Friendships would develop in time, as might a romantic relationship.

Janie had mapped out how Savannah's life would be and how, while the future might seem acceptable once she got there, right now she was on the part of the map next to the inscription "Here Be Monsters."

A guy with a full cart passes her by. She notices the abundance of beer cans and frozen pizzas, as well as the way his eyes flit over her body before landing on her face. It's something she's had since puberty. Her friends got dimples and entrancing eyes, and she developed curves in all the wrong place for an awkward teenager.

"Hey there." The guy's smile is easy and open. He's not what Savannah would class as her type, if she had such a thing. "You're a new face around here." His hand leaves the cart and is held towards her. "I'm Danny."

This is Savannah's first real interaction in town. Her first opportunity to use her new name and to lay out the prepared cover story. A genuine chance to establish herself and set off down the highway towards a new life. She can't do it. She isn't ready. Her brain freezes and denies her the memory of what her new name is. She doesn't want to interact with Danny. Doesn't want to get hit on by him, even if he is cute.

"Sorry, Danny, I'm not interested, okay?"

Savannah tries a gentle smile to go with the letdown, but feels her face pull into a rictus rather than the pleasant gesture she's intending. She has been hit on plenty of times in the past. Often enough that she can read the signs. Danny would chat to her for a little while about Pagosa Springs and then, as she is new in town, he'd offer to show her round. And that would be that. She'd be going on a date with a guy she'd met in a grocery store. Perhaps Danny is just one of those nice guys who welcomes strangers. He might have a wife and kids at home, and he might just be the kind of jerk who lives off store-bought pizzas, drinks too much beer and sleeps around. Whatever he is, she's not interested.

Janie had warned her that in a small town like this, a new female face is bound to attract male attention. She'd even been kind enough to describe Savannah as pretty; but Savannah is enough of a realist to recognize that she's one notch above plain. Two if she spends hours giving herself a makeover.

She waits in line at the checkout. One cashier is scanning goods and there are two self-service stations. One of which has a handwritten sign apologizing for it being out of service.

The squeak of a cartwheel makes her turn. Danny is coming her way, his face set in what she guesses is his attempt at an ingratiating smile.

"We meet again."

"Please drop it, Danny, I've already told you I'm not interested." Savannah folds her arms and looks away, hoping her body language will reinforce her words.

"Drop what? I'm just saying hi to a new face in town. Ain't nothing wrong with that. I mean, it's not like I'm asking you to dinner, is it?"

Savannah's instinct is to let Danny down gently rather than tell him where to get off. To leave him in no doubt that she doesn't want anything to do with him, but in a way that doesn't hurt his feelings. If necessary she can ramp it up a notch or two, but that's not her way. Humiliating and hurting people is something that's foreign to her, but the way her nerves are currently strung out, she knows it would be very easy for her to step out of character. Once again it's Janie's wisdom that comes to her. Janie warned her not to fall out with anyone until she'd gotten a picture of the various connections in Pagosa Springs. Janie explained about small towns having tight communities and the various benefits and downsides of this.

"No, it isn't but, for the record, if you did the answer would be no."

Danny steps round to see her face. "That's fine and fair enough. I got an answer to a question I haven't asked. But in the interests of market research and personal betterment, what is making you say no?"

Savannah steps forward and starts running the groceries in her basket through the self-service scanner. "I'm sorry, but I'm not interested. No means no. Don't you get that?"

"Ouch. You really go for the jugular, don't you?"

Savannah nods at Danny's shopping cart. "Only when I'm forced to. Underneath your beer-swilling, pizza-munching exterior there may be a nice guy. But right now I'm not interested in dating anyone, and that includes you."

"You said you're not interested in dating anyone right now. Does that mean there's hope for me in the future?"

"I doubt it. Right now I'm living day by day and I can't see a time when I'll be living week by week. Do yourself a favor and hit on some other girl, because you're wasting both of our time by hitting on me." Savannah can hear her voice is rising and her tone harshening, but she's unable to do anything about it. Half of the threats she's imagined have involved a guy using the cover of hitting on her.

Savannah reaches for a shopping bag and lifts her eyes from the pile of groceries. All around faces are looking her way with expressions of shocked amusement. She bundles her groceries into a bag and marches out of the grocery store, her cheeks burning in self-recrimination at the way she's drawn attention to herself. Whatever Danny's intentions may have been, she's just made things a whole lot worse for herself.

# CHAPTER SEVEN

The screens in front of Xandra dance a disco beat as she works. They're changing color like a chameleon running across a rainbow, and while the whole process mesmerizes Roche, he can make no sense of what any of the screens are depicting.

A printer whirs to life beside Roche and he takes the paper it spits out. An address is listed on the page as well as Gilmoure's social security number, the vehicles registered in his name, his company's name and the minivan his wife drove. The address is listed as being in Dallas.

"How did you get all of this so quickly? Surely Gilmoure would have covered his tracks, his identity and his whereabouts."

"He has." Xandra stands and points to the door. "Come on, walk and talk. You have a plane to catch. Gilmoure's company has to be registered. He has to have it as a legitimate business to get any government contracts. Sure, he's got a couple of holding companies to distance himself, but they only stop traditional investigators, not digital ones. Once you get past them and get a location, the rest is so easy it gets boring."

"I have a plane to catch?"

"You're on a deadline and that old clunker you're driving doesn't look like it'll survive the trip to Dallas. I booked you on the next flight. Now hurry, we have a half hour to get you to the airport and it's a forty-minute drive."

Roche keeps his mouth shut as he trots after Xandra. He's confident she'll get him to the airport in time. She's driven him before and while she's a fine driver, she considers speed limits to be something for other people to pay attention to.

As they power along the 610 Loop, he deems it's time to resume their conversation. "How much do I owe you for the plane ticket?"

"Not one sweet dime. I haven't paid for a flight or a hotel room in the last twenty years. For some strange reason, their software always gets me a reservation that's free of charge. There's a rental car waiting for you at the other end. Again, they didn't seem to be able to take my money."

"You do remember that I expense this kind of thing, don't you?"

"Expense it. Claim for first class if you like. Consider it a bonus."

Roche casts Xandra a glance and catches the wink she gives him. It's typical of her to do this kind of thing. She's a generous benefactor to several charities and a wealthy businesswoman in her own right. She has no need to pull these stunts. He'd expected to have to persuade her to help him. Digging into the US Marshals witness protection database is the kind of crime that carries a long and stiff sentence. Especially so if they fail to save Savannah but are tracked as looking for her.

He knows why she does it though. The same reason she developed her hacking skills. While it might be a question of pride in her abilities, or pure nosiness, that drove her to hack her way into sensitive digital enclosures, he's convinced she likes the danger. Not the gun-to-your-head or knife-at-your-throat danger he often faces, but the cat-and-mouse tests of skill that come with the risk of imprisonment should she be careless enough to leave a trail back to her door.

Xandra shafting the airlines and hotel chains isn't her being cheap. It's her flipping them the bird simply because she can.

The car screeches to a halt outside the airport twenty-nine minutes after Xandra started its engine.

"You're going to have to run, otherwise you'll miss your flight."

# CHAPTER EIGHT

Savannah walks towards her car with ever-lengthening strides. Behind her she can hear footsteps and Danny's voice, now higher pitched, as he indignantly protests about the putdown she'd delivered in the grocery store.

"Hey, lady. There was no call for that. I was trying to be friendly."

"He was, too."

A glance back shows Savannah one of the onlookers has followed Danny out and is also on her trail. It's a woman, around the same age as she is, with a kid resting on one hip.

Others are emerging from the store and rubbernecking at the free entertainment. As much as she's falling apart inside, Savannah knows she's going to have to put an end to this. To calm things down before they escalate any further. She stops and turns to face Danny and his support act, a hand held up to halt their progress towards her.

"Look, I'm sorry if I was a bit rude. I moved here because I'm trying to put my life back together and make a new start after I got my heart broken. I'm not ready to date again. Not even ready for a platonic relationship. Hell, I need to get myself fixed before I can begin to think about making a friend." A lot of what Savannah is saying is part of the cover story she and Janie concocted as her reason for moving to Pagosa Springs.

"That wasn't rude, that was insulting, what you said to Danny. Ain't no need for you to rail on him for being friendly. All that no means no bull. That's for rapists, not good guys like Danny." The woman with the kid on her hip is stepping forward as she speaks. When she halts she's close enough that Savannah can smell the cigarette smoke on her breath. "You said you need to get yourself fixed. Well, there's a veterinary clinic across the street where you can get that done, and then maybe you'll not be such a bitch."

In times of stress and danger human beings are programed to do one of two things: take flight or start fighting. Savannah's instincts are giving her mixed messages. As much as Savannah wants to get away from the vicious woman, she also wants to hit her. With the kid on her hip and a street full of witnesses, violence of any kind can't happen, but it takes all of Savannah's self-control not to answer fire with fire or dash for the tranquility of her own company. She takes a deep breath and opens her mouth.

"I've apologized for insulting him. I've even bared my soul as to why I'm not going to date him. I'm sorry if that's not good enough for you, but I don't think I can do any more."

Danny steps forward, his face neutral and a hand reaching for the woman's free arm. "Leave it, sis. Like she said, she's apologized."

Savannah sends a look Danny's way. "Thank you, and again, I'm sorry for what I said."

As much as the commotion may now be over, the crowd doesn't disperse until Savannah's car draws away. She's given them a negative impression of her. Instead of being nondescript, as Janie counseled, she's drawn attention to herself and all because she freaked out when a guy hit on her. Houston Savannah, as she thinks of her former self, would be shocked at how badly she handled that situation. Pagosa Savannah is distraught at how badly she's screwed up. Worst of all, she doesn't recognize herself. She's not attuned to the fire in her belly that she's just had to quell lest things spin properly out of control. Hers has been a life of laughter and mediation at awkward situations, yet it had just taken all of her self-control not to rail on Danny in a much worse way. Houston

Savannah would have batted away Danny's advances with a cheery smile; Pagosa Savannah had lost control of a harmless situation.

In her car, Savannah can't help but speculate if this is who she now is. That the ordeal of having to uproot her life and live in hiding has changed her core personality. Houston Savannah worked for good causes and left a positive impression on those she met. Pagosa Savannah is the kind of self-centered bitch she'd cross the street to avoid.

Savannah wants to retch. Wants to expel the bile souring her mouth and gullet. Wants to puke out the nasty and the fear and the self-loathing. She can't though. Not here. Instead, she swallows hard and reaches for the indicator stalk, vowing to work harder to conquer the all-consuming fears that are making her unrecognizable, even to herself.

# CHAPTER NINE

The home of Tomas Gilmoure fits his status as a tech genius. At first glance from the hire car, Roche guesses it has a minimum five bedrooms. There are kids playing in the street and not one of the front yards has so much as a blade of grass that isn't manicured. Everything about the area screams money and respectability.

Roche walks up the path to the front door and prepares himself for what he expects to be an interesting and potentially violent conversation.

Unlike the other homes on the street, Gilmoure's shows no sign of life. The double garage doors are closed, and a look at the windows shows no changing shadows as the house's occupants move around, or the flicker of a TV screen sending different colors into any of the rooms. According to Xandra, Gilmoure has three kids in their teens, so it stands to reason at least one of them would be watching TV or blaring music.

No sounds come from the house. No yelling as siblings fight or argue with their parents. No thumping basslines, screeching guitars or laughter from a family enjoying one another's company.

The doorbell gives a chime that manages to be both musical and annoying. Nothing happens. Nobody comes to the door. No one peers past a curtain.

Twice more Roche presses the doorbell. The second time he holds his finger on it for an ear-assaulting half minute.

When Roche gets no answer he strides round the house. He doesn't believe the Gilmoures will be in the backyard, but he has to try. If they're out of town, his case falls apart and Savannah will die. If they're not, he can let himself in and await their return.

Over the years Roche has let himself into enough houses to have become adept at the practice. Rule one of such enterprises is to look as if you belong so you don't draw suspicion upon yourself as you approach. Rule two is when you're actually breaking in, do it out of sight via a rear or side door.

As he expects, Roche finds the backyard empty. A few chairs and a table are arranged on a patio, and there's a hibachi large enough to cook an entire bison's worth of steaks at once.

Roche tries the back door and finds it locked. Now it's crunch time. Now is when the case can fall apart. He can be inside the house in seconds. The lock picks in his pocket will ensure that. The question he's got to think about is where Gilmoure and his family are. If they're on vacation, the house won't just be locked, it'll be alarmed. Tech geeks are suckers for gadgets, and as someone who made his name from breaching the security of the US government, Gilmoure is sure to take his home security seriously.

A silent alarm will alert the police while he's padding around the house or awaiting the return of the Gilmoures. An active one will alert the neighbors and they'll call the police.

Roche knows all of this. Knows every possible pitfall that comes with breaking and entering. He might have a license as a private investigator, but he's walked in the shadows as well as the light.

The lock picks are set to work. Roche is confident the alarm won't be set. It's early evening on a Sunday, and Sundays are school nights, even if the kids attend a fancy-ass school instead of a public one. The garden furniture is light enough to blow away should the wind pick up; any responsible homeowner would pack it away when they went on vacation. The hibachi is bound to be worth several thousand, and it's left standing against the back of the double garage with nothing tethering it to prevent its theft. All of this tells Roche the Gilmoures are in town. That they might not be at home right now but they're not too far away.

Once inside the house, Roche sees that rare fusion of money and taste. Perhaps they hired an interior designer, or maybe the Gilmoures have a good eye. Either way, it's given them a functional and attractive place to live.

Room by room, Roche searches the house in case one or more of the teens has been left behind. He's got his gun in his hand, but his hand is at his side. Trouble isn't something Roche is expecting. The house is way too quiet for that.

It takes two minutes to search the house. Roche has found no human life; but one of the kids keeps a snake and there's a fish tank whose occupants display every possible color on the spectrum.

Gilmoure has a den, which makes Roche feel a pang of envy. The den has a corner bar, supple leather seats and a TV so huge Roche can't work out how it got into the room. It also has a massive workstation where Gilmoure will be able to indulge his hacking instincts or simply just work from home.

If he knew more about computers, or had Xandra here with him, Roche would have been tempted to power up Gilmoure's system, but he recognizes doing so as a way to waste time he doesn't have. Instead, he goes back to the kitchen, the heart and hub of every home. If there is a clue as to the whereabouts of the Gilmoure family, it will be in the kitchen. A note stuck to the fridge as a reminder, or a calendar entry.

It is a calendar that gives Roche what he needs. As technology focused as Gilmoure himself may be, that doesn't always transmute to the rest of a household. It might be that he or his wife send messages to the household telling of certain events, but that seems too authoritarian for the picture of the laid-back guy Xandra had painted Gilmoure to be.

The calendar has a full list of notes about soccer or baseball practices, a dentist's appointment and this evening's family dinner.

Below the stated time of 6:30 p.m. there is the name "Chez Phillipe."

A check on Google teaches Roche that Chez Phillipe is a French restaurant that holds numerous culinary awards. There is an address listed online, so Roche once again has a decision to make. Does he wait for two or three hours for the family to return, or does he go to the restaurant and somehow extract Gilmoure and then persuade him to give up Savannah's new location and identity?

The answer is simple. He daren't wait two or three hours for the return of Tomas Gilmoure, as it's time Savannah might not have.

# CHAPTER TEN

Roche walks across the parking lot to Chez Phillipe. If the cars he's passing are any kind of indicator as to the restaurant's client base, they're high rollers, the upper echelons of society in terms of wealth and prestige. The restaurant is understated in every possible way. The sign is discreet and there's no huge glass frontage allowing him a look inside. This is a place for the elite to dine in private, rather than the wannabes who desire to be seen by those they want to leave behind.

Roche glances at the sample menu displayed on the wall. To him it seems overcomplicated. His tastes are simple: give him a big chunk of dead animal, a heap of fries and a few mushrooms and he's happy. So far as he's concerned words like drizzled, jus and compote shouldn't describe anything you put in your mouth.

Most telling about the menu is the lack of pricing on it. The old adage "if you have to ask how much it is, you can't afford it" comes to Roche's mind. It's egalitarian and elitist. He's no problem with capitalism and people making money, but the snobbery of such moves has never sat well with him. Chez Phillipe will have a dress code, of that Roche is sure.

All of this gives Roche a preconceived idea about what the restaurant will be like inside. He walks in and finds he's right, although it gives him no satisfaction. A maître d' hovers grandly in the center of the room with watchful eyes, surveying his domain. His suit sharper than any knife Roche has ever owned.

Roche's eyes scan the room. Xandra has furnished him with a picture of what Gilmoure looks like, and it only takes Roche a few seconds to find his quarry among the suited, bejeweled and coiffured customers. Gilmoure is sitting at the center of a long table. He's holding a menu and is speaking to a waiter. With twenty people at the table who'll remember him, and a restaurant full of diners and staff, Roche knows there's no point in approaching Gilmoure. He needs to get the man to come to him.

By standing at the lectern by the door, Roche gets the maître d's attention. The man walks his way with pronounced footsteps chapping on the marbled floor. He has a Gallic nose and enough of the restaurant's inverted snobbery to make Roche feel inadequate as he gets a once-over. Or at least he'd feel that way if he gave the slightest damn.

"Good evening, sir." The smile and polite welcome as genuine as a glass eye. "Do you have a reservation?"

The question is a restaurant's defense mechanism. Undesirable last-minute patrons can be kept out by a booking system. If the maître d' doesn't like the look of someone, he'll claim there are no tables. A place like Chez Phillipe will be exclusive enough that booking will be essential, although regular clients would always be found a table with or without a booking. None of this matters to Roche; he's not looking for a table. He'd rather go hungry than dine in a place with so many pretensions.

"No. That's not why I'm here." Roche gives what he hopes is a helpless and apologetic gesture. "I took a wrong turn, so I pulled into your parking lot to turn around. Unfortunately I dinged one of the cars there. I don't know whose it is, but I'll need to set things right with the owner." He pulls his cell out and shows the maître d' a picture of Gilmoure's license plate. "Is there a way you can find out whose car it is so I can sort this out? The car is a Porsche Panamera, if that helps."

"Of course, sir." The maître d' scribbles down the license number. "If you give me a minute or two, I'm sure I can find the owner for you."

Roche doesn't miss the way the maître d's attitude towards him has changed upon hearing the lie he's concocted. A dinged car with no apology or recompense for the customer will be bad for Chez Phillipe. For the maître d' as well as his customer. Roche is doing him a favor by being a stand-up guy and taking responsibility.

The maître d' works his way around the room. He's all smiles and graciousness and has the people skills to not get sucked into lengthy conversations at any table, yet neither does he appear to rush. Only once before getting to Gilmoure's table does he consult the piece of paper with the license number on it. Roche sees a woman's head shake as her face sheds itself of concern.

Gilmoure stands a second after the maître d' consults his scribble. His face is set to irked rather than anger, but that may be an act for the family. Roche has no worries about Gilmoure getting angry. By the time another hour has passed, Gilmoure will be in the unenviable position of wishing his car *had* been crashed into.

# CHAPTER ELEVEN

Gilmoure is mid-forties, rail thin and carrying enough small man syndrome to give him backache. He marches across the room towards Roche, his face darkening with every step.

"I suppose I should thank you for your honesty, buddy, but I'm not gonna lie. I'm pissed at this. It's a damn big parking lot."

"I know. I'm sorry." Contrition doesn't come easy to Roche, but he's seen it in others often enough to know how to fake it. "I couldn't leave without making things right, though."

"I want to see what the damage is for myself." Gilmoure strides out the door.

So far this is all going to Roche's plan. He follows Gilmoure outside, making sure to only ever be a pace or two behind him. His right hand slipping inside his jacket and nestling around the butt of his SIG Sauer.

"I don't see anything." Gilmoure's finger is aimed at his car and he's looking back at Roche.

"It's at the other side."

As soon as Gilmoure rounds his Porsche, Roche jams the SIG into his ribcage. "Change of plan. There's nothing wrong with your car. I need your help and you're going to give it to me."

"Please, don't shoot me. I don't know who you think I am, but I don't see how I can help you."

"You wrote the software for the WITSEC database. It has information I need. We're going to go to your home and you're going to get me that information. Someone is leaking details of the people who are in the program, and you're going to help me save one who's had a credible threat made against her." Roche bumps the barrel of his SIG into a rib hard enough to draw a yelp. "I could make all manner of threats against you, but I'm holding a gun and you're smart enough to realize I've tracked you down. Not just to your home or office, but to where you were having dinner with your family."

"Please. I beg you. I can't get into that database."

"Shut up, dickwad. You will have a back door so you can get in and work on any flaws the system has or develops. I know how these things work. Now, there's a Chevy two cars over. It's mine. You're going to drive it to your home, and I'm going to sit behind you with my gun pressed against the seat and a fervent hope I neither have to keep making threats, nor get forced to shoot you because you decide to come over all heroic. Once you are in the car, I want you to hand me your cell and then put the GPS on, so I know you're not jerking me around by going the long way."

*

To Roche's mild surprise, the journey to Gilmoure's home is uneventful. He'd expected the man to try something, even if it was pleading for his life or declarations that Roche would pay for kidnapping him like this.

Gilmoure's wife had replied to the message Roche had sent from the geek's cell. Rather than have her raise the alarm when he was delayed in his return, he'd lied that he was taking the incident to the police as he didn't trust the guy who'd crashed into their car, and told her that she and the rest of the family should enjoy the meal without him.

The closer they get to the house, the more agitated Gilmoure becomes. It isn't that he is trying to talk his way out of the situation, more that his driving grows a tad erratic and his hands shake whenever he releases the wheel.

Roche gets the man's worries, they are understandable. Gilmoure will be imagining that once his usefulness has expired, he'll be shot. He'll be thinking that he ought to refuse and will be running his own calculations on Roche's response: whether he'll be tortured with a bullet through a limb that'll render him agonized, but still able to do Roche's bidding, or whether a show of resistance will seal his fate when he otherwise might have been allowed to live.

At the house, Gilmoure parks on the drive and then exits under Roche's supervision.

"Okay, nice and easy, we're going to enter the house, go to your den and you're going to get me what I want. When I've got the information I need, I'll leave and you can go back to your family. No harm and only a very small foul."

Gilmoure's keys jangle as he feeds one into the front door. His body trembles as he swings it open and steps inside. Then he convulses, his body jerking forward and the door slamming shut behind him. Or at least it would slam shut were it not in sudden and violent collision with Roche's gun hand.

The SIG falls to the ground as Roche curses.

# CHAPTER TWELVE

Savannah curls her lip at the offerings from the TV channels and tosses the remote control onto another chair. The altercation with Danny and the woman with the kid on her hip has left a sour taste. There is so much to adjust to now she lives in Pagosa Springs. She'd thought she was dealing with the loneliness and the isolation well enough, but now she's had her first proper interaction with another human being it's left her bereft of confidence.

Back in Houston, Savannah had a circle of friends with whom she could party, dine out with, or simply just hang. Here she has no one and she's blown the first chance to establish herself. One date might not have been too bad. She could have made sure to keep Danny at arm's length and used him to introduce her to some folks.

She gets the hypocrisy of her feelings. She'd told Danny she isn't ready to start building new friendships and her words to him were from the heart: she isn't ready, and she knows it. But that doesn't mean she doesn't want to. She's been a social animal since kindergarten. Part of the crowd. Never the head cheerleader or homecoming queen, just one of the guys.

For the umpteenth time Savannah flicks through the books that had been in the house. Whoever created the library must hold literary snobbishness dear to their heart. The shelf is laden with heavyweight classics and bereft of anything that takes her fancy. Her tastes lie in thrillers, cop books and horror. There's an old Stephen King novel that she might tackle were circumstances different. Right now, there are enough real-life situations to terrify her without sourcing artificial chills.

Janie's words of warning come back to Savannah as she lifts her iPad. She's to make no online contact with her old friends. She can have social media accounts in her new name, but she cannot connect with anyone from her old life. To do so is to put her head in a noose. To possibly put their heads in nooses. It was on this point Janie was strictest. Her friends and family members' accounts may be being monitored for new contacts. Those contacts may be traced.

Savannah has created social media accounts in her new identity. She can't think of it as *her* name yet. Maybe that day will come and maybe it won't. Whatever the case may be, the people she used to chat with on Facebook, those whose tweets she looked out for, or followed on TikTok or Insta, are no longer safe to be a part of her life. Erica Dobbs, as she's now to be known, has none of the real-life background knowledge of her social media contacts that she has. Everyone has to be vetted. Has to be held up for examination of their principles and beliefs before Erica, née Savannah, can begin to interact with them.

The process is wearing away her sense of self. Layer by layer, it's grinding her down and she knows she's only just begun this new life. That she has years of it ahead of her. She's wise enough to know that it will get easier as she finds herself a new gang to hang with, but she'll never stop missing her old one.

Her finger taps the YouTube app, and it opens. She types with rapidity and brings up her digital comfort blanket: Maisie and Steven's wedding. A three-hour recording of their special day. Privately, she'd scoffed at the notion of anyone ever watching the full three hours. Since arriving at Pagosa Springs, she's watched the whole thing thrice. She sees her old self in the video. Dancing, laughing, chatting and having a ball, despite the hideous dresses Maisie had chosen for her bridesmaids. This video is her window, her portal to what once was yet can never again be. She knows she's taking a risk in watching something from her old life, but every fiber of her being is mourning the lost connections.

Lacking a date that week, she'd taken her brother, Richard, as her guest. He'd been his usual self. Full of jokes that were neither cruel nor discriminatory, mindful of others and good company. Richard was the brother every sister wanted. All of her friends adored him, and she wasn't so naïve as to not think there hadn't been couplings between her brother and her besties.

That night they had danced and laughed until the early hours. In another world he would have been her ideal man. He was certainly the yardstick she measured all her boyfriends against. One suitor had even been turned down because she knew he viewed Richard as a goody two shoes.

The screen shows her and Richard dancing away, broad smiles apiece and the sheen of happiness radiating out from them.

As the tears tumble down her cheeks, Savannah isn't fool enough to think the reason she keeps taking the risks associated with watching this video are solely because she misses her friends. The larger part of her compulsion to watch and re-watch the video is because it helps to heal the Richard-shaped hole in her heart.

# CHAPTER THIRTEEN

Roche barges the door with his shoulder. The pain in his wrist from where the door slammed it into the casing both a blessing and a curse. A blessing because without it he'd be outside the house and Gilmoure inside, but a curse because his arm feels numb and he's not got the time to go to the ER and get it checked out for fractures.

The door gives a foot but is then halted as Gilmoure tries to close him out. It's not going to happen. Even though one arm is largely useless, Roche has enough superior weight and strength to gain the upper hand.

The digital world is Gilmoure's playground, it's where he excels, where he'll be able to run any rings he wants around Roche. However, when it comes to rough and tumble, to getting down and dirty, Gilmoure can't begin to compete with Roche.

Roche gets himself wedged between the door and its casing. Gilmoure is now expending energy trying to push the door closed, while all he's doing is using his body as a blocker. Let the little man tire himself out. Then he'll teach him an unforgettable lesson.

Gilmoure either tires or starts to use his brain. The fingers he has gripping the edge of the door move downwards.

To Roche the only reason Gilmoure would move downwards would be to collect a weapon. Roche knows he's dropped his SIG, knows it's not on his side of the door, not between his feet. Therefore, it must be what Gilmoure is after. The geek might be half his size, and nowhere near as adept at fighting as he is. None of that will matter if he has the SIG. He'll control the narrative, and that narrative will be sure to involve handcuffs and a whole lot of unanswerable questions.

Instead of passively blocking the door, Roche now heaves against it, pressing a foot on the casing to give him something of a backstop to push against. The door opens and he sees Gilmoure's fingers reaching for the SIG. They are maybe two inches away, which doesn't leave him much time to react.

Roche's foot launches forward. Its arc accelerating to a peak as Gilmoure's hand grasps the pistol and begins to lift and turn it.

Shoes versus flesh is a fight that's only ever had one winner. Whether it's a new pair of shoes introducing themselves to their wearer, or an aggressor quite literally putting the boot in, flesh has always been defeated by shoes.

Roche's shoes aren't ordinary ones. His have metal toecaps hidden underneath their leather exterior. They have a thin steel plate embedded between sole and upper. The shoes are designed to have maximum impact when used to kick or stamp. With this knowledge on board, Roche has aimed his kick with care. A computer hacker who can't type is useless to him and he knows it. That's why his kick was aimed at Gilmoure's forearm and only given enough force to numb rather than break.

Gilmoure's hand flies back, the gun skittering across the polished timber floor. He chases after it, and Roche goes after him.

The pistol is five steps away, but it's on the ground, whereas they're upright. For either to bend to the ground and lift it when the other is in such close proximity will leave them open to attack. Roche knows this. Gilmoure doesn't.

The computer genius stoops as he runs. His shorter frame means he has less distance to bend. Roche snags Gilmoure's collar with his good hand and adds enough lift to the geek's momentum to prevent him grabbing the SIG.

Once there's no danger of Gilmoure getting the gun, Roche releases him with a shove that sends him careening into a table bearing a vase of flowers. By the time Gilmoure is on the move again, Roche has the pistol lifted and aimed his way.

Roche steps forward, taking care to not get himself into a position where Gilmoure can strike back. "Okay, you tried, you failed. You get an A plus for guts, but a D minus for the way you went about it. All you've really achieved is a sore arm and a pissed me. Otherwise, we're right back where we started. I'd ask if you think trying was worth the effort, but the answer's damned obvious. Now, we go to your den and you get me the information I need."

"No way." There's fear in Gilmoure's eyes and a San Andreas Fault-sized tremor in his voice. "I'm not going to put those people at risk, and you can't get what you want from me if you kill me."

"You're right, I can't." Roche pulls the SIG's trigger.

# CHAPTER FOURTEEN

The vase explodes and showers Gilmoure with fragments of porcelain as the water inside it floods outwards and splashes onto him. Gilmoure has several cuts to his scalp, but they're minor so he needn't worry about them.

Head wounds tend to bleed out of proportion to the damage done. There are a lot of small veins running all over the scalp, which is basically a thin layer of tissue. Folks who have spent their youth playing out are used to seeing head wounds from childhood injuries. The geeks who stayed inside honing their craft in front of a screen aren't generally so experienced in such matters.

Roche knows Gilmoure will be able to feel the blood running across his scalp. That he'll be worried about a piece of porcelain digging into his skull. Gilmoure's greatest asset is his brain and, for a second or two until rationalization returns, he'll be worried about having received a brain injury.

A second shot gets planted into the wood floor between Gilmoure's legs.

"Get up and get yourself to your den. The next bullet is going in your ankle if you don't do as I say. Your legs may not work, but I can still drag you to your den."

Roche's voice is calm, as if he's ordering a coffee. He's been threatened often enough to learn that quiet threats delivered with surety are far more effective than screamed or snarled ones.

Gilmoure's face is contorted with malice as he levers himself upwards. "That vase has been in my wife's family for three generations. It's survived fifteen house moves and more kids running past it than anyone can count."

"Would you rather I'd shot you?"

Gilmoure's answer is to trudge in the direction of the den.

With Gilmoure at his desk, Roche gets another chair and sets it where he can watch the geek's hands and keep the SIG in his line of sight.

"Listen up, Gilmoure. I have a couple of things to say to you, and you need to listen to them. I'm not the bad guy here. I know I may seem that way to you but, believe me, I'm not. Now I could spend the next ten minutes wasting both our time by laying any number of heavy threats on you. You might be resistant at first, but in the end you'd do what I want, so let's save me the time and you the pain. You have a wife and three kids. That's three weak spots, four if you're happily married."

"It's four, you jerk."

"Then I'm jealous. My own private life is best described as tumultuous. Anyway, I need you to find where a girl called Savannah Nicoll, who's originally from Houston, is and what she's now called. The reason I need to find her is because there is a very specific threat against her. Her mother made me aware of this threat and its deadline. The deadline is close. Real close. I'm going to protect Savannah and keep her safe. But first I have to find her. That's where you come in."

"How do I know you're not the one who's trying to kill her?"

"You don't, but you're nobody's fool. Nobody questions that you're smart. Wherever she is within the country, the odds of me getting to her before you raise the alarm are miniscule. You're going to have contacts in the US Marshals Service. Savannah can be getting moved within five minutes of me leaving here. I dare say you've already realized that the counterpoint to that is if I kill you, you can't raise the alarm."

"It has crossed my mind."

"Your wife and kids will be back in an hour or two. They'll find your body, call it in and there still won't be enough time for me or anyone else to get to where she is and kill her." Roche taps his chest. "I'm the hero in all of this, not the villain. If I was the villain, I'd have put a bullet into you long before now. Pain works better than fear as a motivator, yet I've not once hurt you unnecessarily. From my point of view, a bullet in your ankles or knees will have your fingers flying over that keyboard like an F-16 strafing an enemy base. I'm sure that by now you'll have noticed a distinct lack of bullet holes in any parts of your legs."

"You've still threatened it."

"I have. And if necessary, I'll do it. But I don't want to. I want you to co-operate without me having to make or carry out any more threats. Like I said, I'm not the bad guy here. Once I've got what I need from you, I'll be on my way to protect Savannah. You can call the Marshals, but I'd prefer you satisfy that nagging doubt in your brain."

"What doubt?"

"The one you've had since I first told you there was a leak and people in the Protected Witness Program are having their details shared with people who want them dead." Roche tapped a finger against his temple. "That's eating at you, isn't it? You're wondering if your software has been breached. Wondering if you're somehow culpable. I don't need to kill you when I leave here, because the first thing you're going to do is make sure your ass is covered if there is a leak. Once that's done you'll be able to pick up the phone, but then you'll be asking yourself who you can trust. Will telling them about this visit accelerate or remove the threat to Savannah? You'll run the numbers in your head and decide Savannah's best chance is with me, because by then you'll have worked out that if I really was the villain of this piece, all I'd have to do is snatch one of your kids and then I'd be able to get new names and locations from you whenever I wanted."

"Okay, I'll do it." Gilmoure reaches for his keyboard and mouse.

"One last thing. Don't even think about triggering your own User Bomb. I know it's there and what it'll do. You trigger it and we just head to your office and start all over again. Except, when I leave your office, your hands will be so badly broken you'll need years of surgery before they're fit to go anywhere near a computer again."

# CHAPTER FIFTEEN

Gilmoure's fingers tremble as he feeds in a password that's every bit as long and complicated as any one Roche has seen Xandra use. He reasons that because they know how to breach digital security, all former hackers are paranoid about their own.

"Look, dude, I can get in and get you what you want, but to protect myself going forward, I don't want to leave a trail of breadcrumbs back to my door. I'm doing this the long way."

"No. You're doing it the quick way." Roche gestures at Gilmoure. "You're the US Marshals' man when it comes to this system. If there's an investigation further down the line, the chances are they'll need you to deal with the technical bits. Cover your ass on their time, not mine."

Gilmoure turns back to his task without replying, but Roche can see there's a fraction less hunch to his shoulders. The geek has realized the truth of his words.

This isn't the first time Roche has used strong-arm tactics to get what he wants from someone reluctant to give it to him. He knows how these things play out. The quick way to get information is to create pain, or at least fear of pain, and while he's prepared to follow up on any threat he makes, that's always a last resort for him. People like Gilmoure are innocents undeserving of horrendous injury or torture. They may see themselves as a knight or bishop in their own games, but to Roche they are of no greater importance than a pawn. They can be sacrificed, but only if and when it's to his advantage.

Gilmoure is such a pawn, one who needn't become a martyr. This is why Roche browbeat him with the logical outcomes of him sharing the information. Why he outlined what would happen in various scenarios. It's why Gilmoure has chosen to be compliant.

"Come on, Gilmoure, you ought to be done by now. In the back door, run her name in a search bar and then cablammo, you hand over her details to me and we part company."

"Give me a break, buddy. It's not that simple. There is no direct access to the files via the back door; that is something everyone agreed was not needed to be possible when the system was designed. I'm in the system, I've found a user who's offline and I'm currently learning their password. It'll take about five minutes, so chill."

For all he's moved so he can keep an eye on the screens, the images and data are moving far too fast for Roche to make any sense of them. He has a growing feeling Gilmoure has somehow sent a warning or distress call out in among doing his bidding.

"You have those five minutes and then things will turn ugly for you."

Beads of sweat decorate Gilmoure's face as he types with a furious intensity.

At four and a half minutes he pushes back from the desk and points at the screen. "I'm in as the marshal and a search on her name is running. You'll have everything you need in a few seconds."

"Print it for me." Roche would have used better manners, but he's learned the hard way that good manners mean nothing when someone is pointing a gun at you.

With a sheet of paper in his hand, Roche flicks his eyes between the paper and Gilmoure. Savannah is in Colorado. At a place called Pagosa Springs. He's never been there or even known it existed. That's something he half expected. Only a cartographer with a photographic memory would have heard of every town in the whole USA.

"Here." Roche hands the sheet of paper to Gilmoure. "I don't expect to need your help again, but I want your cell number in case I do. For the record, and so I don't have to repeat myself, you ought to consider all the usual threats have been made about non- or false compliance."

Gilmoure scrawls a number onto the paper. "Is this how you live all the time? Threatening people? Breaking into their lives and leaving destruction behind you?"

"Just on a Sunday. Tomorrow is mariachi night, and Wednesdays are when I read bedtime stories to kittens and orphaned dolphins." Roche skewers Gilmoure with a stern look. "I'm going to leave in a moment. You're probably having all kinds of ideas about calling the cops and having me picked up. Those are bad ideas. Those ideas will get a young woman killed. The second you call the cops or the Marshals, this whole thing will blow up. There will be many calls back and forth and Savannah will get moved. But if the person organizing these hits has access to your software, then she'll never be safe no matter where she gets relocated to. First, I have to save her, and then I have to identify how her killers found her. This needs to be stopped at source. You calling the cops means it can't be stopped at source."

Roche leaves the house and calls Xandra. By the time he arrives at the airport, she's got him booked on a flight to Albuquerque and there will be another rental car waiting for him. He looks at his watch: 7:30 p.m. An hour and a half in the air and then another three and a half behind the wheel will see him enter Pagosa Springs. Add at least an hour for delays at the airport, getting a rental car and a quick stop off at a contact to get some weapons and that brings him to a total six hours. He's working on the theory any attack on Savannah will take place between two and five in the morning. With these timings, he ought to get to Savannah in time, but there are too many things that can go wrong for him to be confident in his plan.

# CHAPTER SIXTEEN

Savannah tosses and turns. The mattress is comfortable, but she isn't. She's never been comfortable in the new life that's been created for her. Old ghosts haunt her dreams to the point where she's afraid to sleep. Her nightstand has a glass of water, a lamp and a Glock that rests beside her cell. The nightstand at the other side of her bed has a lamp and another Glock.

This is her life now. Sleeping between two guns so that if she does manage to sleep, she has the reassurance of a firearm close at hand should she be woken by anything other than the latest nightmare. And there have been a lot of nightmares. So many nights spent writhing around the bed as exhaustion and frustration and fear engaged in a three-way fight for supremacy.

Janie had suggested she get a weapon if it would give her peace of mind. She'd gotten two. It's at night when she expects any attack to come. The witching hour is so named for good reason, and Savannah needs a pair of 9mm automatics to face it.

The nights are always the worst. She knows from personal experience people hear strange noises when sleeping in unfamiliar places. Noises that are recognized in your usual environment become foreign and threatening when heard elsewhere. Living on her nerves as Savannah is, there are few nighttime sounds that don't make her heart flutter in all the wrong ways.

As always when trying to snatch some sleep, her mind goes back to the fateful events of that night. Not the night, or another night. *That* night. The night when a bad date had become a life-changing event.

She'd been out with a guy she'd dated a couple of times before. Albie was decent enough and she liked him enough to keep seeing him, although she recognized he wasn't, and never would be, the one. He'd drunk more than was good for him and left her pissed at him when he made comments that jarred against her sensibilities. A guy she'd seen around and knew by reputation but had never spoken to caught her eye. He was looking her way. At the time she'd been flattered by his attention and credited her outfit rather than her looks for the attentions of a solid eight. Whatever his attraction to her might have been, she couldn't help but reciprocate it.

Savannah hadn't wanted to deal with a drunken Albie, but nor did she possess the ill manners to abandon Albie in favor of the enigmatic stranger with the chiseled jaw. When Albie lurched to the men's room, the stranger walked her way. His name was Michel, and he offered her escape from the bad time she was having. She'd defended Albie but had still taken Michel's card when he'd offered it. Albie was that little bit of a bad boy and carried a knife beneath his shirt lest he get into yet another fight. Against her better judgment, she liked that about him, liked taking a walk on the wilder side of life instead of her usual cosseted existence. But Michel, he set her pulse racing for so many other reasons: primal, instinctive reasons.

Michel had slunk back into the crowd, but she'd seen him looking her way three more times in the ten minutes Albie knocked back a couple more shots and suggested they go back to his place. A drunken fool around with Albie held the same appeal to Savannah as a week spent wrestling alligators. She'd gone outside to hail Albie a cab. Michel followed, as she'd hoped he would. So did Albie.

Albie's drunkenness made his interpretation of events wrong. He threw a punch towards Michel who danced back out of the way towards an alleyway. Albie followed, aiming wild swing after wild swing. Once in the alley, Michel stood his ground. Savannah had managed to get between them only to be bumped to the ground by their attempts to get at each other.

From nowhere Albie's knife was drawn and plunged into Michel's chest. Savannah knew some basic first aid and did what she could to stem the bleeding until the EMTs arrived, but she couldn't save Michel. Half an hour later, Albie had been arrested for first-degree homicide and her life had been set on a track she couldn't escape from.

Savannah sees their faces as clear as any movie screen. Albie's, numb and uncomprehending as he clutched the blood-soaked knife. Michel's, paling from blood loss and contorted in pain. She blames herself for Michel's death. Knows that in the darkest recesses of her soul that her actions are what led to his death. That's why she stood up in court; that's why she sacrificed her own happiness and security. That wrongs have to be righted and responsibility taken for the consequences of your actions is a big part of Savannah's belief system. The sole witness to the events of that fateful night, Savannah's testimony was what the whole trial revolved around.

She could have no more slit her own throat than not stand up and give her version of events so justice was served. Doing so has cost her dear. She's given up a loving family and a comfortable, if not opulent, lifestyle. There are no ways back. Her destiny is set to be Pagosa Springs and fear. And yet, for all she's spending every waking moment in terror, she wouldn't change things back. This is a conscious choice she made. Savannah couldn't stand by and let a murderer go unpunished, couldn't not give Michel's family the closure that came with knowing what happened that dreadful night. That they have misconstrued her part in events is nothing more than an unfortunate by-product of her doing what she believed was right.

Savannah hears a noise that has her rolling across the bed and fumbling for a Glock. With it in her grasp she listens again as she slides her cell into the waistband of her pajama bottoms. There it goes again, a scratching sound coming from the back of the house. She retrieves the other Glock and, with one in each hand, she pads her way to the window for a discreet look.

A beam from a flashlight, a human shape or anything that makes her feel threatened will see her dial 911 and prepare to withstand a threat to her life as best the two Glocks will allow her.

Savannah sees a deer silhouetted against the bushes as it grazes in the yard of her house and smiles to herself at the overreaction. "Well played, Bambi. You got me." She sets off back towards the bed convinced there's no way she'll sleep after the scare. Instead of climbing into the bed, she decides to repeat her lockdown routine, if for no other reason than to give herself peace of mind.

The kitchen, lounge and utility room have been checked when the doorbell goes. Its chime both echoing a friendly welcome through the house and twisting a corkscrew of fear through every fiber of Savannah's body.

# CHAPTER SEVENTEEN

Savannah freezes, all her mental preparation should a moment like this arise forgotten in that first second of blind panic. It's five after two in the morning. Nobody knows she's here. Only Janie and others in the US Marshals Service.

Her instincts kick in and she aims the Glocks towards the front door. In her mind questions fight each other for answers. Who rings a doorbell at this time of night? Is there something going on like a forest fire coming their way? Have Janie or a marshal come to move her because they've heard of a threat to her? Have Danny or his vocal sister tracked her down? Is it someone from Michel's family come to exact a proxied revenge on her? There were many accusations in court of her leading him on and therefore being complicit in Michel's homicide. Her lawyer had dismissed such claims, but Michel's distraught father had made enough threats for it to be deemed necessary for her to enter the program.

The one question she can't get past is—what kind of killer rings a doorbell? There is no logical basis for it other than drawing someone to them. It's as she's approaching the door that the answer comes. If she opens the door and stands in the doorway, the potential killer will be able to shoot her without having to breach the security the house offers.

No way should she open the door. No way should she put herself in that position.

Technology saves her. She pulls the cell from her waistband and opens the app that's connected to the video doorbell. There's nothing to see. Nobody stands on her porch. Not a marshal, a hitman, nor even a well-meaning liaison officer.

Savannah notices a rock on her path though. It appears to have a piece of paper beneath it. Her first thought is that it's a form of tethered goat, put there to entice her out and bring her into a position where she can be killed.

Rather than react without thinking, Savannah goes back upstairs. There's a window that overlooks the front door and she plans to use it to scan for anyone who might offer a threat to her. Her hand goes towards the light switch as she enters the room, but stops before it connects. A primal part of her knows that she's safer in darkness regardless of the fears the dark itself carries.

Savannah drops to the floor and crawls to the window. If there is someone out there intent on killing her, she's not going to make it easy for them. A part of her wants to dial 911, but she doesn't want to be the girl who cries wolf. Doesn't want to risk a slower response time when she might really need the cops. She gets to the window and lifts herself to her knees. In slow increments, she moves her head until she can look out at the front of the house. She sees nobody on her first look; her second is a slower sweep that enters parked cars, peers into bushes and examines every line for a human shape.

Not once does she see anything that gives her a reason to feel afraid, yet she's never felt a terror like the one that's gripping her. From this angle, she can see the rock a little better. The paper underneath it flutters in the breeze. She knows she should call 911 rather than go out and retrieve it herself, but the part of Savannah that's seen her join protest after protest for one worthy cause after another is strong. Fears are there to be conquered.

Savannah slinks back from the window and heads back to the front door, heart pounding and pulse racing. It's easy for her to justify a delay in executing her plan. Too easy. She knows that if she doesn't do this now she'll lose her nerve. From the look out of the upstairs window, she's proven to herself there are no obvious threats. The more she tarries, the less convinced she'll become of that observation.

It takes three petrifying seconds for Savannah to undo the bolts and swing the door wide open. Instead of standing in the open doorway, she's cowering behind the door waiting for the thudding impact of bullets into the door. They don't happen. Nothing happens. No gunshots, shouts or running footsteps. A light breeze entering the hall is the only consequence of the door being opened.

Savannah releases the Glock from her left hand and makes a dash for the rock. Terrified as she might be, she has to know what's on that piece of paper.

# CHAPTER EIGHTEEN

Roche watches as the door swings open and Savannah darts out towards the rock he'd left on the envelope. She's fleet of foot and nimble with it. The way she stoops to gather the envelope has him giving her a mental thumbs up. Instead of stopping at the rock itself, she reaches down as her momentum takes her past.

More impressive to him is that with the envelope in her hand she doesn't waste time looking at it. She also carries on two more paces before turning a corner and dashing back to the door. He likes that she has the presence of mind to have a gun in her hand but doesn't waste any time beyond rapid sideways glances to look for threats. Moving targets are always the hardest to hit, and Savannah is in constant motion until she re-enters the house.

When the door careers shut with a hefty slam, Roche pulls out his cell and waits. Savannah will want time to digest the contents of the letter he's left her. She'll need time to recognize her mother's handwriting and convince herself the letter is genuine, and not written under duress.

The letter of introduction had been his idea. There is no point in him arriving to rescue Savannah if she fears him. If he's to keep her alive, he's going to need her complete and utter trust. To get that, he dictated a letter to Mrs. Parker-Nicoll. The wording includes enough details of the threat to scare her into compliance, reassurances that he is on her side and his cell number. The fact it is handwritten by Savannah's mother rather than typed and signed is another way of confirming the letter—and by extension his presence at her door—is a genuine measure of protection being offered. It felt wrong telling Mrs. Parker-Nicoll what to write when describing him and his protective capabilities, but the letter was about inspiring confidence and allegiance, not assuaging any false modesties he possessed.

Ten minutes pass. He understands that she'll be scared upon learning of a definitive and time-sensitive threat. He knows she'll be overloaded with emotion once she sees the childhood nickname her mother included in the letter as further verification.

Xandra's comments about the girl's state of mind are uppermost in his thoughts. He's prepared to deal with a frightened fawn, a wilting flower. Few people are equipped to deal with the knowledge that someone actively wants them dead; fewer still have the strength of character to deal with the fact there is an imminent plan to kill them. Savannah will need time to get her head around all of this. She'll need the strength of her convictions to dial his number. In his mind he's run the timeline of events. Savannah has another five minutes before he's going to be pressing her doorbell again.

He can wait the extra five. He's already scoped out the house from every angle. Weak spots have been identified and in his own mind he's already assaulted the house in several different ways.

His cell rings. An unknown number.

# CHAPTER NINETEEN

Roche answers the call with his name. He's taking as much gruffness out of his voice as he can while also trying not to sound too nice. For Savannah to have faith in him, to trust him with her life, she has to believe in his capabilities. All the same, for the first contact he's trying to strike a balance between nice guy and tough guy.

"I have a letter that's telling me you've been given a password."

"The password is the name of your favorite soft toy as a child. The toy was a blue rabbit and you called it Mr. Pookie Toes."

"Him, not it."

Roche smiles in the darkness. Not only has the password been accepted, but Savannah has just betrayed her inner fortitude with the immediate correction of his pronoun. Yes, it may also be a sign of inward childishness, but after finding someone he shouldn't have been able to find in a mere thirteen hours, he's looking at glasses that are half full rather than half empty.

"Okay. Him. You've obviously read the letter, recognized your mother's writing and convinced yourself that I'm genuine. We wouldn't be speaking otherwise. If I come to the house, will you let me in?"

"I will if you can prove one more thing to me."

"Name it." Roche is smart enough to recognize Savannah will have her own hoops for him to jump through.

"Why you? Why isn't a US marshal here? Or a team of trained bodyguards? No offense, Mr. Roche, but you're only one man and I've never heard of you. What makes you think that you can keep me safe?"

"The US Marshals didn't believe the threat that was made against you. They dismissed it as being made just to scare your mother. I am here because since meeting your mother at noon yesterday, I've managed to track you down. You're in witness protection; you're supposed to be untraceable. Unfindable. Yet, here I am, having not just found you, but traveled to where you were hidden until I'm sitting in a car a hundred yards from your door. I operate in the no man's land between the cops and the criminals. I have connections on both sides of the street. If there is a rotten apple in the US Marshals, you don't want to rely on the US Marshals for protection. A team of bodyguards who can't find you are no protection at all. Enter me, stage right. The white knight who isn't afraid to ride into the darkness to protect your life. I'm not going to lie to you or give you any soft-soap version of events. If the threat made to your mother is credible, then some men are going to try and kill you in the next ten or eleven hours. If they succeed, I don't get paid. If I can find out who sent them, I get a bonus. Now are you going to open the door and let me in, or should I say goodbye instead?"

"I'll open the door." Savannah's voice is soft, as if she's been chastised. It wasn't in Roche's plan to spell out the facts of her current life in such a brutal fashion, but if it earns Savannah's compliance, her mother or the government can afford the therapy she'll need to set herself straight once the case is over. As much as he's being paid to protect her and is subsequently prepared to risk his life on her behalf, he needs to get her on the same page as him and quickly. Someone else can deal with the handholding. His job is the prevention of homicide, both in the short and long term.

"Three knocks, then two, then one. That way you'll know it's me."

# CHAPTER TWENTY

Savannah opens the door and finds herself looking at a strange man. He carries a heavy bag with him and doesn't waste time on pleasantries. His suit looks as though it's spent the first years of its life being worn by a wild orangutan, and his face has a battered and lived-in look about it that makes it a caricaturist's dream.

"My mom's letter. It said there's been a threat made. That I'm to trust you. That you'll save me."

Roche sets his face into as gentle an expression as he can manage. "That's right. I'm Kyle Roche, call me Roche or Kyle. I'm going to call you Savannah. I'm here to look after you and keep you safe, but please don't get me wrong if I'm brusque. I get you're scared. I get that me appearing here has made any threat you've imagined become real. We have a lot of work to do and not a lot of time to do it. So until we're set, don't speak unless it's necessary and then say what you need to say in the fewest words possible. Now, go to the kitchen and get every piece of crockery and glassware you can find and take them to the bottom of the stairs. Take pots and pans as well. Work in the dark without putting a light on. I'm sure you've already done it, but for my own peace of mind, I'm going to check the doors and windows."

It takes Savannah five trips to carry everything to the foot of the staircase. Why he wants them there is beyond her, but as the plates and glasses are solid and heavy, she guesses he plans to use them as missiles.

As he passes the stairs she hits him with a question. "Why aren't you just moving me to a different location?"

"Because it wouldn't be safe. There would always be a trail back to you. Your real name and your assumed one are known to anyone in the US Marshals Service who may have sold you out. Your family can afford a new identity for you and probably to set you up somewhere else, but that'll leave another trail to be followed. Unlike the Witness Protection Program, time won't make you feel safe. You'll spend the rest of your life visiting chiropractors to get rid of the crick in your neck that comes from always looking over your shoulder. For you to ever have a decent quality of life, I need to protect you tonight and then work back up the chain to find out who's sold you out."

"Are you always this full of comfort and good cheer?"

Roche whirls to face her, his face screwed tight with suppressed anger. "I'm expecting a hitman to arrive any time within the next hour or two. If we get through the night, then you may see a sunnier side to me. Until then I'm doing everything I can to make sure we both see the sunrise. You're not the first girl in trouble that I've helped, and I dare say you won't be the last."

Savannah gestures at the pile she's created at the bottom of the staircase. "What do you want me to do with these?"

"Nothing. Go get the bag I dumped in the kitchen and take it upstairs. Then wait there. I'll be with you in a minute."

The bag is heavy and cumbersome. She's tempted to see what he's brought, but he doesn't seem the type to be impressed with snoopers or anything that wastes time, so she stands at the top of the landing with her Glocks and waits for him. For all he's behaving like a complete ass, there's something reassuring about his take-charge manner; and she realizes that if she's to survive the night then he, not some soft-spoken and long-winded wuss, is the kind of man she needs on her side.

A light on the staircase has always been on, so she can watch him as he lifts the piles of crockery she brought from the kitchen. The largest plates get stood on end against each step. Bowls, glasses and cups get positioned at the front of the steps. She gets what he's doing now she sees it. He's creating obstacles on each step. None will stop an intruder from coming up, but there's no way that anyone could creep up the stairs at them.

Roche is here to save her life; the least she can do is pitch in. "What do you want me to do now?"

He points at a doorway leading to a spare bedroom that faces the top of the stairs. "Go in there and drag anything you can find away from the door area. I'm talking three feet clear on either side. When you've done that, there's a window above the porch. Open it and open it wide, that's our escape route."

"Won't the attackers try and get in that way?"

"They'll need ladders, and the window is at the front of the building." Roche never stops laying out the crockery as he speaks. "No attacker worth their salt is going to clamber up a ladder at the front of a building. It's asking to be seen and spotted. Unless you can rappel down a building and smash through a window, gaining access via windows is a good way to get yourself splatterated."

Savannah falls silent as she enters the bedroom and checks that either side of the door is clear. Roche's term "splatterated" is a new one on her, but there's no mistaking what he means by it. Somehow the fabricated word gives a glimpse into the man himself. He's comfortable in his own being. Confident enough to use his own terminology and not worry what others think. In some people it might be construed as arrogance, but from a man who's working feverishly on ways to keep her alive it's almost endearing.

It takes her less than a minute to follow Roche's instructions and prepare the doorway. "What next?"

"Go and get properly dressed. If we have to make a run for it, I want you in outdoor clothes. Put a pair of sneakers or boots on your feet. Something that you can run in. If we have to leave, we'll be leaving in a hurry. You have approximately one minute before I remove the door to your bedroom, so be quick. Also, pack yourself a small bag of toiletries and toss it into my bag. Whatever happens we won't be staying in this house tonight, and as I've already said, the chances are that when we leave we'll be doing so in a hurry."

As Savannah emerges from her bedroom, she sees Roche has already removed every upstairs door save the one on the bathroom. He uses a drill to remove the screws at the hinges of her bedroom door, then adds it to the stack he's created by the door into the room at the top of the stairs.

"We hole up in here. If you need the bathroom, now's the time because we might not be leaving this room until morning."

"I'm good."

Savannah watches as Roche lays the first of the five doors he's collected across the doorway. Next he stands two more on either side, then steps over the makeshift barricade he's created.

She understands that he's using the solid wooden doors as bulletproof screens. That their purpose is to absorb the energy of any shots fired at them. "Why are they outside the room instead of inside? Won't anyone who comes in be able to just toss them out of the way?"

"Of course they can. But if the bad guys get to the top of the stairs, we'll have bigger problems than them being able to move our barricade. They're on the outside of the door so that any bullets that hit them will push them into the wall instead of away from it. They're no use to us if we have to hold them up."

Savannah sees Roche's logic. Despite her fears for what's about to happen, his matter-of-fact ways and practical fortification of the house are reassuring. He knows what he's doing, or at least he's certainly giving her the impression that he does.

He lifts his bag onto the bed and opens it. From it he pulls a pair of automatic pistols and another two guns.

"These are Mossberg shotguns. Special Forces and SWAT teams use them for clearing houses. I'm going to have one and so are you. You are *not*, and I cannot stress the 'not' strongly enough without cursing, to pick it up unless I go down. I'll be at the door." He points to the far corner of the room. "You'll be over there. The spread from it will hit me regardless of how good your aim is. It's got six shots plus one in the barrel. If you have to use it, put it hard against your shoulder and point it in the general direction of anybody you want to shoot. It kicks like a furious mule so it'll hurt, but if you have to use it, it might just save your life."

Savannah nods, her mouth dry at the thought of a close-confines battle. "Where did you get these from? You said earlier that you're from Houston. I can't believe you were allowed to have them on a plane?"

"In my line of work it's always helpful to know people who can get you things. I arranged to collect them when I got to Albuquerque."

Savannah realizes Roche is a lot more than just a battered man in a badly fitting suit. She points at the Glocks. "I have these as well."

Roche's eyes narrow. "I saw that. Have you ever shot them?"

"Only at a range."

"This will be different. It's one thing shooting at a paper target, another altogether shooting at someone who is firing back. If necessary you can use them to cover me, but otherwise leave the shooting to me. Friendly fire is every bit as deadly as enemy fire."

"Sure." Savannah gives him a look. "The big brave man will do all the shooting and the woman will stay at home baking cookies and cornbread."

"The bodyguard guards the principal. The principal doesn't guard the bodyguard." His tone is mild, but his face carries the same amount of criticism as a drill sergeant trying to mold raw recruits into killers.

It's easy for him to tell her not to shoot, and she gets that—as he doesn't know how good she is with a gun, he doesn't trust her not to shoot him by accident—but should an attack come, she's not sure if she can cower in a corner rather than try to defend herself.

"Here." Savannah shows Roche her cell phone. She's activated the app that connects to the internal cameras. "You need to see this. We'll be able to watch them and prepare for their arrival as they move through the house. That way they won't get the jump on us. On you."

Roche takes the cell and peers at it. "As much good as it may be in some situations, it's largely useless to us tonight. The stuff on the stairs is our early warning system. No way can they get past that lot or move it without making a sound." He scans the room. "Have a pen or paper in here?"

"No. What for?" Savannah doesn't get why he needs them. Who uses pens and paper these days anyway?

Roche pulls a face. "Okay, here's the deal. You keep an eye on the screens. Use the fingers on your left hand to indicate how many of them there are. With your right hand: One finger is the hallway. Two, the lounge. Three, the kitchen. A clenched fist is the bottom of the stairs. Two clenched fists is halfway up."

"I got it."

"Good. Now quickly, signal me a few things so we get it right."

Savannah takes him through the house, putting no more than two attackers in the house at any time. The idea of more is too much for her to contemplate.

"See?" Roche pulls a set of car keys from his pocket and lays them on the windowsill. "If we have to leave in a hurry, I'll yell 'abort.' If I do that, grab these, get out onto the porch roof and hang down before dropping. That will give you a four-foot drop, so you shouldn't hurt yourself. Get the car, it's a blue Impala parked along the street to the right; if anyone but me comes out of the house, step on the gas and get out of town. If I'm not with you and you don't hear from me within a couple hours, find a cop and tell them everything."

# CHAPTER TWENTY-ONE

Roche runs over his mental checklist of everything he can do to prepare the house for assault. He's created a strong defensive position, set up a warning system and secured an exit should it be needed. The biggest worry he has is Savannah. There's a wildness to her eyes that speaks of numbing terror. He needs her to be calmer than she is. It's good that she's had the sense to get her own weapons, and the pair of Glocks she carries are what he'd have chosen for her. What is a greater concern is the idea of her using both at once. Movie heroes who use both hands to fire separate weapons at differing targets have a lot to answer for. The reality is that unless a shooter is highly trained, or their target almost upon them, trying to shoot two guns accurately at the same time means neither gets aimed with the necessary care to hit the target. As he's going to be in a position where Savannah is shooting from behind him, he really doesn't want her to provide anything other than covering fire.

All of this would be fine if he could trust her to obey his commands. Even highly trained and experienced soldiers can lose their way when bullets are pinging around. Savannah is a civilian. A scared, frightened civilian who has no experience of battle. The odds are that she'll panic at the first shot, grab one of her guns and then fire wildly towards the attackers. Once that happens, all bets will be off. He expects her aim to be erratic, unfocused and more of a hindrance than a help.

"Listen up. I get that in your modern world you've got issues with traditional gender roles. I'm telling you right here, right now, that bull stops when you are talking to me. Forget man and woman. I'm here to save your life. You're not used to this kind of thing. I am. Because this is my playing field you will do as I say, when I say it and you will not question what I say. The guns you have are not, I repeat not, to be used unless I tell you to use them or I get shot. If you shoot me by mistake, then you've got much less chance of surviving the night. Do you understand what I'm saying?"

"Yes."

"Are you okay with that? Because if you're not then we got a problem. To solve that problem, I'll drive you round until the noon deadline has passed. Then I'll kick you outta my car and collect the payment from your mother for keeping you alive past the deadline. After that you'll be on your own." Roche has no intention of following through on his threat, but he has to have complete and utter compliance from Savannah if he's to keep them both alive. Hurt feelings are nothing compared to a bullet wound.

"I'm okay."

It's good to get confirmation she'll do as told, but he still doesn't trust her to maintain her discipline. Everyone can be brave until they hear the first gunshot.

"I've got these to help keep us safe." Roche reaches into his Bag of Plenty, as he thinks of it, and draws out two bulletproof vests. "They're heavy and cumbersome, but they stop bullets, which means they save lives."

Roche opens the side straps of one and drops it over Savannah's head. She goes to fumble with the straps but he beats her to it. He wants to make sure the vest is on as it should be. Killers aim for center mass, and he doesn't want a bullet sneaking past the vest because she's not pulled the straps as tight as they need to be. As he always does when handling a client, he makes sure that he only makes physical contact when necessary and that contact is limited to areas of the body where impropriety cannot be claimed.

They settle down to wait. Thanks to his barking orders, there's an atmosphere in the room. Roche could care less about any bad feelings from her, but he needs her onside and not feeling resentful that her mother has hired the wrong guy.

"Look, I'm sorry if I came across as brusque, but we were up against the clock and I didn't have time to waste trying to pick the right words. I've done this before and I'm guessing you haven't. As the most experienced person in the room, it's better that I take the lead."

"Really? You've done this before?"

"Yeah, really. I've worked plenty of cases where I have to protect someone from harm. None were quite like your situation, but once I'm with the principal, the basic requirements are the same. Prepare to repel boarders and make sure the principal survives."

"You have protected others?" Something shifts in Savannah's eyes. Hardens as she searches for reassurance. "You ever lost a client?"

"A client, no. Someone I shoulda saved, yeah." Roche doesn't know why he's made the admission. A therapist would point at something, some fancy term like latent guilt, and they'd be right. It's a stick he beats himself with, even though he knows no real blame can be attached to him or his actions.

Pammy died many years ago and, as her elder brother, he should have stepped in sooner. Should have noticed the signs and protected her. He hadn't noticed any signs and, as far as he's been concerned ever since she died, thanks to his inattentiveness, her blood has always coated his hands.

Savannah's hand tugs at the vest. "You lost someone who wasn't a client? So it was a loved one you failed to protect. Want to maybe offer me a reason why knowing this is supposed to make me trust you? Make me feel safe, because right now I'm losing all confidence in you."

"Quit it. We get through tonight, maybe I'll tell you what happened and maybe I won't. But if it makes you feel any better, I lost Pammy more than twenty-five years ago and no one since."

The lack of losing anyone else does make Roche feel better. It's the salve for his conscience, but also the chink in his armor. When he's protecting any client, he goes to places most people would run from. Doubly so if the client is a female and younger than he is.

"Twenty-five years, huh? I don't know if that means you're due another loss or if it means you've learned from your mistakes."

"I've learned, now drop it and hush up. We need to be listening for intruders."

"Don't you tell me to hush. I'm the client here and I can fire you at any time."

"Your mother is my client. As the person I'm paid to protect, you're the principal and therefore can't fire me. I don't want to, but if I have to bind and gag you to protect you, so help me I'll do it. Now please, be goddamn quiet."

Roche can hear Savannah's snorting breaths as she gets her head around her new reality. As much as he understands her fears, now isn't the time to play mother hen and make her feel all warm and comfortable. Now is the time to protect her. Succeeding for Savannah can never make up for failing Pammy, but he's made many vows to himself regarding the people he's paid to protect. Not once has he broken those vows regardless of the risks to his own well-being. He's killed to protect his principals, and he's prepared to kill again if it's necessary to protect Savannah. Likewise, he's taken bullets for his clients and is prepared to do so again.

Time passes slower than a tortoise relay. Shadows cast by the streetlights remain static as the seconds tick past at a pace a sloth would be ashamed of.

Roche's hand shoots up when he hears a noise. He casts a glance over at Savannah to make sure she's on message. Wide eyes tell him she's heard it too. Roche pulls out his SIG and gets himself ready. He's got his SIG pistol in his right hand and one of the Mossbergs hanging from his left. Normally he'd have the guns the other way around, but his wrist aches from where Gilmoure trapped it in the door earlier. The SIG is far lighter than the shotgun and therefore easier to handle. He's also afraid that if he fires the shotgun with a damaged wrist his aim will be off, or that he'll drop it if the recoil jars him too violently.

# CHAPTER TWENTY-TWO

Savannah's eyes peer at the screen. She sees movement. With the lights off downstairs, she sees human shapes rather than defined outlines. Height and weight are hard to judge, but there's little mistaking the fact the intruders are carrying weapons.

Roche gives her a thumbs up as she signals there are two in the kitchen. It makes sense they've gained access from the rear door into the utility room.

She drops a finger from each hand to show one has moved into the hallway, then replaces one on her right hand to show the other is still in the kitchen.

Another thumbs up from Roche. He seems so calm. How he can seem so Zen-like at a time like this is beyond her. His position by the doorway means he will have the stack of doors to protect him from any bullets that come his way. All the same, the doors will only protect him if he stays behind them. The moment he tries to return fire through the open door, he'll be putting himself in the firing line.

The intruder in the kitchen enters the lounge, and she updates Roche. The intruders might be little more than vague shapes, but there's no way she can miss the way they're moving through the house. It's like every action movie she's ever seen where troops of good or bad guys are storming a building. The efficiency they're displaying is enough to make her breath feel lumpen in her throat.

Savannah doesn't know what she expected when she imagined a killer coming for her. In her mind it was always a lone figure, slipping ninja-like through the house, a silenced pistol in their hand. What she's seeing is a military assault by a pair of trained professionals.

Every fiber of her being is telling her to stop goofing around with hand signals and pick up the guns that rest on the bed beside her. She exhales and crushes the primal instincts down. Roche's plan has some merit. If he pops out when the attackers are halfway up the stairs and opens fire, he'll be able to shoot them. Should they manage to return fire, she'll still be able to leap out of the window and make her escape if Roche falls. He's told her she is his principal. Therefore, he's here to defend her; and if her best chance at survival means leaving him behind, then that's what she must do.

The cell's screen flickers a different shade as the attackers team up at the bottom of the staircase. Her right hand clenches into a fist she shakes at Roche. He nods, licks his lips and nods again.

On the screen the attackers pause. Their heads turn to look at each other as they remove what she guesses are night-vision goggles. It's now and only now she realizes the flaws in Roche's preparations.

The stacked doors, the staircase littered with things that don't belong there, they are all signs of fortification. Instead of the intruders thinking they had a clear run, they're now forewarned of a reception committee. Instead of their planned stealth assault, they have a decision to make. Proceed at greater personal risk, or abort and come back another time.

One of the intruders aims a pistol up the stairs as the other bends down to clear a foot-sized space on the second and third steps. Savannah watches as he places the plate and glass he's removed onto the wooden floor with exaggerated care. As careful as he is, there's still a slight scuffing sound that carries up to them.

Roche tosses a questioning look her way, so she holds a palm up to tell him patience.

The intruder's next move is to lean forward, place a hand on the clear space of the third step and collect objects from steps four, five and six.

With the objects deposited on the floor, he ascends the steps until he's standing on the sixth step. He lifts a dish from the seventh step then aims his pistol at the doorway with the dish held behind him for the other intruder to dispose of.

Savannah realizes that regardless of all Roche's planning and defensive measures, their immediate survival rests on her shoulders. It's she who must call the timing, she who will give the instruction to Roche that it's time for him to shoot. She also realizes that if she'd made Roche aware of the cameras when he'd first arrived, he might have planned his strategy differently. The cameras give them an unknown advantage, and the same plan could have been put in place without the forewarning provided to the attackers by Roche's defensive strategies.

Something on the screen catches Savannah's eye. As the intruder on the sixth step is closer to the camera and now illuminated by the landing light, she can make out more detail about him. He's wearing the same kind of body armor she's seen on SWAT teams. That's concerning enough, as it'll make it a damn sight harder for Roche or her to score a telling shot, but of greater worry is what's hanging from his belt. Grenades.

Savannah uses silent steps to get to Roche and show him the screen. He nods and points to his Bag of Plenty and then the window. She gets the message. He wants her out of here, and she's only too happy to comply. One of those grenades tossed through the doorway will kill them both in an instant.

As Savannah makes her way to the window with Roche's bag, she looks back at him. His face is grim and he's clutching his guns as if they are life rings.

# CHAPTER TWENTY-THREE

The grenades are a game changer, and not in a good way. It doesn't matter whether they are fragmentation, incendiary or simple flashbangs. The second that one of them comes sailing through the doorway, it's game over for anyone inside the room. He'd expected body armor and the possibility of night-vision goggles, but not grenades.

Roche adjusts his position and holsters the SIG. His plan has changed and, with the inclusion of grenades in the battle, it's time to bring in the largest firepower at his disposal.

He sets up the Mossberg to use left handed and tucks it into his shoulder. As much as he wants to hurry so he can strike before a grenade is thrown, he still needs to calculate the correct angles. He aims the Mossberg at the drywall and lowers its muzzle until he figures he's got the angle right. He's also got to shoot from a position that will allow the shot to fly past his makeshift barricade and down the staircase.

The Mossberg booms when the firing pin connects with the primer and kicks back into Roche's shoulder. A rapid pump and he's got its muzzle aimed at the hole in the wall the first shot made. Another boom. Another kick and a muffled yelp combines with a faint clatter of crockery being broken.

Roche knows the noise from the crockery should be a darn sight louder, but the twin discharges from the Mossberg in a confined space have left his ears ringing. Bullet holes pock their way into the drywall beside where he'd shot from, so he ducks back to where he figures the stacked doors will protect him. Now it's a question of guesswork, which is never good when there are guns drawn.

He doesn't know what success he's had with his shots. The bullets fired his way could be from one man with two guns or two firing one each. There was a yelp and a fall, but that doesn't mean he's scored a fatal or even debilitating hit. In the glance of Savannah's cell, he picked up that the intruders are wearing full body armor. He's outmatched in terms of firepower, numbers and probably training. The smart move is to get out. Getting out might mean the difference between life and death. It also means that he can't ask the attackers any questions about who sent them. Until he gets those answers, this case will never be over.

The first thing he has to guess at is the attackers' whereabouts. There have been no thudding footsteps to indicate they've gotten to the top of the stairs. That suggests they've retreated to the bottom of the staircase and are planning to try sniped shots. A shotgun such as the Mossberg is deadly at close range, but as the range increases its effectiveness drops.

The attire and behavior of the attackers suggests they're professionals. They'll have seen the damage caused by his shotgun and will have worked out he's using a short-barreled one. Therefore, they'll know that if they stay put at the bottom of the stairs, the shotgun will be much less of a threat to them. What they won't know is what other weapons he has.

They'll expect him to fire from one of two points. Either through the hole in the drywall, or out of the doorway. If there are two of them still active, they'll each cover an option. If only one, then it's a case of guessing and second-guessing which one he'll go for. Get it right and he can pick off the attackers. Guess wrong and he will feel the impact of a bullet.

To confound them, Roche drops down and crawls across the doorway, making sure to stay below the top of the horizontal door he's used as a barricade. Roche stands. His body frozen as he listens for any noise the attackers may make. He can imagine their thought processes. They'll be thinking of tossing a grenade through the doorway. An easy enough proposition on a level field, but with the stairs and his makeshift barricade providing obstacles, the odds of the grenade sailing through the opening are diminished. The last thing the attackers will want is for the grenade to miss the doorway, bounce off a wall and come back towards them.

It's this hesitation to use the grenade that Roche is banking on as he swirls into the doorway and fires both pistols down the stairs. He's not expecting to score a kill shot; instead, he's keeping the attackers back so he can work out a way he can gain the upper hand.

Over the sights of his SIGs he sees the attackers as two dark shapes. His aim is drawn automatically to center mass, his bullets slamming into the chest of the attacker on the right.

The man doesn't go down. He rocks back from the heavy impacts, but he doesn't slump. No blood appears on him. The body armor he's wearing is doing its job.

Roche feels a torturous thump in his own chest as the other attacker opens fire at him. Even as he's ducking back, he's aware of the attacker trying to adjust his aim upwards to go for a head shot.

Bullet after bullet crashes into the barricade. Roche is listening to the pattern and he recognizes that the two attackers are working in unison. One firing as the other reloads. Between them they're keeping him pinned down, unable to return fire.

Rather than make a heroic but suicidal last stand, Roche crouches down behind the barricade and adopts the position of a sprinter in the blocks. As a distraction, he tosses the gun in his left hand out through the doorway and sets off the SIG in his right hand, firing blindly towards the stairs as he sprints across the room and dives through the open window.

# CHAPTER TWENTY-FOUR

Savannah throws out a hand and grabs Roche's arm. His momentum jerks her forward, but the extra weight she adds is enough to stop him from rolling off the edge of the porch roof and plummeting to the ground.

His instant reaction is to throw an elbow her way. The angles are on Savannah's side and the elbow sails past her chin, but she's sure it would have done a lot of damage had she been within reach.

Roche's eyes are wild, but they calm when he sees who has a hold of him. "Sorry, didn't know it was you." He gestures to the edge of the porch. "We need to get out of here. Do what I do and roll when you hit the ground."

Savannah watches as Roche slithers his legs over the edge of the porch. His body follows until his fingers grasp the gutter. He maintains the grip for less than a second before dropping.

An instant later he's waving her down. With gunfire exploding in the house, Savannah doesn't waste time. She drops her legs over the gutter and uses her hands to slow her descent, just as Roche had used his. Her attempt to grab the gutter isn't as successful as Roche's; her right hand gets a good hold, but the fingers of her left scrabble at thin air.

Savannah hangs by one hand. Instead of her body being properly vertical, it's tilted at an angle. If she drops from this position, her feet won't land flat. She'll land on one leg and only if she's lucky will she be able to land that foot square on the ground. At best, she's looking at a turned ankle, but she knows she could be looking at a broken ankle or leg. To make matters worse, the efforts she's made to grab the gutter have left her spiraling. The gutter is digging into her fingers, but there's no way she's going to let go of it.

In the bigger picture, getting away from a murderous attack with only a broken leg or turned ankle can be considered a win. However, Savannah sees her immediate future involving a wild dash across the lawn to Roche's rental car as the attackers shoot at her from the window. The idea of being hobbled or broken as she has to do that is too scary to contemplate.

Savannah feels strong arms encircling her calves.

"Let go."

Upon hearing Roche's command, Savannah's fingers release the gutter. The grip around her calves loosens and she finds herself scraping down Roche. Her back to his front.

The pressure on her calves eases and she slithers to the ground. Roche lets her go a fraction after her boots reach the grass. He doesn't bother telling her to run, as she's haring off towards the rental car as soon as she feels his embrace slacken.

He gets to the vehicle first and heads for the driver's side. "Keys?"

Savannah fishes them from her pocket and tosses them over the hood as a shot whistles past her. Roche catches the keys with one hand and returns fire with the other. The attackers are coming from the front of what was briefly her home. One is offering the other a supporting arm but they both have guns aimed at her and Roche.

The attackers cower down under Roche's barrage, and she uses the moment to clamber into the car. Roche has his own door open and is sliding behind the wheel as he's shooting.

Five seconds later, the engine is roaring and Roche has the car moving off.

"Why the hell were you not off the porch and in the car?"

It is a question Savannah has no good answer for. Roche may have just saved her life, but that doesn't mean he gets to treat her like a naughty child. It had been all she could do to get herself out of the window when bullets were flying her way. Once atop the porch her imagination had kicked in. She'd pictured other attackers waiting for her on the ground, saw herself falling in a crumpled heap of tangled and broken limbs. She'd be at the mercy of anyone who wanted to harm her. Yes, she may have tucked a Glock into her waistband, but there would be precious seconds between dropping and landing when she wouldn't be able to feel the weapon's comforting shape in her palm.

"I asked you a question, lady."

"And I didn't answer it. Man."

Savannah gets that his emotions will be running high after being in a firefight. It's not something she's experienced before, but she can feel herself reacting as her body dumps different batches of hormones. She's getting shakes, feeling sick and yet there's still remnants of the adrenaline that had made her want to join the shooting and unload her pistols at the attackers.

"Listen up." Roche's voice may be a low growl, but it carries enough menace to give her gooseflesh. "When I tell you to do something, you do it. You do it at once and without question. I'm here to save your life, and if you disobey me, your life may well end up not being saved. That means you get yourself thoroughly deaded. I don't know about you, but that's not what I want to happen."

"Screw you, Roche. There's no need to ram your point home quite so hard. I get it."

"You need to." Roche jerks a thumb over his shoulder. "Because we've got ourselves some company."

"Company?"

"Yep. Black SUV. As we left your place, it drew up behind us and my guess is that it was there to collect the gunmen."

"Shit." Savannah glances back. The SUV is a hundred or so yards behind them, but it fills the quiet street with a brooding threat.

"You could say that. Personally, I'd say a whole hell of a lot worse than that and then garnish the curses with a rant full of invective but devoid of repetition."

Savannah glances across at Roche. She can't believe how centered he seems, how calm in the face of adversity. The rental car is a generic sedan. It's got plenty of spec designed for comfort, but for all Roche's efforts to wring a decent speed from its engine, it's sluggish under acceleration and she can't imagine the bulky SUV having the same lack of power.

"Slide your seat back as far as it'll go and get down into the footwell." Roche's hand points as if she's too dumb to comprehend what he's saying. "When you get there, get yourself as low as you can. Chances are they won't fire in a public place, but if they do, they'll be aiming for either the driver or the tires. Take them out and any vehicle stops."

Roche's matter-of-fact way of detailing things irritates Savannah more than she'll ever admit. The complete lack of sugarcoating from him is somehow both terrifying and reassuring. It's clear he knows what he's talking about, and everything he's saying makes practical sense; it's just that she doesn't want to hear it in such precise detail.

Savannah hunkers down in the footwell and, against all of her instincts, puts her entire trust into Roche to keep her alive.

# CHAPTER TWENTY-FIVE

Roche is wringing everything he can from the rental sedan, but he knows it's not enough. The SUV is larger and more powerful. Any advantage he gains from the sedan's more nimble cornering is eaten up the moment he's on a straight road.

Had he arrived in Pagosa Springs earlier, he'd have studied a map and learned the major routes in and out of town. He'd done his best to research Pagosa Springs on the plane, but the Wi-Fi had been patchy and he'd only had his phone, which meant he had to keep zooming in and out. A nice twisty mountain pass would be ideal, but while he sees plenty of road signs, he doesn't know whether they lead to a dead end in a residential area, or a road so twisty he'd be able to outrun the SUV.

Roche considers asking Savannah for directions, then dismisses the idea. She's only been in Pagosa a week and he reckons she'll have spent that week cowering in her house, afraid to go to even the most mundane place like a grocery store.

Another idea is to haul ass to the nearest police department in the hope that the presence of cops will deter the attackers. This idea gets rejected as soon as it enters his brain. First off, there's no guarantee the tactic will work, and they'd be sitting ducks the minute he drew to a halt. Second, the fact the Witness Protection Program has been compromised, suggests that someone in the US Marshals is corrupt. It could be that that person places witnesses in locations where he has contacts in the local PD. Third, Pagosa Springs is a small town in the middle of nowhere. There would be cops, but they'd be minimal in numbers. In the middle of the night, there might only be one on duty. Weekday night shifts don't get handed to the best officers, because the square root of diddly squat is likely to happen; instead, they get passed on to rookies with little experience, or old-timers who've got one hand on their pension and the other resting on a box of donuts. Leading trained killers towards such a cop would merely result in adding another potential fatality to the situation.

He takes a turn, the sedan offering up protests via the screech of its tires. As he always does, he'd gotten the most powerful rental car he could; but there was little on offer from the rental company, and he'd had to sacrifice his desire for a big engine in order to get on the road at the earliest possible moment.

The more he drives the sedan hard, the greater Roche's understanding of the vehicle is. Because it's outmatched for straight line speed, he's making constant turns in order to try and increase the gap between the sedan and the SUV. He's learned that turning it too hard will see the sedan understeer and fail to turn. By the same token, he has to feather the gas pedal if he takes a corner too slowly, as the rear-wheel drive sedan has a tendency to kick its tail out. With every corner he takes, he has to judge the perfect speed to get the sedan round it as fast as possible. As both the car and roads are new to him, he's batting a fifty percent success rate. The one thing he can claim as a definite advantage is the lack of traffic on the roads. The early hour means that save for a very odd truck, he doesn't have to worry about other vehicles being obstacles to his wild attempts to lose the SUV.

A glance down at Savannah shows wide terrified eyes as she hunkers down.

Roche takes a turn and lets out a curse. The turn was good, one of the best he's made, but the road in front of him is long and straight with no side roads he can take. It's a mistake, and he knows it may cost them. He presses his foot harder down on the gas, but the sedan is already giving its all, so the extra pressure on the pedal yields no discernible result.

In the mirror he can see the SUV closing in. In his mind he can hear the roar of its engine, imagine the smug satisfaction of its occupants as they realize the advantage is about to swing back into their favor.

He's damned if he's going to make it easy for them. Ahead of him, the road stretches out in front of the sedan. It's straight, uncluttered and bereft of any possible ways to evade the SUV.

The SUV is closing in at a rate that demonstrates its superior engine. The time from it shortening the gap from a hundred to twenty yards is so small as to be negligible.

Roche is spending as much time looking in his mirrors as he is looking ahead. Neither sight pleases him. In the mirrors the SUV is now large enough to loom, while ahead of him there is not one single thing he can use to his advantage. He knows what the guys in the SUV will be thinking. He recognizes their options as clearly as he's aware of his lack of choices.

The first thing they can do is lean out of the windows now the gap is closed and empty their guns into the sedan. Sooner or later one of their rounds will strike a tire, the gas tank or a human. A second tactic is to run the sedan off the road and into one of the front yards of the houses lining either side of the road. With trees and parked cars littering most yards, there's little chance of Roche and Savannah surviving any such crash in a condition that will allow them to defend themselves. The SUV has a weight and power advantage that will make forcing them off the road easy. Once the sedan crashes, they'll be picked off with ease.

Roche calculates what he'd do if he was in the SUV. It's critical he gets this right as it will define his entire defense strategy. Weaving across the road will offer a good defense against pistol shots, but it will also bleed speed from the sedan. The counter point to this is that a straight course is the best defense against attempts to run you off the road. A straight hit can be bad, but if the wheels are turned even a fraction, then a straight hit takes on a different meaning, forcing the driver to take rapid countermeasures to retain control. If an attacking vehicle is able to hit your rear wing, it has the potential to spin you off the road, or to execute the Precision Immobilization Technique law enforcers use to stop a vehicle by pushing sideways on a rear wing until the car ends up facing the direction it was traveling from.

It's the houses lined at the edge of the street that help Roche make his decision. They're all big houses with tidy yards and good-quality cars on their drives. It's a respectable area, the kind where lawyers, accountants and other professional people live. Gunshots in a part of town like this will result in 911 calls. Far better for the attackers to force them to crash, kill them while they're still dazed from the crash and then make their escape. It's only in Hollywood where shots from one moving vehicle to another have any level of accuracy. A machine gun would do some damage, but if the attackers had a machine gun, it would have been used by now.

The SUV closes to within five yards of the rear fender. It sits square behind the sedan and when it jukes left, as if to draw alongside them, Roche matches its movement. Their fenders kiss, but it is more a peck on the cheek of a great aunt than a lover's snog.

"Change of plan, Savannah." Roche keeps his eyes where they are. One on the rearview mirror, the other on the road ahead. "I need you to lay your seat back and then shoot at the SUV through the rear window. You're not trying to kill the driver or anyone else, just put as many bullets as you can into its front grille."

"Okay."

Roche hears rustling beside him as Savannah moves into action and feels the SIG he is handing over being pushed back at him. "I've still got a gun."

"Be quick. As soon as they see your gun, they're gonna start shooting back."

Savannah's answer comes in the form of a gunshot that is followed by a second. Another pair of shots ring out and the wheel jerks violently in Roche's hands.

The sedan slews under the impact from the SUV. Savannah squeals and falls into his shoulder. Roche ignores her. Such is his focus on keeping control of the sedan he doesn't even look in the rearview mirror to see where the SUV is.

As she rights herself, Savannah pushes on his shoulder, the sudden pressure enough to force him towards the door until he braces himself. Beneath him the sedan squirms, but its tires are good and they bite the asphalt hard enough to allow him to regain full control of the vehicle.

A flick of his eyes towards the SUV shows it has steam coming out from under its hood, but seems otherwise unharmed. It is ten yards behind them and closing in.

Savannah releases four more shots before the SUV thumps into them for a second time.

This impact is far greater than the first and enough to send the sedan on a course Roche can't correct. The sidewalk rushes towards them despite Roche's best efforts to stay on the road. A dropped curb for a driveway saves the sedan's wheels from a hard impact, but the grassy verge offers no traction as the sedan careers towards a white picket fence in front of a sturdy oak tree.

# CHAPTER TWENTY-SIX

Roche feels the sedan go into an inescapable drift and does what he can to counter it, but there is little to no grip to be found on the short grass. The sedan smashes broadside through the fence and keeps thundering towards the tree when the tires find a rogue slither of traction.

Instead of a full-on collision with the oak tree, the sedan's rear wing clatters into the trunk and bounces off on a new heading.

Without stopping and reversing, there's nowhere for Roche to go but into the next house's yard, so that's where he points the hood of the sedan. He skirts a playset and aims the sedan between two trees as he navigates a way back to the asphalt.

A rapid glance over his shoulder shows the SUV has kept pace with them and is some forty yards back. Steam gushes from its radiator, giving Roche hope the SUV is catastrophically damaged.

Once back on the asphalt, the sedan builds speed, but the SUV is a long way from out of the game and it powers forward, its body filling Roche's mirrors with its menacing shape.

Roche spies a side road and takes it. It heads roughly north, but he's confident from its width that it will connect to somewhere a lot farther away than a residential part of Pagosa Springs.

As the SUV takes the turn, Roche pays attention to how quick it catches him up. Before Savannah had put rounds into the SUV's grille, it had oozed power and had made up ground at a frightening rate. Now though, while still faster than the sedan, it is noticeably slower in closing the gap.

With this knowledge at the forefront of his mind, Roche changes his plan again. Instead of using the north-traveling road's twists and turns to open out a significant lead on the SUV, Roche does just enough to keep the SUV on his tail until the sedan passes the town boundary.

For a further five miles he tempers his speed to keep the SUV a hundred yards behind him and then starts to open out a lead.

"Keep going. I think you can lose them." Roche doesn't miss the tension in Savannah's voice. On balance, he's pleased with how she's held up so far. The only real worry he's had about her was the disobedient way she'd remained on the porch roof.

"I could have lost them by now if I'd wanted to."

"What? Why haven't you lost them?"

"Losing them doesn't end this. It's like removing a leg from a starfish: another one will grow back. Wherever you end up, they'll find you. The Leaker is a snake we need to decapitate, and to do that we need a trail to follow." Roche jerks a thumb over his shoulder. "The guys in that SUV, they're the trail."

"Are you for real? There's three of them. How are you going to beat three of them?"

"By fighting smarter than them. As soon as we come to a wooded area, I'll pull over. You jump out and hide in the trees. Once I've dealt with them, I'll shout you."

Roche turns his mind to the problem at hand. Savannah's point about there being three attackers isn't wasted on him. He's going to have to outsmart them to have any chance against their superior numbers and weaponry.

As the sedan powers through the darkness, he refines his plan as best he can until they enter a wood. He pulls over after a hundred yards, and Savannah jumps out and runs off into the darkness.

Roche drives on until he comes to a sharp corner a quarter mile on. Rather than take the corner he runs the sedan off the road and down a bank until it crashes into a tree. With the sedan at a standstill, he thumps the heel of his hand into his nose and snorts blood spatters over the inside of the sedan. Before exiting, he leans across and throws the passenger door open.

He runs from the sedan, making sure to leave a trail of scuffed footprints.

After traveling fifty yards, Roche slows and takes careful steps in a wide arc that will route him back to where he can monitor the SUV's arrival. His trap is set and baited. All he needs is for his prey to step into it.

# CHAPTER TWENTY-SEVEN

Savannah keeps her back against a tree and peeks round the trunk. Her eyes are focused on the road back to Pagosa Springs. No lights come. No racing engines cut through the night. No sudden gunshots ring out.

Roche repeating his point about this not being over until the leak from the US Marshals office is plugged is at the forefront of her mind. She recognized the truth of his words the first time he'd said it; she just didn't like hearing it again.

The idea of him dealing with the two attackers and the driver by himself is alien to her. She saw the attackers as they came for her house, saw the body armor they wore, and recognized the professional way they moved through the house and then made their assault. The attackers are well-trained, not just random hoods.

As she works all this through in her mind, Savannah's senses remain on full alert. Eyes and ears strain for sight or sound of the SUV. Her hands grip the Glock tight enough so that she can use it at a moment's notice, but not so tight cramping becomes an issue. Her nose is attuned to the woodland smells of decaying leaves and pine needles, but searching for something that shouldn't be there: cologne, cigarette smoke or body odor.

Not one of her senses is triggered. She pumps her knees forward one by one to maintain circulation in her legs, but nothing happens that requires her to take a step.

Savannah would take out her phone to check the time if she wasn't afraid its glowing screen would pinpoint her location. Off in the distance a rustle in the darkness has her snapping her head. For all she's developed some degree of night vision, Savannah can only see blackness beyond the first few yards. Her ears strain to pick up more sounds, but the thing she hears loudest is the beating of her heart. As much as she can, she tries to calm herself, to slow the thudding in her chest and quell the tremor in her every muscle.

Time ticks past with a glacial slowness that stretches her already-taut nerves to breaking point. There's no easing, no end in sight to this torment. How long Roche is prepared to wait is unknown to her.

The more time passes, the more she begins to think the SUV isn't coming. She'd dinged it good and the last she'd seen of the vehicle, it hadn't looked healthy. Steam or smoke was pouring from its hood, and while Savannah would be the first to admit she knows nothing about engines, it stood to reason that hard driving wouldn't do a damaged engine any favors.

Maybe the SUV has packed up, or perhaps the attackers have realized they were losing their prey and have given up in preparation to strike again. Whatever the case is, it doesn't look as if they are coming.

The thing Savannah fears the most is that the attackers have anticipated Roche's move and are coming across country on foot. That they're already creeping up on her. They'd worn night-vision goggles in the house. Out here in the darkness of the woods, those night-vision goggles will afford the attackers an insurmountable advantage.

Her body shakes as the act of keeping still robs her of any body heat. It might be warm during the day, but in the middle of the night with no sun to offer warming rays, the temperature isn't far above freezing and she isn't dressed for a hike in the woods.

Savannah clamps her mouth shut to prevent her teeth chattering. This turns into a grind when she hears a noise. It's off to her right, the opposite direction to where Roche had gone, but the very direction she's expecting the attackers to come from if they're on foot.

The noise repeats itself. It's the rustle of leaves and branches being disturbed. Savannah's grip on her pistol tightens as she raises it towards the noise. Her eyes pick out no shapes. No movement registers. Only blackness and fear.

There's a grunt. Not a human grunt, the grunt of an animal. Savannah has no idea what animals may be living in these woods. It could be nothing more than a deer, or something like a cougar or jaguar. Whatever it is, for all she's prepared to defend herself against it, the idea of shooting an animal goes against every one of her beliefs. She'd climb a tree if she could, but there's no easy way to do that and she daren't turn her back on whatever's out there.

The rustling increases and she hears the sound of rapid movement followed by a brief animal squeal. Savannah pulls her shredded nerves back under a semblance of control as she realizes that she's not the prey that particular hunter is after.

"You can lower your weapon. They're not coming."

Savannah whirls round, annoyed with herself for the panicked yelp she lets out. Roche's voice is calm and low. How he'd found her in the darkness. How he'd managed to get so close to her without her being alerted to his presence is beyond her, but instead of reassuring her about his skills, it strikes a shard of fear into her.

"How do you know that?"

"Trust me, I do." He points in the general direction of the road. "Come on. We'll have to get the car back on the road and then find a motel to hole up in."

# CHAPTER TWENTY-EIGHT

When Roche tries to back the sedan away from the tree he finds the back wheels just spin. His fingers cut the engine at once. The last thing he wants is to dig the wheels in and beach the vehicle. He points to Savannah. "You get some small branches and push them in behind the rear wheels. I'll see what I can find by way of a branch to act as a lever."

Five minutes later he's ready to try again. The ground behind the rear wheels is now carpeted with traction-enhancing branches and he's holding a sturdy branch. He digs the end of the branch into the ground under the front fender and raises it until it makes contact with the fender. It's now at a forty degree angle. Savannah is in the driver's seat. A look of disgust adorning her face at the blood he'd spattered in there earlier.

Roche puts his shoulder against the branch, flexes his muscles and sends a nod at Savannah and heaves. The front of the sedan lifts a little, but the more he heaves, the more the angle of the branch increases. As well as his levering putting more of the sedan's weight onto its rear wheels, it's also pressing the sedan backwards.

Savannah follows the instructions he'd given her. She's got the sedan in reverse but with the engine barely ticking over. As it starts to claw its way backwards, she feathers the throttle a fraction then stomps her foot down when it starts to move.

A minute later, Roche is driving them onward along the road. He'd like to push the sedan harder, but it's been through the wars and he's sure at least one wheel is rubbing the wing surrounding it.

"Where are we going?"

"Wherever this road leads us. We need to find somewhere to rest up and I need time to think."

Roche keeps his mouth shut. He's already done a lot of his thinking, and he's not comfortable with his thoughts. Most of this discomfort is centered around Savannah, but for the time being he has to park that. He needs to work out the details of his plan. To finesse the finer points. First though, Roche pulls over and gets his Bag of Plenty from the trunk. From the bag he pulls a burner cell that he hands to Savannah. "Here, use this to call your handler in the Witness Protection Program. Tell them that you escaped from a potentially deadly attack and fled fearing for your life. Don't mention me, and for God's sake don't tell them where we are now."

Savannah takes the burner and pulls her own cell out. "Why can't I use this?"

"Because it's possible that's tracked. I want you to take the SIM card from it and toss it out the window. The next time we pass any kind of gulch, river or ravine toss the cell itself."

"Why not just toss the cell now?"

"I want to separate the two of them, and a ravine or gulch or river will do far more damage to the cell than the soft shoulder will. It's amazing what you can get back from those things if you know how."

Roche watches as Savannah swipes her way into her cell and then types a number into the burner. For this simple act, he places a mark in the negative column of his suspicions about her.

She makes the call and ditches her SIM card as ordered, but Roche doesn't speak to her again and nor does he answer any of the questions she puts to him.

A half hour's drive sees them enter a town. It's not one of any great size, but it has what they need: a motel.

Roche hands a sheaf of notes to Savannah. "Here. Go across there and book us a room. Book it for two nights and make sure you use whatever name you're supposed to go by now."

"You're joking me?" Savannah's eyes are wide. "Surely we should be using a false name. Your name would do. All you're doing is giving them a trail to follow."

"Exactly. Do I have to mention the starfish or the snake again? To make sure you're safe long term, we need to have contact with them."

"This is stupid. You'll get us killed."

"No, I won't. We're not going to actually be in the motel room. We'll be elsewhere, watching it to see if they come."

"And then what? We can't exactly sit in a car they've been chasing. This might be a crappy rental, but it's beat up enough to be memorable."

"Agreed. You book the motel. I'll sort us out some new wheels. Once you've got the room booked, go to it and put the burner under the mattress. If they're tracking the number, they'll go to it thinking we're there. Once you've dumped the burner in the room, make your way to the grocery store over the street. There's an alley beside it. Wait for me there."

Roche drives off and moves aimlessly around the town until he finds what he is looking for: a bar. The bar is closed, which suits him just fine. Outside the bar is a parking lot that sports three vehicles. A modern truck, a sleek Mercedes and a pickup that looks old enough to have arrived in America aboard the *Mayflower*.

He parks the sedan beside the pickup and looks it over. For all it's ancient, there are no evident oil leaks from it, the tires are new and the interior shows signs of care rather than neglect. Old vehicles don't have alarms. Nor do they have tracking devices. Vehicles left at bars aren't needed first thing in the morning. In a town like this, when you leave your wheels at a bar overnight, it's because you've properly tied one on; therefore there's no way you're going to be retrieving it any time soon.

Roche tries the door handle, it's open. Of course it is. Nobody would worry about someone stealing this pickup. To anyone but its owner, and someone with shares in a junkyard, it's worthless.

The other thing about old vehicles that makes them easy to steal is they're easy to hot-wire. For someone with Roche's skills, stealing the pickup is easier than boiling an egg.

*

Savannah emerges from the alleyway and climbs into the pickup when Roche pulls up. She doesn't comment, but there's enough derision on her face for there to be no doubts about her thoughts on their new transport.

Roche doesn't speak until he's got the pickup parked on a side street that lets them observe the motel's sole entrance. He's had enough time to go over things in his head and every thought he's had has raised a question.

"Okay, Savannah. We've got some time on our hands and we need to talk, and talk big. First off, tell me why you didn't get off the porch roof and get into the car like I instructed you?"

Savannah doesn't speak at once, but Roche hears the rustle of her shifting in her seat as she composes her answer.

"I was scared there may be more of them waiting on the ground." She turns her head and looks at him with venom. "Which there was. If I'd done as you said, then the driver of that SUV could have drawn up alongside and shot me easily."

"Bull. If he was an active combatant, he'd have been in the house instead of stationed along the road. He was a driver, nothing more. The delay in getting you down from the roof meant they could close in on us. It could have been enough to let us get away scot-free."

"Get away? The minute we did get away, you stopped and waited. You set an ambush, damn you. That's not getting away."

"I turned things to our advantage once I knew the initial risk had passed and I'd made my assessment of our foes. If they'd had an automatic rifle in that SUV, we'd be getting fitted for a toe tag right around now. We didn't know that when I gave the order for you to get to the car. I can't stress this enough, lady. You'll get yourself splatterated if you don't do as I say, when I say."

"Please, my name is Savannah, not 'lady.' Could you remember that when you're addressing me? It's the twenty-first century, so it'd be nice if you treated me like a twenty-first-century citizen."

Roche keeps his face neutral. Savannah has just waltzed into his trap and made another black mark in the negative column of his thinking. He's starting to believe that she and her mother have held a lot back on him. Savannah should be freaking out about the attempt on her life: she isn't. She's riding him about how he's addressing her. She's not protesting enough about the fact she's in constant danger. He's been in this situation before and, every time, the principal was begging to be placed somewhere safe, pleading with him to protect them. Savannah ought to be doing those things, but she isn't. Sure, she's making protests about him following the trail back to the person who's leaked her information, but she's giving in far too readily for his liking. When he'd given her the burner, she'd had to look up the number to call her US marshal handler. To Roche's way of thinking, that number should have been burned into her memory within three seconds of her being given it.

"What about the gun you had? Why didn't you tell me you were armed? What if it had gone off when you were jumping down from the porch? It could have shot either of us if the safety got knocked off."

"It's a Glock. The safety is in the trigger mechanism."

Roche lifts an eyebrow. "If I'm not allowed to call you 'lady,' then you're not allowed to speak to me in a tone that implies I'm an idiot. How do you know about the safety on the Glock?"

"I got the guy at the gun store to teach me about the gun. I know how dangerous they can be and I didn't want to shoot myself or anyone else by accident. Have you finished with your questions, because I have some for you?"

"For now I have, fire away."

"Don't tempt me." Savannah huffs out a breath and lets her shoulders slump. "Those attackers at the house, they were wearing body armor and carried grenades as well as pistols. There were two of them. I thought that if anyone came it would be a single person, dressed normal and carrying a pistol. They looked like they were part of a SWAT team. Why? What's so dangerous about sneaking in and killing me, a defenseless woman?"

Roche drums his fingers on his leg and makes a point of trying to keep his tone gentle. "You weren't defenseless though, were you? Forget about me being there and the stuff I did. You had a pair of guns in the house. If I was in their position, I'd have wanted someone I trusted with me. I would sure as hell have worn whatever body armor I could source. As someone who's just been inserted into the Witness Protection Program, you'd be terrified. I don't expect you've been sleeping well. I'd anticipate you waking at the slightest noise. I'd expect that every time you got scared you reached for the comfort a weapon in your hand gives. If I was taking on a target who was scared, jumpy, alert to new and foreign sounds and likely to have a weapon to defend themselves, I'd be heavily protected and armed too. It might sound foreign to someone with your background, but to me it's basic common sense."

"Well, if you understand all that and pass it off as basic common sense, why do you have to be such an ass to me all the time?"

"I'm here to keep you alive, not hold your hand. You want your hand held, go call mommy. If you want to see your next birthday, stop holding out on me and start doing as I tell you."

"Bite me."

Roche lets the insult slide. He's still not broached the one point that's raised his suspicions more than any other. Savannah had fired eight shots towards the grille of the SUV. They'd been in four pairs. Two pairs before they got bumped the first time and two more before the collision that had almost put them into the sturdy oak. He doesn't think of them as four pairs though; instead, he's thinking of them as double taps. The kind of double taps used by someone who's been properly trained in how to use a pistol.

He's chosen not to bring this suspicion to the table yet. He wants to keep his powder dry before making any accusations about Savannah's ability to shoot, or the way she'd been calm enough to score successful hits. Most of the principals he's protected in the past would have done well to hit the SUV once; yet, by his count, Savannah had scored five telling shots.

A large black SUV slides hesitantly into the parking lot of the motel, draws to a halt and then reverses so its hood is pointing at the street. Two dark clad figures climb from the passenger side, but the driver stays put. The fact one of the figures has a pronounced limp is all the proof Roche needs that it's the same hit team they tangled with earlier.

Roche glances at his watch, a battered Timex given to him by Leigh on their first Christmas together. "They got here within an hour twenty of you making the call. That's quick. Whoever is leaking is on the ball and actively overseeing things."

"Does that surprise you?"

"Nope. It just means things are gonna be harder than they need to be."

# CHAPTER TWENTY-NINE

"Here's the plan. You take the wheel; when I wave like Forrest Gump, you bring the pickup over. I'll do the rest."

"You're taking them on alone?"

"Of course. You're the principal. No way am I going to risk getting you involved. If things go bad, haul ass to the nearest police station and kick up as much stink as it takes for you to feel safe."

Roche doesn't waste time giving further instructions to Savannah. He needs to catch up with the two attackers before they discover the empty room.

To retain the element of surprise on the driver waiting in the SUV, he leaves the alley and immediately takes a right so he's out of sight of the motel. There's no way for him to know if the driver is in radio communication with the two gunmen, but he takes it as a given considering how well-equipped they had been earlier.

Roche crosses the street and puts his back against the wall of the motel. The motel is L-shaped with the parking lot in the center. Four steps get Roche to the edge of the building. He could peek round the corner and take a look. He doesn't. Instead, he buttons up his coat to hide as much of the blood from the nose he'd burst earlier and lurches round the corner in his best impression of a drunk.

Step by uneven step he moves forward in a series of drunken sways. His head is down as if he's looking for dropped money. When he gets within five feet of the SUV, he fakes a dramatic stumble and uses the move to disguise his true intent.

In a swift movement he whips the SUV's door open and puts a pair of silenced bullets into the head of the driver. The driver doesn't have time to register anything more than momentary shock before being shot. Roche feels nothing about the man he's killed. So far as he's concerned, anyone who is involved with hitmen deserves everything they get. Had the driver been competent enough to lock the SUV's doors, he might have lived a few seconds longer, but he wasn't.

Roche approaches the reception area. It's in the join between the motel's two wings and shows signs of impending crumminess, unless there's an imminent refurbishment program in the works.

Behind the chipped counter an aged receptionist is slumped in his chair. There's blood on his chin and holes in his chest. The death of an innocent like the receptionist means far more to Roche than the driver's untimely end. A part of Roche's brain is already working out that as he's heard no shots, the gunmen must have also fitted suppressors to their pistols.

Savannah has given him a description of the motel. Told him where the room with the hidden burner is.

The room is halfway along the corridor to his left. A5. Roche throws a rapid look at the panel supporting a bundle of keys on hooks. Things are as he'd hoped. The motel's down-at-heel appearance means there are vacancies. Not knowing how the numbering is laid out, he scoops the keys for A4 and A6 into a pocket and moves down the corridor quieter than a wisp of smoke and carrying a SIG in each hand.

With there being no sign of the gunmen he's ultra-cautious. He can guess what they're doing. Upon finding no sign of him or Savannah in the room, they'll be having a quick decision-making session. They'll be wondering if they've been led on a wild goose chase, or whether they should lie in wait. Sooner or later one of them will realize that if they're to lie in wait successfully, they'll have to dispose of the receptionist's corpse. It could be they've put in a call to their boss for instruction. Whatever they're doing, they won't be doing it for long. Any second they'll leave the room for one reason or another.

Roche is twelve feet from the door of A5 and two from A6. He puts the SIG in his left hand under his chin and fumbles the key into the lock by touch alone. Not once does he allow his eyes to stop peering over the sights of the SIG in his right hand.

He gets the door open and makes his play, his voice deepened and given a drunken slur. "Hey, sweetcakes, Daddy's back and he's ready for some of that good lovin' you got goin' on."

It's a calculated risk that Roche is taking. While the gunmen have proven they're willing to kill innocents, he's confident they'll want to limit the number of kills. A murdered receptionist is one thing: suspicion will land on the guests. A pair of drunken lovers being added to their tally will only increase police pressure. By the same token, the presence of awake witnesses will limit the gunmen's options. The receptionist would have been killed because he'd seen their faces. The supposed lovers haven't, and therefore offer no threat.

Roche keeps the handle turned as he bangs the door closed. As soon as the timber hits the frame he opens it again and lies in wait, with both SIGs aimed along the corridor towards the door of A5. Positioned as he is only Roche's head and hands are showing. He's a small target, but when the gunmen exit A5, they won't be small targets: they'll be life-size. Except they won't be. They'll still be wearing their body armor. Shots at their center mass will be absorbed. To be certain of surviving this encounter, Roche knows he must go for head shots. His target: the faces of his aggressors. Tactical helmets only protect from the sides, behind and above.

The problem with shooting the men in the face is that they'll be too dead to answer his questions. This means that Roche has to kill one of the men but disable and then disarm his buddy. No matter which way up he stands it, Roche knows that he's going to be damned lucky to kill one gunman and disable the other without any shots coming his way.

As the seconds tick past, Roche begins to wonder if he's made a mistake. The gunmen might not even be in the room. They've maybe checked it and moved on. They could be scouring the streets looking for an all-night diner where their prey might be refueling.

Roche hears a hissed whisper and footsteps. The SIGs in his hands are gripped that fraction tighter as he starts to take up pressure on their triggers. Over their sights he's focused on the corridor. It's tempting to aim at the doorway, but by the time he registers his targets are out of the room, he'll have to adjust his aim. The pistol in his left hand is aimed five feet from the ground and three feet from the door. The one in his right is aimed waist-high and is eighteen inches from the door, which means it's close enough to be retargeted should a head pop out for a peek before the men exit the room.

No head pokes out from the room. Instead, two men wearing body armor walk out at pace. Each has a gun in his right hand, but the gun is pressed against their thighs in a compromise between discretion and protection. The first guy makes a simple mistake. It's a fifty-fifty toss-up and he chooses wrong. Upon exiting the room he looks right first. Maybe it's a throwback to being taught road safety by his mom, or because he's right-handed. Whatever his reasons for the choice, it means he doesn't get even the slimmest chance of identifying the threat from Roche before his face is struck by the first of two bullets.

The second guy fares better. He was always going to. The fractions of a second Roche has used to make sure his aim is true on the first guy have given the second a chance. His gun comes up as Roche's rounds thud into his legs. He goes down screaming, but his gun never leaves his hand as he pumps rounds Roche's way. As much as Roche wants to put a round into the guy's gun arm, he doesn't.

Roche's next shot hits the guy in the upper thigh. The body armor covering his thigh will absorb the bullet, but it'll feel like the leg has been hit with a sledgehammer.

"Stop shooting or you die just like your buddy." Roche's aim is adjusted until it's square on the guy's face. "Drop your weapons and clasp your hands together above your head. I won't shoot you unless you make me. Understand?"

The gunman nods, his face tight with pain. Fear dances in his eyes with all the grace of a drunken uncle at a wedding. He takes care to make a show of not aiming his pistol Roche's way as he drops it then laces his fingers together above his head.

Roche steps out from the room and keeps his guns aimed at the guy. When he's within reach, he kneels down and presses the barrel of the SIG in his right hand underneath the body armor at the guy's groin. The SIG in Roche's left hand gets holstered and he goes on to strip the guy of all his weapons.

"What are you going to do to me?"

"We're gonna play a little game. It's called Question and Answer Time."

The guy's eyes close and he gives a huge swallow. "Then you better just kill me now, because there's no way I'm going to talk. They know where my family is."

Roche has expected some form of resistance and here it is, right on cue. His boot lashes out and catches the guy in the jaw. Hard enough to stun, but not hard enough to break bones. He rolls the gunman over and slips a pair of Plasticuffs onto him.

With the gunman now groggy and disarmed, Roche gathers up the weapons, grabs the collar of the guy's shirt and drags him out to the parking lot. As soon as he's outside, he gives a big wave and waits for Savannah to come across. He raises a finger to his lips. "No names."

Savannah has to help him lift the gunman into the pickup's load bed; but less than a minute after exiting the motel's reception, they're powering out of town as fast as the ancient pickup will go.

# CHAPTER THIRTY

Savannah's head is in a whirl as Roche drives out of town. She'd expected Roche to be brutal, but the way he'd executed the SUV's driver was something else. The guy she'd helped put in the back was alive, but she doesn't expect he'll stay that way. Every one of her thoughts is centered on wondering if her mom made a mistake selecting Roche as her savior.

A glance across at him shows his face set hard. She gets that. He's just risked his life. Committed at least one instance of first-degree homicide. All to save her. The presence of the guy in the load bed needs no explanation. Roche has lured the potential killers to a trap and then captured one of them. This is something else she gets. The gunman in the load bed is the key to Roche identifying the Leaker. The man will be questioned and, after seeing how ruthless Roche can be, Savannah is fearful for the man's immediate health.

Or at least she would be, could she not feel the burning rage inside her. As with every moment of passionate feeling she's ever experienced, the strength of her emotions are threatening to overwhelm her. The guy in the back has tried to kill her. He may have killed… No. No way can she think those thoughts. She needs to stay focused. To stay in control. Since Roche arrived there's been a gunfight and a near-deadly car chase. After that she witnessed a man being killed and another taken hostage. This is so far away from her usual world of garden parties, charity events and social functions she's struggling to make sense of anything. The only other time she's experienced anything like this was the night that prompted her to have to join the Witness Protection Program, and that happened in a few blurred seconds. This has taken place over a couple of hours.

Roche hauls the wheel over and sets off along a forest track. He's making no concession to the ruts and the potholes left by loggers and is bouncing the pickup over every obstacle. The thud from a pothole both jolts her spine and lifts her out of the seat.

"Jeez, Roche. Can you not slow down?"

"Nope. There's some meat in back and I want it nice and tender."

Savannah turns her head, braces herself against the next violent movement from the pickup and takes in the gunman as he rolls around the load bed. Roche has stripped him of his tactical helmet and she can see blood on his head from where he's slammed into the side of the load bed. As Roche fords a small stream at pace, she sees the gunman jolted into mid-air before slamming down into the load bed as it shoots up from the next bump. With his arms tied behind his back, he has no way of protecting himself from impact after impact.

It's a purgatorial experience for the gunman, and not one she fancies for herself, but it doesn't mean she feels pity for him. At one point she gets a look at his face. It's knotted with pain, but she can see the blue of his irises. His ears protrude from his head in a way that's sure to have earned him a lifetime's teasing. None of this matters to Savannah; this is the first time she's looked into the face of a murderous enemy, and all she feels for the man is hatred.

Savannah isn't naïve enough to think that Roche is bringing the man out into the woods for a nature ramble. His comment about tenderizing meat is a sure signpost to his intentions. Roche plans to torture the guy, or at the very least threaten torture until he learns what he wants to know. She knows she ought to be aghast at such a concept. Torture happens in movies. In places like the Middle East or Guantanamo Bay. Torture isn't something that happens in her world. It's a remnant of bygone days, like slavery, or leaving home without your cell phone.

Dawn is breaking, a new day full of promise and here she is, traveling with a guy who's killed at least once in the last hour and a prisoner from whom he wants information.

Savannah is sure that within a matter of minutes she'll not just be witnessing actual torture, but will actively be complicit in it. Inside her head, Savannah is arguing with herself. Being kind to others at all times is a tenet she's tried to live by since she was old enough to understand how kindness engendered people to her. Until recently, she's lived a good life, helped others. Maybe she hasn't always made the difference she's wanted to, but she's tried her best. That's the good part of her brain speaking; it's her true self being appalled at the idea of deliberate actions that have no purpose other than to inflict pain on another human being. Rather than being scared all the time, as she has been since entering witness protection, she wants to go back to being her former self. Wants to not lash out with words for no reason other than her own strung-out nerves.

Her primal brain has other thoughts. They are relishing the idea of seeing the man who'd tried to kill her screaming in agony. The prospect of him begging for his life gives her shivers of anticipated pleasure. Her instincts want the man to be torn limb from limb for what he's attempted to do to her. For what he may have done to others. He is not a man who deserves pity. No pleas for mercy can save him from this part of Savannah. She might not help Roche harm this guy, but nor will she feel inclined to stop him. A part of her primal brain wants to get involved, to dish out punishment to this monster who's invaded her life with the aim of murdering her. She wants to lash out at him, to punch and kick and shoot the guy, but deep inside her consciousness, she knows she must stay in control. If she loses it with the guy, she might kill him before he tells Roche what he needs to know. Savannah doesn't want the gunman's blood on her hands. Not when he's helpless. If it comes to a fight situation, she's confident she can kill and live with herself. To execute a prisoner is wrong on every possible level, and it's at this point she realizes that she has no idea what Roche will do to the guy once he's learned what he needs to know.

Roche pulls into a clearing and stops. His next move is to gesture at the bag he's stowed by her feet. "Pass that up, will you?"

Savannah watches as Roche retrieves a length of rope from the bag and climbs into the back of the pickup. He lashes one end of the rope around the gunman's wrists and gives him a nudge with his boot.

"Am I going to waste my breath asking your name?"

A small shake of the head. The guy is wise enough to know which battles to fight and which to concede. "Everyone calls me Wingnut."

One look at Wingnut's protruding ears explain his nickname.

Roche leans over and drops the tailgate of the pickup. "Okay then, Wingnut. It's time to go for a little walk. I need hardly remind you that we have guns. You know I'm prepared to kill, and you know why I've kept you alive. You can survive this without any further hurt. You can go home and see your family again. Or you can do something stupid that will end up with you screaming in pain. It's your choice, but just so you're making an informed decision about your levels of co-operation, the longer I believe I'll get what I want from you, the longer you don't have to worry about the sudden onset of rigor mortis. All I want from you is the code to get into your cell and a few questions answered. Give me them and I'll be happy to release you, alive and well."

"Screw you, asshole. I'm a dead man. I know it. You know it. And that blonde bitch with you knows it."

Something in Savannah snaps and before she can get control of her emotions, she's stepping forward and slamming her hand into the side of Wingnut's face. "Don't call me a bitch, you murdering douchebag."

"Enough of that now, children." Roche grabs the back of Wingnut's shirt, hauls him off the pickup, then jumps down and drags him off into the woods. Wingnut is squirming to break free, but Roche's grip is strong and the curses that spill from Wingnut's mouth are ignored.

The sun has risen enough to lift the darkness, although it's not yet high enough to fully illuminate the forest to daylight levels.

Fifty yards into the wood, Roche releases his grip on Wingnut, trips the man and throws the coil of rope over a sturdy branch that's as thick as Savannah's waist. She watches as Wingnut tries to rise to his feet while Roche gathers the loose end of the rope and walks towards a fallen tree.

Savannah steels herself for what is about to come. It's obvious Roche has a plan in mind for Wingnut, and that plan doesn't involve anything remotely kind.

# CHAPTER THIRTY-ONE

Roche has tied many knots in his time. Sometimes just securing a load to a truck, or a sail to a boat. That's one of the things about living in a port city like Houston, you get used to there being a certain nautical element to your life and Roche's life has been rich and varied.

More than once he's used rope to bind a prisoner, but zip ties and Plasticuffs are what he uses now as they're much quicker and easier to apply.

The knot he's tying now is a simple clove hitch that he uses to secure the end of the rope for a moment. So long as that knot is in place, he's able to release his hold on the rope and go over to where Wingnut has risen to his knees.

"Last chance to not feel any more pain, Wingnut. I know you reckon you're a dead man, but I swear I'll release you if you tell me who hired you. If you tell me where I can find them, you'll be able to go home and make sure your family is safe. You and your buddy tried to murder me and my principal earlier. You came back for a second attempt. I'm still willing to let you live if you give me the name of whoever hired you. Hell, even the code for your phone will do. But, and this is a huge but, if you resist me, if you don't talk to me, even after encouragement, then one way or another, I'll find out who hired you. And before I take them down, I'll make sure they know that you talked. That you led me to them." Roche raises a hand as Wingnut's mouth opens. "Don't bother cursing me out. I've heard worse. My father was the first man I ever wanted to kill, and there's no insult you can throw my way that he hasn't already bettered. Now do you want to talk to me?"

Even the mention of his father in this context raises a long swell of hatred within Roche.

A bead of sweat runs down Wingnut's cheek then flies off as he shakes his head.

Roche doesn't speak again. Doesn't utter another sound as he steps behind Wingnut, pushes him so he falls face down in the mulch of the forest floor and strides back over to the fallen tree he's secured the other end of the rope to. Not once does he look at Savannah. She's off to one side, and while her reaction to the forthcoming events is sure to be revelatory, he's got other things to deal with right now.

With the clove hitch loosened, Roche clambers onto the fallen tree and starts to tie a whole different kind of knot. A trucker's hitch was used to tie loads onto flatbeds before the advent of straps. It works like a block and tackle, and once tied, leaves a loose end that can be hauled upon to increase the pull of a rope. With this knot, Roche can exert far more than his own strength on the rope that loops over the sturdy branch and ends at the wrists tied behind Wingnut's back.

A trucker's hitch isn't hard to tie for someone with Roche's experience, but as Wingnut is currently face down and trying to rise, there's going to be several feet of slack once he gets to his feet. This is the reason Roche is standing on the fallen tree; it means he can start the hitch at a higher point in the rope. In turn, this means that when Wingnut does manage to stand, there will be enough distance between the knot and the broken branch, where he plans to loop the bottom of the hitch, before he continues to pull Wingnut's arms upwards until the gunman feels compelled to talk.

It's a close thing. Wingnut has risen to his knees and is bracing a foot flat on the ground ready to stand when Roche loops the bottom part of the hitch around the broken branch.

Wingnut grunts as he gets upright. His first thought is sure to be to run, to try and escape. That's understandable. Anyone in his position would be trying to abscond. He'll be expecting to die. Better to die trying to escape a torturer than to be executed after suffering.

Roche slips his fingers from the loop as he hauls downwards on the free end of the trucker's hitch with his right hand. He gets two feet of pull before he encounters any real resistance. Wingnut is perhaps four feet away from the point where the rope drops from the high branch.

Another haul has Wingnut backpedaling and gives Roche eighteen inches. The trucker's hitch is now four feet from where its lower part is looped around the broken branch. Wingnut hasn't got four feet of freedom. He's now below the branch and is positioned like a grotesque plumb weight. He's leaning forward, both to alleviate the pressure on his arms and because the rope is lifting him that way. His feet are still flat on the ground, so there's another few inches of tippy-toed balancing he can do before the real pain starts to kick in.

Roche gives the rope a hefty haul and claims those inches along with a couple more. Wingnut lets out a yelp that's followed by a low moan, so Roche ties off the knot with a simple hitch and walks across to see what Wingnut has to say for himself.

Rather than get straight to the point and start asking questions, Roche decides to turn the screw on Wingnut. The pain he'll be in will be agonizing but tolerable. However, the promise of far greater pain to come might be enough to turn him all chatty.

"You know something, Wingnut, you're almost to be admired for not screaming. For not begging me to untie the rope. The defiance that's still in your eyes is commendable. You're a brave man. A proper tough guy. But, and I say this with no sense of pride, I've broken tougher men than you. One guy I had trussed up like this was a real powerhouse, even his eyelids were ripped with muscles. I lifted him clean off his feet and he never said a word. At least for the first hour. After that he started to curse me out for a while. I waited. You'll discover soon enough that I'm good at waiting. Anyway, his curses soon stopped, but he still wouldn't talk. He was hanging there for two hours. His face one big knot of gritted teeth and furrowed features, but he didn't talk. Can you imagine that? Two hours suspended with your whole weight tearing at your shoulders. All those tendons and ligaments and joints and muscles strained beyond breaking point and still the guy was silent. Sweat poured off his face. His breathing got all ragged and I thought he was going to die from the effort of resisting me. Want to know what I did?"

Wingnut grunts a nothing answer, but Roche can see the defiance in his eyes has been tempered with fear at the imagined pain.

"I hoisted him up another few feet and then jumped up and grabbed his ankles. His shoulders were too muscular for his weight to do the necessary, so I added my own weight. Needless to say, once Mr. Muscles had finished screaming, he talked. Now I'm not going to pretend I can tell you with any great medical detail what damage was done to him, but his shoulders would never work again properly. So, do you want to try and beat Mr. Muscle's record, or would you rather start talking? You see, that's all you need to do to end this pain and prevent yourself feeling any more. Give me a few words and your pain will be over."

Roche watches as Wingnut's eyes close in defeat. He's bought the lie about what he'd done to the fictional Mr. Muscles. "I can't. I wouldn't dare. They'll go after my family. My mother's eighty-two. I have three kids. Good kids. Do what you have to do to me, but don't expect me to talk. I'm not risking anything happening to them."

"To hell with this." Savannah strides forward, her face set harder than the oak Wingnut hangs from. When she gets within a pace of Wingnut, her right foot swings forward and buries itself in the man's groin.

Wingnut's instinctive reaction is to double up. The way his arms are tied prevents this and all he achieves is the lifting of his feet from the forest floor. His body sags for the brief moment he's suspended by the arms tied behind his back, and then his feet shoot down as the pain in his shoulders supersedes the agony of his bruised groin. A howl falls from his lips as his face tightens.

"Enough, Savannah." Roche holds up a hand to stop her attacking their prisoner again. He understands why she's lashed out. For her, Wingnut will be the public face of the forces who want her dead. He gets that she wants to hurt him. That she wants to punish him for his role in the attempt to assassinate her. All things considered, he's glad that she has enough restraint to only deliver a kick to the nuts rather than pull out her gun and shoot Wingnut. He puts this down to her upbringing. Had she been from the other side of the tracks, he'd have had to make sure to relieve her of her gun, because a dead Wingnut would be useless to him.

Savannah's tone is that of a sullen teen. "Douchebag deserved it."

"No arguments from me." Roche moves until he's right in front of Wingnut. "How are your shoulders? Do they feel like they're on fire yet? Like they're being pulled apart? You got a little taste of what Mr. Muscles went through. With you though, I'm going to do something different. Instead of hoisting you up and letting gravity do the work for me, I'm going to speed things up." Roche pulls one of the pistols he'd gathered from the gunmen at the motel and shows it to Wingnut. "I've checked the ammo. You loaded this with hollow points. I know you'll know what a hollow point does when it makes contact with its target. How it mushrooms and destroys whatever it hits."

Wingnut doesn't speak, but there are rivulets of sweat forming on his brow and there's enough fear emanating from him to attract every predator within a twenty-mile radius. His jaw clenches and he looks into Roche's eyes. "Go ahead, shoot me. I'm not going to talk, so you're wasting your time making any more threats."

Roche would believe Wingnut's words if it weren't for the wobble in his voice. All the same, he maintains the eye contact Wingnut has initiated and returns the stare. "Oh, don't worry, I'm not going to kill you. Not at all. What I'm going to do is shoot you in the kneecap. The hollow point will, of course, smash your kneecap into splinters. You'll find yourself in agony as you stand there on one leg. If that doesn't make you talk, one minute later, I'll shoot your other kneecap out. Then you'll be hanging by your arms. When your shoulders give out, your body will slowly lower until you're resting on broken kneecaps and being supported by shoulders that have been wrenched out of alignment. If you talk to me then, I'll release you and you'll be able to survive, but at least the next six months of your life will be spent in a hospital. If you're still dumb enough to be stubborn, I'll just walk away and leave you to die in agony. Maybe you'll get lucky and be found by a hunter. Or perhaps some of the animals local to the area will rip your throat out as they eat you. That won't be a good way to go, as I doubt they'll start on your throat." Roche drops to one knee, taking care to keep out of kicking distance and takes aim. "By the way, just remember, talking to me is your best option for protecting your family, because I *will* make sure your boss knows it was you who talked whether you do or don't. Now, shall we dispense with the clichéd countdown and just get to this?"

"No. Please. Wait." Wingnut's head droops forward. "The code for my phone. It's 983466. The person who hired me though. I don't know his real name, but he's known as the Wraith."

"Tell me more about this Wraith character." Roche keeps the pistol aimed at Wingnut's kneecap.

"There's not a lot to tell. He's someone who sources guys like us for hits. There's a board on the Dark Web where he posts hits for us. We get the details from there and, well…"

"How do you get paid?"

"He sends crypto to our accounts."

Roche nods. What Wingnut is saying makes sense on every level. He's sure the Wraith will have a variable IP address and that, coupled with using the Dark Web, will make it damned near impossible for him to be traced digitally. By paying Wingnut in cryptocurrency, he's doubling down and making sure that not even the money leaves a trail. It's a sensible approach and exactly how he'd do things if he were in the Wraith's line of work.

The Wraith will only be an intermediary, too, between the person who's doing the hiring and the person who's leaking the details of the protected witnesses. Roche knows all about intermediaries. He has one who sends him work from time to time, and while he's never taken a contract to kill someone, his intermediary has asked the question.

"Okay. Now tell me about this board and where to find it."

Wingnut closes his eyes and begins to speak in a voice that's strained with fear and pain.

When Wingnut is done talking, Roche walks over to where the rope is tethered and undoes the knot. It will take Wingnut a few minutes to ease the pain in his shoulders enough that he can pull the rope over the branch and then set off on his way to wherever he deems freedom lives.

As Roche sets off back towards the ancient pickup, Savannah grabs at his arm. "What? You're just going to leave him there?"

"Totally. He's no threat to you now."

"But he came to kill me. Surely you're not going to let him go."

"What do you suggest? That I kill him too? Trust me, that's not something we need to do. He knows he's given up the Wraith. He'll know the consequences of that. His immediate priority will be to get himself and his family somewhere safe. By the time he's done that, I'll have already knocked on the Wraith's door, so to speak."

"But…" Savannah tails off and flaps her arms. "You killed the driver back at the motel. Why aren't you killing Wingnut?"

"But nothing. The driver had to die because he would have warned Wingnut and his buddy. There is no need to kill Wingnut. He's neutralized." Roche grasps Savannah's shoulders and looks deep into her eyes. "I'm comfortable in taking lives when it's necessary. But I don't kill for no reason and I don't kill for revenge or any kind of misplaced idea of vengeance."

# CHAPTER THIRTY-TWO

Roche's mind is only half on the conversation with Xandra. He's already plotting his next moves as he relays the details of the board on the Dark Web.

Despite the early hour of the call, Xandra's voice is clear and bright. "You want me to track the board back to the person who posted the jobs. You don't ask much, do you, Roche?"

"If anyone I know can get that intel, Xandra, it's you."

"Oh, how you flatter me. Never has a girl felt so loved."

Roche lets her sarcasm slide. Xandra will be up for the challenge. Past conversations he's had with her have revealed her fascination with tracing the untraceable. He knows her well enough to suspect that she's already had several attempts to breach the *omertá* provided by the Dark Web's protocols. For someone who's never given up a chance to test her abilities, she's bound to feel a pull, a compulsion to break the unbreakable.

"You've got my number. Call me when you have something." Roche cuts the call and climbs into the pickup.

As they drive back to town, Roche keeps his counsel to himself. He's still thinking about Savannah and how she isn't what she seems. The way she'd stepped up and nailed Wingnut with a boot to the groin had been her only real loss of control when confronting a man who'd twice come to end her life. The problem was, she'd not really lost it. Not properly. In such a situation, most people would have gone to town on Wingnut with fists, feet and any other weapon they could find.

Savannah had a gun on her. She could have pulled that and blown Wingnut's brains out. She hadn't. She'd been too controlled for that. Even her one brief lapse had been halted with a two-word instruction. The disobedient Savannah had obeyed him despite her fury.

He's noticed other things about her too. When they're walking anywhere, she has a tendency to fall into step with him. Her back is always kept straight, and while that may be due to backache, coupled with her ironclad self-control, he's beginning to wonder if she's had some kind of military training. Although, considering her family, it's possible she's had ballet lessons.

The more he thinks about it, the less he's inclined to think she could have, although it's possible her mom sent her to military-style boot camp to rid any teenage rebellion out of Savannah's system. It doesn't fit with her background, though. As a matter of course when taking on a new client, he'd done his homework. The Nicoll family aren't the type to send their kids off to war. There's the mother, a stepfather, Savannah, and a brother who disappeared into the depths of the San Jacinto River after an auto accident. While not old money, there's more than one generation's wealth in their coffers. Savannah's birth father was in real estate before his untimely death. When she remarried, Savannah's mother chose a lawyer who was tipped for governor and had a fortune all of his own. Savannah had a brother, Richard, who died two years ago. He'd been driving drunk and had plunged his car off the road and into the San Jacinto River. There had been heavier rains at the time and the river was swollen. When the rain ended and the San Jacinto receded enough, authorities had dredged for days, searching for the car and Richard, but neither were ever found. The only way the Nicoll family knew what happened was from the testimony of the friends who'd been following a half mile back. According to them, Richard had been showing off and driving fast. They'd seen the smashed barrier and, when Richard hadn't been contactable again, had put two and two together.

Savannah's life had taken a path that was so common it was a cliché. She'd studied social issues at college and had spent years bouncing between jobs at one charity or another. The only real change to her life had been when she'd had a stint as a publicist for a Houston publisher. That foray into the unknown had lasted less than a year and afterwards she'd returned to familiar territory.

So far as Roche is concerned, each of Savannah's jobs represented tasks that needed doing, but for him they weren't real jobs. They were holding pens to make her feel good about herself rather than a required source of income. Savannah's finances are another matter. There is a seven-figure trust fund, meaning she didn't need to work; therefore she'd taken the jobs because she was fueled by a social conscience or boredom. Now he is getting to know her a little, he'd bet on the former. Nowhere in her background was there any mention of the military. At no point had she been recorded as even going to military summer camp. Therefore, any suspicions Roche has about her having military training are unfounded. He reasons that she's playing up to him. Trying to fit in as despite the clash of their personalities, she sees him as her protector. She's got to be scared. Terrified even. It makes sense she's putting a brave face on things and trying to fit in with her new reality.

"I said, where are we going? What are we doing now?"

"We're going to swap this pickup back. Get the sedan and then prepare for the next step."

"And how do we do that?"

"We get some food. We rest. We learn."

"You're jerking me around. After watching what you did back there, I don't think I'll ever be able to eat or sleep again. And learn? I heard your call. You've got someone doing the learning for you. All we can learn is how to wait on your contact."

"You'll eat soon enough. Your body's desire for sustenance will override any disgust you feel right now. Likewise with sleep. Right now you're fueled by adrenaline and fear. When they both subside you'll crash. Hard. Your body needs it. As for the learning, I have more than one iron and more than one fire to put said irons in."

*

An hour later they are back at Pagosa Springs. Roche has paid cash for two rooms at an out-of-the-way motel and they're sitting in a diner attached to a truck stop. The sedan is parked in the lot in such a way as to hide as many of its wounds as possible. To Roche's way of thinking, none of the diner's other patrons are likely to recognize Savannah. Even so, he's positioned their seats so she's facing a wall and he can observe the entire diner, including all its entrances and exits.

Savannah sips at her coffee as Roche shovels food into his mouth. He's got his go-to meal of ham, eggs and toast. Protein and carbs. In front of her is a bowl of cereal. It has nuts and fruits in it. Compared to the contents of Roche's plate, it's a lesson in healthy eating, but he's sure it won't taste anything like as nice.

"Did you really do that?" Savannah lifts a spoon and scoops up a little of the cereal. "Did you really jump up and grab that guy's ankles?"

"Who, Mr. Muscles?" She nods. "Of course not. I made him up." Savannah's eyes widen. "Torture isn't so much about creating physical pain, it's about breaking spirit. It's about winning a battle of wills. That's why I made up the fictitious Mr. Muscles. I wanted to show Wingnut that however much pain he was in, things could get so much worse for him. Wanted him to fear that pain." He points his fork at Savannah. "You kicking Wingnut's balls actually helped. It gave him a brief taste of what it would be like to have his feet off the ground."

"Yeah, well. I want no credit for it. I'm ashamed of myself for attacking a prisoner. Even though he was trying to kill me, I shouldn't have kicked him when he couldn't defend himself." She lays down her spoon and looks straight at Roche. "What would you have done if he hadn't talked? Would you have shot out his knees? Hauled him up then added your weight to his?"

Roche gives a shrug as he loads his fork. "I'd have done what was necessary. He's a killer. A hitman. To him the taking of your life was nothing more than another payday. When you live by the sword, you have to be prepared to die by it."

"And are you? Are you prepared to die by the sword? You risked your life for me. You could walk away now and get the first part of your payment. Lots of people would do that. It's probably the wise thing to do."

"No one ever accused me of being wise. Stubborn, yes. Pig-headed, many times. Rude, on a daily basis. But wise, nope, never been called that." Roche lays down his cutlery and reaches for a glass of orange juice. "I'm not one for giving up. Call me a sucker for a damsel in distress or an idiot, whichever fits your view of me is cool, but I don't do half a job. I see things through to the end, whatever that end may be. I have my reasons for being the way I am. Reasons I'll never share with you."

Roche puts the juice glass down with enough force to suggest the conversation is over and pulls out his cell. His own intermediary isn't likely to know the Wraith. It's not like there will be a club where intermediaries meet. All the same, if you don't ask…

# CHAPTER THIRTY-THREE

Savannah yawns and stretches to alleviate the numbness in her body. Somehow she's managed to sleep for more than two hours. Roche hasn't rested, but considering how he looked when he'd first arrived at her house, his battered face shows no obvious signs of fatigue. She gives him the hardest look she can muster. The dynamic between them seems to have shifted while she slept and she can't figure out why. He is never going to get his name on her Christmas card list, but even so, his behavior towards her has changed. Instead of frank looks, he's now giving her sideways glances. It's like he's observing a captive animal in a zoo. She feels his scrutiny at all times. His face doesn't give much away, but she's learned enough about him to know when he notices something.

"We need to split up." Roche opens his bag, pulls out an envelope and hands her a wad of cash followed by a cheap cell phone. "I'll hire you a car, you take it and find a motel in the middle of nowhere. Hole up there and wait for me to phone. Watch TV, sleep, eat, but whatever you do, keep a low profile and only ever use that cash. If you haven't heard from me in three days, assume I'm dead and go to the cops."

"No way." Savannah tosses the cell and money back into his bag. "I'm not going to sit in some motel room waiting for your call. I'm not one of your dates. You said I'm your principal, so stay with me and protect me."

"That's not going to happen. I'm hunting down the Wraith. He's the next link in the chain, and there's no way you're coming with me. It's too dangerous."

Roche's tone is final, but Savannah is used to final tones. She's also used to getting her own way.

"Is it more dangerous than defending the house against attack? Than outrunning a faster car than yours? Than asking me to shoot into their radiator? Is it more dangerous than setting a trap for the killers?"

"Who knows? I sure as hell don't."

Roche's voice is starting to rise and, to Savannah, it's as pleasant a sound as the tinkling of a stream over rocks. Angry people say the wrong thing. They are easier to back into a corner hamstrung by their own words.

"My point exactly. You've done wonders so far, but think about your next steps. This Wraith character, if he was a killer, it'd be him who'd come for me. He's got to be some kind of middleman. A broker or whatever. He's not a threat, not to someone like you. Maybe you'll need me in some way. A lookout, backup. You're after someone whose name is the Wraith. He's going to be hard to find. What's wrong with having some help?"

"You're the principal. It's up to me to keep you safe. It's a golden rule of protection."

"Golden rule?" Savannah loads her voice with every drop of scorn she can muster. "Not six hours ago you had me make a call to draw the killers to me. For all you've observed that rule it might as well be made of lead. Face facts, will you? I'm safer if I'm with you and, you never know, I might just be useful to you."

"How do you figure that? You claim to be a lookout. To offer backup. If I need a lookout, I want one who's trained to spot things, to observe and read between the lines, not to just see what's happening and accept it. What backup can you provide me? I don't want some amateur as backup. That's often more dangerous than not having backup. Are you holding out on me? Do you have some training?"

"Of course I'm not holding out on you. I haven't any training."

"Really? You don't seem as scared as you should be. When I got you to shoot at the SUV, you scored at least five hits from eight. You shot in pairs. A double tap, and if you're unfamiliar with the term, it's used to describe a pair of deadly shots. Usually used when executing someone. You want me to go on? To point out all the other anomalies between a little rich girl and you?"

"You're so far off the track you're practically crossing the border. I had a boyfriend who was into action films. He talked about double taps and strategic moves all the time. To hear him speak you'd think he was Vin Diesel or Dwayne Johnson. I loved him and I listened to all his macho bull right up to the point when I learned he was cheating on me. If listening to him has made me better able to deal with this nightmare, then it's the one good thing to come out of that relationship. He'd gone through basic with the army but got invalided out when a training exercise went bad and he got shot in the leg."

Roche's nostrils flare, but Savannah can tell from the way he's not speaking that he's going over her words. Testing them against whatever suspicions he has about her and coming to his own conclusions.

Rather than answer her, he reaches for his cell. As soon as he's keyed in his code she sees a shift of his face. It's fractional, but his pupils focus with a new intensity and his finger moves over the screen as he controls the cell.

"Want to tell me what you're looking at?"

"Two things. I've got a location for the Wraith." Roche's hand rises to quiet any comment she might make. "He's in Denver, which will save us from schlepping across the country. So far the data is imprecise, but fixed locations are to follow. My contact has a tag on his IP address, but says it must be being used by a tablet or cell as it's frequently moving."

"The second thing, what's that?"

"I've been asking around about this Wraith. He's well-connected, but is relatively new on the scene. Nothing is known about him, except that he's got a fantastic network of contacts and there's nobody that he can't find."

Savannah purses her lips and makes a show of thinking about what Roche has said. She's got one point in her favor and it's a point she intends to ram home.

"So there's nobody he can't find. How do you think that piece of knowledge is going to sit with me as I wait for your call in some crummy motel? What if you can't find him and he ends up learning your name? Do you think he won't come for you?"

"My father started coming for me when I was eight. I'm still around. He's not."

Savannah lets those words and their unspoken implication pass without comment. She's got an advantage and she's not going to surrender it over stories of childhood woe. "Would I be right in saying that the best way to pinpoint a moving IP address would be triangulation? And by that I mean triangulation in the field and not remotely. That you'll find this Wraith much easier if you and I work together from different points to do the triangulation?"

Roche gives a reluctant nod. "You would be right on all counts. Are you sure you want in? And before you answer, bear in mind that I may have to resort to heavy-handed tactics to get what I need from the Wraith."

"Listen, Roche, this guy paid people to kill me. I want to see his face. Look into his eyes and see him for who he is. I want to put a gun against his head and see fear. You might think of me as a little rich girl, but there are times when even little rich girls want to fight back."

"Not how I think of you." Something on Roche's face changes. "You're tougher than I expected, but all in all, that's a check in your plus column. You're in for now. The first hint of any danger and you'll be packed off. Understand me?"

"I got you. Loud and clear." Savannah makes a conscious effort not to look pleased about Roche allowing her to tag along. She also refrains from saluting him lest he again prod at the idea she's had military training.

# CHAPTER THIRTY-FOUR

Roche steers the rental SUV towards the cloverleaf and chews things over in his head. He'd swapped the sedan for the SUV at a rental place in Pagosa Springs and hadn't bothered answering any of the salesman's questions about how the sedan was so beat up.

Xandra has come through for him on several counts. She used her digital skills to trace the Wraith's IP address and gave him two locations where the tablet or cell phone—that was used to post the hits on the Dark Web—has spent the most time. One is a plush house, the other an office building. Her initial attempts to identify the home's owner have drawn a blank as it is registered to an offshore company. Given more time she could have dug deeper, but she's had to abandon Roche's request as she has a meeting she can't skip or rearrange. The last thing she'd told him was that she'd sent him an app and, if he opened it, the app would give him the current location of the tablet or cell belonging to the Wraith.

He gets Savannah to google both locations and show him the street views. The house is a plush effort in what looks to be an excellent neighborhood. The office building looks modern and runs to several floors.

According to the app, the Wraith is at the office building, but when Roche drives past, the app doesn't give them any kind of clue as to which part of the building he's in.

"So what's your plan?"

"Not sure yet." It's an admission Roche doesn't like to make. He's not used to having a principal with him on an investigation, let alone one who he's convinced is hiding something. "We don't know his name or what he looks like, so trying to flush him out with a fire alarm or something similar won't work. The office isn't the place to question him, but I do want to find out who he is."

"Why not just go to the house and wait there? The Wraith's bound to return at some point soon."

"He is. But you've seen the house. I imagine you grew up in a similar sized place. Tell me, do you think he lives alone in such a big house? My guess is he's got a wife or girlfriend, possibly some kids. I'd bet a buck to your dime he's got a maid or some other staff there. What do we do with them? Kill them? Tie them up? If I have to get rough with him, I don't want any witnesses, but I'm sure as hell not going to harm any innocents. I may walk the line between good and evil, but I won't harm a single person I don't feel deserves it."

"I get what you're saying. What about staking the place out and when the Wraith gets home, you go in and get them to talk?" Savannah shoots him a glare. "And why do you assume the Wraith is a man? The Wraith could just as easily be a woman. Have you any idea how sexist that assumption is?"

"I'm not being sexist. I'm being a realist. I've had years of experience of dealing with the criminal classes and I've learned that the bad guys are generally guys. Sure, I've met some women who are every bit as evil as some of the guys, but I can count them on one hand. Anyway, don't be giving me any of your bull. I'm here to do a dirty job and I don't have time or brain space to worry about your woke sensibilities."

Roche sees the glare from Savannah and goes back to his thoughts on how to identify the Wraith. If he can identify the man, there's a chance he can be ambushed. The office building has a parking garage, and he knows from a painful episode fifteen years ago how good parking garages are for ambushes.

"Savannah, how brave are you feeling? I have an idea on how to identify the Wraith, but it will involve a slight risk on your behalf."

"I thought you said you'd be packing me off at the first hint of danger. Now you're asking me to take a risk and not even telling me what your plan is."

Roche drums his fingers on the wheel. "We need to get this guy alone. That's not going to be easy at his house. The best place I can think of for doing it is in the parking garage, but first we need to know what he looks like. We can't identify him, but we can make him identify himself."

"How?"

Roche points at a Nordstrom across the street. "We get ourselves suited up like a businessman and his assistant and we go looking for the Wraith. I'll make myself out to be an ass and you'll get sympathetic looks. Your hair will be in a ponytail so that unicorn tattoo below your ear is visible. When the Wraith sees you he'll react. He won't be able not to. He thinks you're dead. Even if he doesn't think you're dead, he won't be expecting you to pop up at his work."

"So then what happens? Do you think he'll just brush off seeing me? By seeing me in his place of work you're as good as threatening him. What if he pulls a gun and shoots me? Even if he misses, he might kill someone else."

"I can't see that happening. One, he's not a killer, he's an intermediary. He pays others to kill for him. Two, killing you in a public place like an office is a monutastically stupid thing to do. Whatever else he may be, the Wraith hasn't got where he is by being stupid. Three, he's only going to get seconds to react and then we'll be gone. We're going to be quick and we're going to be loud. Shock and awe are our bywords. What we're doing is trying to get him to make a mistake. He's at work. He'll have a cover to maintain, but he'll be desperate to get a level of control.

To manage the situation. My guess is he'll feign illness and then hole up somewhere while he calls in another hit team. I'll snatch him in the parking lot, take him somewhere quiet and have a polite conversation with him."

"Like you did with Wingnut?"

Roche catches the sarcasm in her tone but doesn't react. "Will you do it?"

"Why do I have to be the assistant? It's the twenty-first century, for God's sake. I could just as easily pose as your boss. Why do you always have to conform to gender stereotypes? First you insisted the Wraith must be a man and now you're going down this route. What's wrong with you?"

"Nothing's wrong with me. I just understand what the vast majority of people are unconsciously biased to accept. I'm not saying it's right, but it's the way it damn well is. Plus"—Roche points at his face—"I've got twenty years on you. Do you think I look remotely like someone who'd take crap from a younger female boss?" Savannah doesn't speak, but Roche notices the slight shake of her head. "And, think about how we're doing this. The boss strides into the middle of the room trailed by the secretary—or aide if that makes you feel better—and then draws every eye in the room. Do you want to be in the middle of the room, or are you happier being on the fringes?"

"The fringes. I don't like the gender stereotyping though. I want that on the record."

"You want it on the record, fine, put it on the record. Take it to Memphis and have it recorded onto a CD with a full-scale orchestra for all I care. Are you gonna do this, or do you want to swap a little fear today for a lifetime of being terrified?"

"Do I have a choice?"

"Of course you do. But until the snake is beheaded it can still bite you. The quickest way to activate the guillotine is what I'm suggesting."

"You're forgetting something."

"If you're going to make me ask nicely, consider it done."

"What happens if he does draw a weapon?"

"I'll shoot him."

"Before he shoots me?"

Roche flashes a grin at Savannah. "That's the plan."

"My, aren't you so very, very reassuring?"

"I do my best. Now let's go and get some new clothes. And, Savannah, at the risk of yet again offending your delicate sensibilities, I want your clothes to be functional and practical. Flat shoes so you can run if needs be. Pants for the same reason. And a blouse that hangs loose and buttons to your neck. I want people's eyes on your face, not any other part of you. And get something to put your hair in a ponytail. That unicorn tattoo below your ear is a real identifier and I want it visible. Got that?"

"Yeah, I got it."

Roche parks the SUV and sets off to Nordstrom with Savannah at his side. He doesn't fail to notice how once again she's fallen into step with him.

# CHAPTER THIRTY-FIVE

Savannah has to lengthen her stride to keep up with Roche's march as they enter the Wagner building. All around her she sees threats, people she imagines could be the Wraith. There's a man on a stepladder fiddling with a light fitting; he could pull a gun from his tool belt and shoot her. Or the woman behind the desk could drop the telephone from her ear and send 9mm parcels of death her way.

"Come on, girl, keep up. How many times do I have to tell you that time is money?" Roche seems oblivious to the threats she's imagining as he breezes past the reception desk and down the sole corridor leading from reception.

On the right of the corridor are bathrooms and what she guesses will be a storage area for janitorial supplies; there's certainly the smell of cleaning chemicals in the sanitized atmosphere of the white corridor. The left wall has a glass partition on its top half and Savannah can see there's a cubicle farm stretching the length of the building.

Roche blasts through the door into the cubicle farm and claps his hands good and loud. When he speaks his voice has enough boom about it to reverberate around the room. "I'm looking for a Nigel Timmins. My dumbass secretary"—a thumb jerks over his shoulder in Savannah's general direction—"arranged a meeting with him at some networking event, but didn't make a note of the goddamned company or even think to get his card. All she could remember was that he worked out of this building. Is he here?"

Heads appear over and around the cubicle walls. Most are wearing inquisitive expressions, but she can see pity on a few of the female faces. Roche might be a jerk, but he seems to understand people and the way things work. Most disconcerting about the heads popping up is the fact she can't see what a lot of the men's hands are doing. Her mind has them drawing weapons and while this makes her heart race, the logical part of her brain is agreeing with Roche's thinking. Anyone who's known as the Wraith isn't going to break cover and start shooting in such a public environment. Not only would it blow their cover, it'd leave a multitude of witnesses.

A woman of around the same age as Roche levers herself from her seat and blocks Roche from walking farther into the room. She's not a tall woman and has to crane her neck back to look at Roche's face. "Ain't nobody of that name here. This is a workplace and I'll thank you not to disturb my team any further. Please leave."

"Yeah, yeah, whatever." Roche twists and looks at Savannah. "Well, do you see him in here, girl? Does anyone in here look familiar to you?" He snaps his fingers at her. Once, twice, thrice and layers a menacing growl into his tone. "Come on, girl. Time. Is. Money."

Savannah keeps her head down and shakes it as if shy and embarrassed, but her eyes are scanning the room through her fringe. Her muscles tensed ready to leap to one side in case the Wraith is here and makes a play.

"Are you going to leave or do I have to call security?" The woman all but stamps her foot.

Savannah can see all eyes in the room are on Roche, the boss lady and herself. The women in the room are sending empathetic looks her way while also reveling in the standoff between Roche and the boss lady. The guys largely ignore her, but a couple do send sidelong glances her way. Their faces are all the same. They might be relishing the clash between two dominant personalities, but there's also apprehension in case she picks any of them out and they have to deal with Roche.

Most of the male faces she sees waste no time in slinking back to their workstations. For them it makes sense to not get drawn into things. As Roche will be doing, Savannah is searching for any hint of recognition, any sign that one of the guys looking her way knows who she is. She doesn't see anything that triggers her senses, but that doesn't mean she's at ease. She could have misread the signs.

*"Sir."* The boss lady's arm points at the door.

Savannah falls in behind Roche as he leaves. The sooner she can get out of the cubicle farm, the sooner she'll feel a sense of release as the fear strangling her heart is allowed to loosen its grip. She also wants to know what Roche has seen. He was farther in the room than she was. Closer to the people occupying the cubicles and therefore better able to see the nuances of their expressions.

She's wise enough to wait until they get to the corridor before asking. "Well?"

"Nope. Not even a flash of recognition."

"What if the Wraith's the janitor or someone like that? Someone who'd be overlooked."

"You make a good point, but think about the house. No way could a janitor afford a house like that, and I'm sure the Wraith will be far too smart than to live so obviously beyond their means. Unless we find a hedge fund working out of here where even the interns are millionaires, it's executive or upper-level workers who are in my sights."

"What if it's the Wraith's partner who paid for the house? Their wife or girlfriend. Husband or boyfriend, maybe."

"Good point." Roche leads the way to the elevators. "Although I'd still say we're looking for someone who's at executive level. Think about all the couples you know. Sure, opposites may well attract, but how many truck drivers do you know who date lawyers? People tend to gravitate to partners who enjoy a similar social status, education and career trajectory to their own. Trust me, we're looking for someone who's at least a manager."

Rather than argue with Roche's immutable logic, Savannah keeps her mouth shut and prepares herself for another round of insults as the elevator doors open.

# CHAPTER THIRTY-SIX

Roche strides up the stairs to the third floor with a feeling of anticipation pumping his legs. The second floor was every bit as much of a bust as the first, but the way he's looking at it, he's already eliminated two possible options. There are only five more to go and he's confident he'll have a bead on the Wraith within the next half hour at most.

Savannah is playing her part better than he's expected of her, although he's sure that she'll vent her feelings for the way he's been speaking to her so far. From what he can tell, Savannah is holding up well enough against her fears, but as each floor is crossed off, her terror is sure to be heightened. As much as circumstances will allow, he plans to not tell her that he's spotted the Wraith until they're well clear of the man. Roche has already made sure Savannah has handed her gun to him, so he's not worried about her pulling out a gun and shooting the Wraith in front of witnesses, more that he expects her to freeze, or worse, call the guy out and create a scene where guns have to be drawn. If he believed the Wraith was the end of the trail, he'd be the first to pull a gun on him, but there's the guy feeding details to the Wraith to catch and there's no way of getting to him without the Wraith.

When guns are drawn on a man facing life imprisonment or the death penalty if he's taken in, then desperate measures come into play. The Wraith will do whatever he can to save himself including killing innocents and the taking of hostages. That's the kind of situation Roche wants to avoid more than any other. Plus, the minute he takes down the Wraith in a public setting, the cops will become involved and that means that he won't get the bonus payment for stopping the leak. Most of all though, he wants to get his own hands on the guy leaking the details of people who are protected witnesses. The Leaker, as Roche thinks of the US marshal who's likely revealing the location of witnesses, is breaking justice with his actions. On top of the horrors of good, law-abiding people having to uproot themselves and start a new life in fear after doing the right thing, the Leaker is selling them out and setting them up for death. It might be that the Leaker is being blackmailed into helping by a third party, but Roche cannot comprehend a level of personal threat that would make him leak that same information.

Like the two previous floors, the third has a white corridor, but rather than the windows showing cubicle farms, this floor has a multitude of doors. At first glance the doors are open and as Roche marches along, he's flicking glances through the windows. Each of the windows he looks through shows only women in the room, so he doesn't bother entering them. As much as Savannah might argue the Wraith could be any gender, his gut is telling him the Wraith is a man, and he expects that man to be of a similar age to himself. A young buck may well be involved, but he's convinced the hand on the Wraith's tiller belongs to someone who possesses the wisdom that comes with age. Four of the rooms they pass have no occupants at all, so if the floor proves a bust, Roche plans to loiter for a few minutes in case the Wraith has gone to the bathroom.

The next room has a male occupant, but he's late teens, so Roche discounts him and moves on. There's one final door on the floor and no windows allowing a peek into it. From the door's position in relation to the building, he guesses it leads to a boardroom. That explains the empty workspaces.

"Change of plan. Roll with me here." Roche takes Savannah's right hand in his left, whips the door open and bursts in the room at a run. "Come on, sweetie, we'll be alone in here."

As he's anticipated, it's a boardroom. It's decked out with an overhead projector, a table that's all cool lines and style without possessing any soul and a clutch of people sitting on chairs around the table.

There's an even split between the room's ten occupants. Five men, five women. Six of them are at one end while the other four are at the other. Roche's best guess is that it's a pitch meeting of some sort, as one of the four is a woman standing with a laser pointer aimed at the projector screen that hangs from the far wall.

All ten heads in the room turn their way. Their faces show a mixture of amusement, disgust at someone engaging in office-based conquests and anger at the disruption of their meeting.

"Oops. Sorry, folks." Roche shuffles his feet and scans the room as if seeking absolution for his faux pas. "Guess we won't be alone, honey."

A smattering of laughter rattles around the room, although there are two people who aren't laughing: one is the woman with the pointer and the other is a man sitting at the far end of the table. There's a name card in front of him saying only "Francis," but coupled with the spark of recognition in his eyes when he looked at Savannah, Roche knows he's just locked eyes with the Wraith.

Roche backs out of the room and makes his way back along the corridor, his eyes scanning the nameplates on the doors of the four empty rooms. Two have the letter "F" before a surname, but a glance through the windows shows a pair of feminine sneakers beside a large purse in one and a set of golf clubs and sports trophies in the other.

"Got him." Roche points to the nameplate of the room with the golf clubs. "He's Francis Kempe."

"You saw him? He was in there? We were only in there a few seconds. Are you sure?" There's incredulity and apprehension in Savannah's tone. "Oh my god. What does he look like? What do we do now?"

"We stay calm. I'm sure. He was on the left at the end of the table. He's in his forties, early signs of male-pattern baldness, a goatee that'll be gray in a couple of years and around a hundred seventy-five pounds. Hard to judge his height as he was sitting down, but I guess he'll be around six feet tall."

"You got all that from a quick glance?"

"Of course." Roche tosses a cheeky grin Savannah's way. "It's what I do. This might all be new for you, but it's my job. What kind of investigator would I be if I didn't notice things?"

"Is that what you are, an investigator?"

"It's one of the things I am. Now let's get moving. I want to run Kempe's name through the DMV so I know which car is his, so we can set a decent ambush for him."

# CHAPTER THIRTY-SEVEN

Savannah crouches behind a Chevrolet alongside Roche. Thanks to Roche's hacker contact, they've identified the Wraith's vehicle as a BMW M5. As nice as the car is, Savannah hates the fact that it backs up Roche's insistence that the Wraith holds an executive position in the company. Now that she's gone through the ordeal of being a tethered goat, Savannah has a bunch of questions traveling through her brain faster than any spaceship has ever gone.

She leans forward and puts her lips to Roche's ear. "What if the Wraith is so spooked by seeing me up there and he runs? Maybe he's whistled up some backup. What if another hit team is on their way here right now?"

"Who says he's going to be spooked? Put yourself in his position. He expects you're dead, or running for your life." Roche's voice is as low as hers. "Wingnut sure as hell won't have dared tell him of the failed hit. He'll be hightailing it home to protect his wife and family. Therefore Kempe, because that's who the Wraith really is, will be trying to organize his thoughts. He's got to be questioning what he's seen. You have a look that's fairly common, and that unicorn tattoo you have looks to be the kind of design that's in every tattooist's sample book. He'll be calculating whether his eyes have played tricks on him. If he's seen the real you, or has appropriated your image onto a lookalike because he's been thinking about you"—Roche falls silent as footsteps ring out, but they are the pocking sound of high heels moving fast—"he's going to think you appearing in that boardroom *must* be a coincidence.

He's the Wraith. A man of mystery. A shadowy figure. He deals out death via the Dark Web and keeps himself well removed from any dealings with the killers he hires. He's got to be thinking there's no way that anyone could find him. Could track him to his workplace. Sure, he'll take a precaution or two, because it'd be dumb not to, but by my way of thinking he's got to be itching to get somewhere private. To get some time to try and contact Wingnut and his buddy for a status report."

"I get all that." Savannah's mouth is arid as she whispers. "But what if he does believe it's me he saw? What if he figures his home and car are compromised? And you never answered my question about another hit team."

"If that's the case, he'll run. But when he runs he's sure to take his cell or tablet with him as that's his way of contacting Wingnut. He leads, we follow. If he goes to a hotel, we'll track him down. If he goes to some place remote, we'll find him. You are in a Witness Protection Program and I found you. Kempe is carrying around a tracker. He'll be easier to find than a donut in a police station. As for your worries about another hit team. It's late afternoon. Kempe was in a meeting. The office will close in an hour's time. Two, at most, and he'll have to leave. The odds on there being a hit team he can scramble and have here before he has to leave the office are so small they're negligible."

"I still think he'll dump the tablet or cell. In his position I would."

Savannah sees the narrowing of Roche's eyes and chastises herself for the mistake she's just made. Roche misses nothing, verbal or visual; he catches every nuance and interprets it at a lightning pace.

A woman's voice rings out over a jumble of footsteps. Brash and earthy, it carries across the parking lot. "Did you see that woman who burst in? Man, was she embarrassed. And that dude she was with. He's got to be old enough to be her father. What do you say to that, Francis?"

Savannah stiffens when she hears the name. The Wraith is with the woman who's speaking. Roche doesn't move. She can tell he's poised for action, but is awaiting the optimal moment.

"I say the world is full of couples attracted to each other for reasons that make no sense to anyone except them. Whatever they are to each other, they're both adults who can bed whoever they like. So long as neither of them is cheating on someone else, it's all fine by me. Having said that, maybe I'm a little jealous as he looks older than I am and she's about half his age."

Regardless of how hard Kempe might be trying to act normal, Savannah can hear the tension in his voice that underpins the jokey tone he's attempting to portray.

Several voices all pile into the conversation. They're laughing at Kempe's words and piling in with gentle ribbing.

In a flash it becomes clear to Savannah what Kempe is doing. He's surrounding himself with innocents. A protective detail comprised of unwitting colleagues. It makes sense to Savannah. No move had been made against Kempe upon discovery, so he'll have reasoned that she and Roche are either unwilling to harm nonparticipants, or that he was mistaken but is taking this precaution anyway.

"You joining us for a drink, Francis?" It's the brash voice that asks the question.

"Not tonight. I've a couple errands to run and my wife is away with the kids, meaning I have the house all to myself, so I'm going to grab a takeout and then binge on *Breaking Bad*."

As a rash of cheery goodbyes ring out, there's the slamming of a door and they hear the rumble of a powerful engine starting. Roche slips Savannah a look and then leans forward as if to kiss her. The footsteps are getting closer, so she leans into Roche to keep up the pretense. She doesn't want to kiss him, but as she's expecting bad things to happen to Kempe in the next hour or two, she'd rather be remembered for having loose morals than as someone who is a perpetrator of bad things.

Roche breaks the kiss before it happens, much to Savannah's relief and the amusement of the women who've found them jammed behind the Chevrolet that was parked beside Kempe's BMW.

Typically it's the brash one who speaks first. "Oh, honey, if he ain't gonna spring for a room somewhere, you need to dump his sorry ass and dump it quick."

Savannah copies the embarrassed grin Roche paints onto his face and lets him lead her off.

"I'm guessing that we follow the tracker you planted on his car and you try again."

"Correct. You heard the man. He has errands. Let's see where his errands take him?"

*

Savannah sits in silence as they follow the tracker. Its signal is being picked up by Roche's cell, so she punches in Kempe's zip code to their car's GPS. The route they have to take to get to Kempe's house is the same as the one they're being led by Kempe.

"He's not sure." Roche points at the GPS. "He's questioning himself like I said he would. He's going home. I bet he'll lock himself in his den, and will try to get to the bottom of things. He'll be reaching out to Wingnut. To the other guy. He's maybe going to access a stash of money and weapons he has there. He could be getting ready to go on the lam, but I don't think so. I reckon he's still unsure enough about seeing you, that he doesn't fully believe it was you, and needs to do some fact-checking. The big question is, how long will he stay in the house when he doesn't hear back from the hit team? That is the million-dollar question and our window of opporchancity."

"You do know you can't just make up words, don't you?" Savannah doesn't care about the snort in her voice.

"They don't count as made up if people can understand them. Anyway, language evolves."

"What about the wife and kids? The staff? You were worried about them earlier."

"My contact did some more digging. The wife and kids are on vacation at the moment. We have a clear run. He may have been telling the truth about the house being empty, but even if he wasn't, after potentially seeing you, you can bet he'll send his staff home so he has absolute privacy."

As Roche drives past Kempe's house, Savannah takes a good look through the wrought-iron gates. It's a beautiful two-story building in excellent condition, except for the roof. The shingles are being replaced, and there's a scaffold running along half the frontage and one side. As soon as she sees the scaffold, she knows that if Roche is going to get into the house, the scaffold is sure to feature one way or another.

# CHAPTER THIRTY-EIGHT

Roche parks far enough along the street to be out of sight from Kempe's house. As he'd seen Savannah do, he'd gotten as good a look at the house as he could through the ornamental gates without slowing down to the point where he was conspicuous.

None of what he sees pleases him. The scaffold that's erected to facilitate the replacing of the shingles is a bonus, but there's a long way between the perimeter walls and the house. Save a few low flowerbeds in which flowers cling to their last bloom, there's nothing that could be described as cover. In fact, the whole area would best be described as a killing zone.

Worse, he spots security measures atop the walls. Alongside cameras there are sensor beams and motion detectors. He's sure the gate will be alarmed and were this not a respectable residential area, he'd expect it to also be electrified.

These setbacks aren't anything he hasn't encountered before, but anytime he's circumvented them before he's done so on an unsuspecting quarry, rather than one who may well be preparing for an assault.

Roche hauls his Bag of Plenty from the backseat and equips himself with what he thinks of as his breaking-and-entering kit. He adds two fresh clips for his SIGs and contemplates the wisdom of donning his bulletproof vest. In a street such as this, the sight of one will have the residents scrambling over each other to call 911. On the other hand, not wearing one to cross the forty yards of open ground can be the difference between life and death.

He resolves to take the bag with him and slip the vest on at the last second before he breaches the security.

"So." Savannah's gaze is direct and her face is set hard. "How do we get in there?"

"We? There's no we. This is very much an I situation."

"Bull. I'm coming with you. I can act as a lookout, or provide covering fire if needed. Besides, are you really going to leave me sitting in the car where I'm a sitting duck? I'd guess you don't want me to drive round and round the block in case you need a rapid exfiltration."

"I very much doubt that you'll be able to do either of those things. However, I know what a stubborn little madam you can be and that you'll just follow me anyway. Here's the deal. You come with, but you do as I say at all times. The first time you disobey me, I'll shoot you in the leg and then haul your sorry hide to a nice public hospital, where I'll register you in under your own name. After that, I'll go home and leave you to your own devices."

Roche says nothing more as he zips up his bag and reaches for the door handle. Savannah's insistence on coming along doesn't fit with the scared victim. Neither does the terminology she's using. Providing cover could well be something she'd learned from the boyfriend who was an action movie buff, but exfiltration is an army term. Civilians would use terms like getaway or scram. She hasn't. She's used a word only soldiers would use. Roche closes the car's door and makes a mental note to get Xandra to do a much deeper dig on Miss Savannah Nicoll.

Rather than approach the front of the house, Roche walks in the opposite direction until he finds what he's looking for: a lane between two properties. It has a beaten track that shows two worn ruts and a grassy central strip.

"What are you up to? The house is that way." Savannah takes his arm and points along the street.

"Really? You think I don't know where his house is? You need to sharpen up and have a little faith in me." Roche punctuates his words with the most withering glare he can muster. "Okay, then, here's the kindergarten version. In any security system, there is always a weak spot, an Achilles heel. The trick is finding and then exploiting it. This is something I've become adept at, and the scale and scope of Kempe's house is playing into my hands. While Kempe's house isn't palatial, it's certainly well above the normal footprint and will have run him over a million bucks. When people can pay that amount of money for a house, it's unusual for them to manage all the upkeep. Therefore, they'll have staff. A cook and a maid are the main staff. We heard him say it's the cook's night off. I'll bet a dime to a dollar they'll also have a gardener swing by a couple times a week. If they have a pool, then there'll be a pool boy." Roche lifts a finger as he strides along the lane. "And please don't give me any of your gender politics about the term 'pool boy.' Some terms just are what they are, and we don't need to have a battle over every one."

"I wasn't going to."

Roche can tell from Savannah's sullen tone that's exactly what she was about to do. "Anyway, you've seen the gravel drive. You'll also have seen the lack of cars on the sidewalk. The staff won't be live-in, unless there's a nanny, though Kempe's kids are too old for one of them any more."

"What are you getting at, Roche? You're saying a hell of a lot without actually telling me anything."

"The drive goes to the garage and no farther. There's no staff cars to be seen anywhere. Not at Kempe's place, not at any of the other houses around here. The people who hire household staff on streets like this want their staff to be discreet and unobtrusive in all aspects. To do this, they'll have their own entrances. These are generally at the back of the house where they can't be seen.

Look ahead, this lane intersects one that runs right along the back of the houses. The staff won't be expected to climb over the wall. That means there'll be a gate somewhere. Fair enough the gate may be alarmed, but one alarmed gate isn't going to worry me."

"Damn you, Roche. Why do you always have to be so clever about things?"

"I'm not clever, not in academic terms, but I know how the world works. Really works, not so much about the life that you live, but how things are for regular folks. For all you're this woke warrior or however you see yourself, you're sticking to me, a stranger with a gun, a man you've seen kill another man and use torture to get information, because it makes you feel safer with me than anywhere else. That, that is the real world and the sooner you stop being woke and actually wake up to reality, the better this whole mess will straighten itself out in your head."

Roche gives her a look and tries not to think about his reality. Of having to drop out of high school to support his mother and youngest sister, Harriet. They had been tough times. His mother had become a cowed shell of her former self thanks to his father's abuse, and the knowledge of what her husband did to his eldest daughter shamed her to the point where she'd retreated turtle-like into an impenetrable cocoon of alcohol abuse. Pammy turned fourteen the day before she'd left a suicide note on Roche's pillow and then stepped in front of a big rig traveling along the I-10 at pace. Then fifteen, Roche had gotten himself a gun and, upon learning his old man had burned Pammy's note—thereby destroying the evidence of her accusations against him—used the gun to run his father out of town. Leigh is the only person he's told the full story to. Of how he'd made his father kneel in the dust at the edge of town so he could take repeated kicks at his groin. To this day Roche isn't proud of his actions back then. Whenever he looks back, he aims the finger of blame squarely at himself. He should have protected Pammy the way he did Harriet, by recognizing the cause of the problem and exorcising his father from the house much sooner. If put in that situation again, knowing what he now knows about the long-term effects Pammy's death had on himself, his mother and youngest sister, he'd handle things in a different way. A patricidal way.

Leigh loves and accepts him for who is, but as much as he loves Leigh, Roche never feels worthy of that love. No matter how he might fight it, how he might try and rationalize the past away and lay the blame on his father, the abuser, he can't ever unburden himself from the guilt he feels at not realizing what his father was doing to Pammy and intervening before she sought her ultimate escape.

Even though they are polar opposites in every way imaginable, he sees Pammy when he looks at Savannah. He's always seen Pammy's face when he's had a female principal to protect. A part of him recognizes he ought to seek therapy, but men like him don't cry on a shrink's couch. Men like him have fights, crack wise and drink too much as they try to bury their woes deep enough to extinguish the pain and the self-loathing.

# CHAPTER THIRTY-NINE

Roche snaps himself back to the present. He can fight his demons at another time. Memories of, and guilt over, Pammy will still be around long after he's finished this case.

The gate isn't hard to find, and thanks to the nameplate on its wooden boards, it's even easier to identify they're at the right gate.

Roche's first move is to run a sweep over the lock side of the gate with a scanner. The scanner detects no electrical impulses, so either there's no alarm sensors on the gate, or they're switched off. His next move is to try the handle. He's learned that while a house's owner may be uptight about security, their employees can be lax or downright lazy in their attitudes. The gate doesn't open. The lock on it is a standard mortise model. It will have three, five or possibly even seven levers inside. To Roche's eyes it looks old, which means he guesses at three, perhaps five levers maximum.

The picks he inserts trip the three levers and there's a click as the lock slides back from its housing in the gate's frame.

Savannah goes to reach for the handle, so Roche swats her hand down and pushes her to the side. "Do you know what's on the other side of that gate? Do you realize that Kempe could be lying in wait for us with a rifle?"

Roche accepts the paling of Savannah's face for an answer, fiddles with his scanner and runs it over the lock side of the gate once more.

"You've done that."

"I was looking for an alarm the first time. Now it's set to detect metal. Compared to the rest of Kempe's setup, this is as secure as a prom queen's virtue. If I had a gate like this, I'd have bolts securing it."

"And then what? You'd get up early every morning to let the staff in? Trust me, there won't be any bolts on the inside of the gate."

The scanner finds no traces of metal to indicate the presence of bolts. Savannah has been proven correct, which doesn't surprise him. As a rich kid, hanging out with rich kids, there's a good chance she has more experience of gates such as this than he does. Which begs the question: why didn't she suggest the gate to him?

Roche puts the scanner into a pocket, retrieves his bulletproof vest from the bag and hands Savannah hers.

"Here's the plan. We stand either side of the gate. I'll swing it open. Three seconds later, I'm going to swap to your side. If Kempe has a gun trained on the gate, he might take a shot at me as I appear. He'll be aiming at center mass. Probably around four to four and half feet high. He'll be centered on the gate. If he's quick enough to get a shot off and hit me, the vest ought to catch it. The impact will likely knock me off my feet. If that happens, I'll need you to grab my wrist or ankle, whichever's closer, and drag me back to cover." Roche doesn't say what to do if Kempe has armor-piercing bullets. Nor does he entertain thoughts about the prospect of Kempe being confident enough in his shooting abilities to go for a head shot.

The gate swings open without even the tiniest squeak. Roche steps into the gateway for the briefest second, his eyes scanning for any sign of a potential ambush, then continues over to Savannah's side.

No shots ring out. No shouts challenge him. He'd seen no sign of any hidden gunman, so he does his best to ignore the trickle of sweat running down his back and drops into a sprinter's crouch.

"We're going to make a run for it. I'll lead, then you come after me. Right after me. Zig and zag as you cross the lawn. Your destination is underneath the scaffold against a wall. I'll be veering off to the right. Don't follow me exactly as any shots that come my way may get you. Instead, go a little to the left then start the zigzagging. When you get to the house keep your back against a part of the wall that has no windows." Roche doesn't give Savannah time to get nervous. "Okay, let's do this."

Roche bursts through the gateway, SIG in hand as he battles his own fears and the desire to waste time trying to spot a hidden attacker. Breaths thump in and out of his lungs as he races for the sanctity of the scaffold while making sure to alter his course every three or four strides.

He arrives at the scaffold the same time as Savannah. She's less breathless than he is, and he's sure the sheen of perspiration on her face has more to do with fear than the exercise she's just done.

One thing he has noticed when dashing across the yard is that the roofing contractors have stripped the shingles from the rear of Kempe's house. There is a row of skylights cut into the roof and he's spotted that one of them is open. That's how he plans to get into the house.

The scaffold surrounding the house is a kind he's seen many times before. On the vertical sections there are four lugs for braces that are spaced every eighteen inches or so. The lugs point in all four directions of the compass and make for great footholds.

Roche makes sure he selects an upright that allows him to keep his back to a walled area and starts climbing. It's an easy climb, but all the same he makes sure to take a good look around him before cresting onto the top level, which is boarded out to create a safe workspace.

He crouches down and waits for Savannah to join him. Heights have never been his favorite thing, but the scaffold is well braced and sturdy as Savannah clambers up. Roche wasn't sure she'd follow him up the scaffold, but the way she's tackling the climb tells him she has far less problem with heights than he does.

Once Savannah is at his side he creeps forward, taking care not to make any sound. The metallic flooring of the scaffold is a worry as it's not at all sound absorbent, but he makes it to the vicinity of the skylight without incident.

This is the sticky part. Kempe could well have opened the skylight as an invitation, a trap. He now knows Savannah is alive. He'll have worked out that if she can find him at work, she can find him at home. Therefore, he's got to be cautious, got to have taken some precautions with his safety.

A plus for Kempe is that the law will be on his side if he shoots them inside the house. Out in the garden, or at work, he'd have a far harder task to justify using a firearm, but in his own home all bets are off.

Roche scouts the area by the skylight. He's checking for obstacles, anything that will impede his progress or hinder a sudden retreat should he need to make one. Next he scours the view through the skylight. It's a typical upstairs room that hasn't yet been designated a meaningful purpose beyond storage. There are boxes around the walls, neutral colors, and a lack of carpeting that means any noise he makes dropping to the floor might well echo throughout the house.

Step by step he works his way along the scaffold until he's seen all of the room that can be seen. The part that worries him is the part he can't see, the part below the skylight. If he was hiding in the room ready to ambush an intruder, that's where he'd wait.

There are two ways to address the problem. One is to creep up the roof and peer in, pistol at the ready. That's a dangerous option: anyone lying in ambush only has to shoot through the roof's sheathing boards to hit him.

The second option is even less safe. It will see Roche clamber onto the roof until he reaches the ridge, then make his way along checking for anyone lying in wait. The problem with this is that any potential ambusher is sure to hear him scrabbling his way up, and then he can either move himself to a different location, or pick Roche off while he balances on the roof. Even if neither of these things happen, the near-horizontal position of the open window will obscure his vision, and if he slithered down the roof to make a quick assault by dropping through the open skylight, there's every chance he'd either get hung up on the raised waterproof top of the skylight, or his feet would cause the hinged skylight to rotate back upwards. This would either trap him or slam him into a potentially broken window.

A third option was discounted before he'd even reached the window. A row of bullets stitched through the sheathing boards below the window would eliminate any potential ambusher, but if it's Kempe, Roche needs him alive to provide answers and there's every chance shooting through the sheathing wouldn't leave the man fit to talk.

Roche puts a foot on the roof. He's four feet to the right of the open skylight and his boot rests on a nail head to give him the illusion of traction. As gently as he can without being overly slow and deliberate, Roche aims his pistol through the skylight at the area he hasn't been able to check out. He's waiting for the pain of a bullet hitting his hand. A shot exploding out of the sheathing, or strong hands hauling him into the house.

None of these things happen in the first second. Nor the second, third or fourth. He risks a rapid peek.

Roche releases the breath he doesn't know he's been holding. The room is empty.

Ten seconds later he's inside and ready to start searching for Kempe.

# CHAPTER FORTY

Roche pads his way across the uncarpeted floor. His every sense attuned to the possibility of discovery. A waft of something meaty carries on the air, and there's a stillness about Kempe's house that borders on unnatural.

Something is off about the house and it's triggering Roche's sixth sense. There ought to be the sound of a TV, or footsteps. Kempe tossing clothes into a case or moving around as he prepares to run.

The only reason Roche can think of for the utter lack of sound is that Kempe is lying in wait somewhere. Poised to spring out and attack. To fire shot after shot at Roche and Savannah.

When searching a building for a potentially armed foe, the recognized method is to have a team of operatives sweep through the building. By working in pairs, the searches can provide cover for each other as each new room is designated to be clear. The presence of a large force also deters ambushes from behind.

This is Kempe's house. His home. He'll know every point where he can circle back and approach their rear. Roche doesn't have the luxury of a team to help him search this house. There's no backup for him. Only Savannah. He fires a glance at her, sees that she's got her gun aimed skywards as she brushes her back along a wall. It's how he would have her position the weapon; no harm can be caused by friendly fire that's aimed at the ceiling. Her face is tight and there's a shine in her eyes that isn't fear, but Roche doesn't waste time questioning it. Right now the search for Kempe requires every shred of his focus.

The most perilous part of hunting Kempe is that when they find him, they need to take him alive. They can't kill him. Killing him will halt their investigation. Cut off their route to the person who's leaking the new identities and locations of those in witness protection. This means that while Kempe will be shooting to kill, any shots he fires will have to be non-lethal, or at least non-lethal in the short term.

Roche leads Savannah out of the room and into a space that has a descending stair and a doorway. It's the central part of the roof space, and while he assumes the other side of the stairwell will have an identical room, he still has to check it out so he's not ambushed.

Savannah understands his gestures and stays back with her gun aimed down the staircase as Roche creeps his way to the other room. As suspected, the other room turns out to be little more than storage space, and he's relieved to find it empty.

Now for the tricky part. As they descend into the main body of the house, anyone lying in wait for them will be able to shoot their legs and torsos long before they can be spotted. If there wasn't a safety rail surrounding the stairs, they'd be able to lean over the opening and scout it out first, but that option is denied them. To do that at the head of the stairs would be nothing more than an invitation to put a bullet in their brains.

To maintain any element of stealth, they need to creep down these stairs, but creeping is a slow process that will leave them wide open to a hidden shooter. A headlong rush down the stairs will perhaps throw off the aim of any hidden shooter, but if Kempe is elsewhere in the house, the noise made by a rush down the stairs would be sure to alert him of their presence.

Roche knows his options are limited, but the way he sees it they're not exhausted. To go for the best of both worlds, he steps forward at pace, cocks one leg up and slides down the bannister. It's not something he's done since he was a kid, but the familiar thrill of doing something he'd always gotten into trouble for hasn't left him.

As he slides down he's got both guns aimed in front of him. He checks out anywhere Kempe may be lying in ambush and finds them all devoid of human presence.

At the bottom of the bannister, he straightens his resting leg and trusts the plush carpet to deaden any thud his boots make.

The carpet does its job and Roche's first instinct is to check out every open doorway. He finds a bathroom, three bedrooms and no Kempe. A closed door reveals a linen closet packed with towels and sheets.

Roche pads forward towards a second staircase at the far end of the hallway. The stairs swoosh down to the left, but there's a door on the right. It's closed and there is the faint sound of a TV emanating from the room. He positions himself in front of the door with his SIGs aimed dead center and signals for Savannah to open the door.

She grasps the handle, twists and pushes. Roche lets out a breath and fights the urge to grip his SIGs like they are a safety rope.

Even as the door is curling open, a scent he knows all too well begins to prickle his nose.

# CHAPTER FORTY-ONE

Savannah doesn't have to be bosom buddies with Roche to recognize that something's wrong. His face says it all.

Roche steps into the room, his guns still raised, but as he passes her she can see the frustration in him. The anger that's bubbling lava-like and looking for a crack it can force itself out through.

She follows him, her own gun held in the two-handed stance she was taught. She repeats the arcs Roche has already covered as a precaution, but when she sneaks a look his way she sees the reason for Roche's distress.

Francis Kempe is slouched in a wingback chair. The bullet hole in the center of his forehead an acceptable reason why she no longer need fear him. It's obvious this is his den. His place of sanctity. The walls are covered with posters depicting classic 1980s action movies. The shelving is laden with sports trophies and guy gadgets, and there's a desk with a laptop and iPad on it.

"What the…?"

Roche doesn't finish his thought, and Savannah can't begin to guess at his thinking. What question he was going to ask.

Savannah can pretty much work out the sequence of events. After seeing them, Kempe contacted the person who hired him to have her killed. Whether he was issuing a shared warning or looking for instruction doesn't matter, he'd have reached out. Kempe's contact had obviously decided the best way to protect himself was to terminate Kempe. What doesn't make sense is that Kempe's communications devices are still here.

Anyone killing Kempe to cover up their involvement would make damn sure any electronic trail was taken away with them, or destroyed beyond repair. If they were so confident of their own security, they didn't feel the need to steal or trash Kempe's devices: there is little need to kill Kempe unless he knew their real identity. To her it seems unlikely. Kempe was known as the Wraith, so he's not going to breach his own security by working with someone he knows on a personal basis.

Savannah steps forward, tucks the pistol into her waistband and reaches for the laptop. She doesn't know what to look for, but she has to try looking anyway.

Roche flashes an arm in front of her blocking her hand. "Don't touch." His voice is tight with suppressed frustration and despite all they've been through, she's never seen him look so grim.

"Why not?"

"They might be booby-trapped."

"What? Connected to a bomb?" Not that she cares about Roche's feelings, but Savannah cannot keep the sneer from her tone. "You've seen too many movies."

"And you haven't seen enough. You don't know how the world really works." Roche stabs a finger at the desk. "If Kempe has been killed to stop him talking, and thereby protect the guy who's leaking details, then only a complete moron wouldn't steal or destroy his computers. Look at them. They're here. They show no signs of attack by a physical object. But, and I repeat myself, they're here. That tells me whoever killed Kempe, or had him killed, isn't worried about them revealing his identity."

"Yeah, I'd gotten that far myself." Savannah is trying not to rise to Roche's patronizing words, but she doesn't like being treated like a fool by anyone, let alone her loathsome savior. "So then, Mister Know-It-All, how are they booby-trapped?"

"Electronically. Either they've been wiped clean and their hard drives are back to factory settings, or there's something been added to them that will trash their memories when they're switched on."

Savannah withdraws the hand that was reaching for the laptop. "So they're useless to us?"

"Not necessarily." Roche fishes a complicated lead collection from his bag and plugs it into both the laptop and the iPad at the same time. The other end of the lead collection gets attached to a flat box around the size of cigarette packet. This in turn gets plugged into his cell.

Roche accesses an app on the phone, keys in a complicated code and then presses a green icon on the screen.

"What's that? What are you doing?"

"I'm sending the entire contents of these devices to a friend who can bypass anything that may be on them and get me the information I need."

Savannah can feel her back straighten. "*We* need. I'm involved in this too."

"You're the principal. You're here on sufferance, so if I was you, I'd keep my big bazoo shut and shut tight."

"Screw you, Roche. You're not always right, you know."

Roche's hand flies up in a "halt" gesture then places a finger to his lips. Savannah strains her ears as her hand reaches for the gun she's tucked into her waistband.

She catches what Roche had. The wail of sirens; and even in the second it's taken her to hear and recognize the sound, it appears to have gotten louder.

Roche's voice is filled with tense insistence as he points at the door. "Quick, get yourself gone. I'll handle this from here and call you when I can. Find a motel on the edges of town and stay out of sight until you hear from me. Here"—Roche shrugs off his bulletproof vest and stuffs it into his Bag of Plenty—"take these with you."

Savannah glances at Roche's phone. The status bar of the app is showing progress of forty-eight percent.

"You're waiting for that thing? You'll get arrested for Kempe's murder."

"Arrests are temporary things. It's only being charged that lasts. Now get moving."

# CHAPTER FORTY-TWO

Roche watches Savannah dash away and curses to himself. The arrival of the police is a complication he could do without. He's sure they'll be coming for him. It's a nice touch by whoever killed Kempe. His presence at the scene of a homicide will see him arrested within seconds of the police's arrival. They will figure him for the killer and at the very least will spend hours grilling him. If he's unlucky and gets the wrong kind of cop, the evidence won't save him.

He glances at his cell and sees the status bar is now at eighty-seven percent. He needs that to be finished before the cops arrive. In preparation for the arrest he knows is coming, he waits until the app finishes its task, unplugs the devices, wipes everything down and, after pressing Kempe's fingertips against his box of tricks, adds it to the drawer. Next he picks up his cell and makes his way downstairs as he deletes the illegal app.

A banging on the door is followed by shouts of "police, open up."

"One moment." Roche doesn't open the door. Not yet. Before that door opens, he has to make sure he's offering as little threat as possible to any trigger-happy cop who may come through it. He slides the magazines from his SIGs, removes the bullets from their chambers and lays them on a hallway table. By removing any weapons on him, he's limiting the reasons the police have for shooting him.

More thumping on the door and another round of shouting.

"I'm coming."

The Denver cops aren't patient people, which bodes ill for Roche. The door crashes open and he's faced with a pair of cops. Both are brandishing drawn pistols, tense expressions and finger-on-trigger stances.

Roche's hands are up and away from his body as he drops to his knees. "I'm unarmed. There are two SIGs on the table behind me. Their magazines are out. I offer you no threat."

"Stay right where you are, buster." It's the taller of the two cops who issues the order. His voice is strong and commanding. As it should be in this situation.

"Don't worry, I'm staying here. Do you want me to put my hands on my head?"

"Keep 'em where they are, where we can see 'em."

"Sure." Roche has been arrested enough times to know that complete and utter compliance with cops always yields the best results. "I'm guessing you're here because of an anonymous phone call. That shots were heard. If you go upstairs, there's a den. In it you'll find the homeowner. One Francis Kempe. He's been shot once in the forehead. I did not shoot him. He was dead when I got here. I'm a private investigator from Houston. In my wallet, which is in my left inside pocket, you'll find my ID and a license that allows me to operate in Colorado. I also have a license that covers the two guns I mentioned before. Mr. Kempe was someone I needed to speak to with regards to a case I have been investigating. He dodged me at his workplace, so I came here to speak with him."

"That's enough, buster." Tall Cop extends his arms the final couple of inches that lock them in front of him. "I don't care what you have to say for yourself. You're under arrest."

Roche stays quiet and listens as Tall Cop reads him his rights. It's a perfect arrest with no wiggle room for even the most cunning lawyer to find a loophole. When Tall Cop and his partner cuff him, Roche offers only compliance. The two cops are rough with him, but he gets why. They think he's a murderer. That he's dangerous, and they're tense and scared and probably that bit jubilant about catching him. They'll see career advancement, maybe even commendations, and they'll want to make sure they don't screw anything up.

As much as Roche is tempted to further protest his innocence, he knows this isn't the time. These guys are beat cops, not detectives. All he can hope is that when handing him over to the detectives, they'll give an accurate account of what they found at the scene and that they don't mess up any evidence that's present at the crime scene.

# CHAPTER FORTY-THREE

The two detectives sitting across the table from Roche wear cynicism like a second skin. One is a slouched woman in her forties with diagonal cornrows, the other an upright guy in his thirties wearing a suit so sharp it ought to come with a government warning.

Detective Ubuane shakes her head as she looks at Roche. "Do you really think we believe you just happened to be there at the time Francis Kempe was murdered and you are not his killer? That we buy your story about how you broke into his house just so you could speak to him regarding a case you're working? That you just so happened to have two guns on you when arrested?"

"We have, of course, looked into you and your background." Herron picks up from Ubuane's lead like a good tag team partner. "That while you've never been indicted, you're suspected to have been mixed up in several homicides in Houston and two in Dallas."

"I've led an interesting life." Roche makes a point of speaking to Ubuane. She's the elder of the two detectives, so she'll be the senior partner. She'll be the most experienced; she'll have encountered the wildest situations, and met more coincidences than the preening Herron. "But I wasn't arrested so you could ask me about my life story. Maybe you ought to look at the evidence. You swabbed my hands for gunshot residue. The tests will come back negative because I never fired a gun." Due to many late-night drinks with Zimm, Roche knows gunshot residue is undetectable after a few hours, and he's showered and changed his clothes since the gunfight in the middle of last night. "Your officers seized both my guns, which I'd placed on the table so as not to offer them any reason to shoot me. Both guns had full magazines and a spare round that I'd removed from the chamber. I had no other weapons, nor rounds on me. Therefore, all the evidence in front of you will be telling you I couldn't have shot Kempe, ergo, I didn't shoot Kempe, and while you're wasting time with me, his real killer is getting away. I'm sure you're well aware the first few hours are critical in a homicide inquiry."

Ubuane lets Roche's sarcasm slide right past her. "Other officers are looking into the possibility you're not the killer. Personally, I think you're involved. If you didn't kill him, you know who did and I'd bet a dollar to your dime you know why he's dead."

"I am sure you have lots of theories, Detective." Roche makes sure he maintains eye contact with Ubuane. "And that in all of them I'm a major player. But, and this is a big but, you don't have a scrap of evidence against me. I'm sure that in time you'll do a ballistics test with both of my guns and you will find *neither* of them match the bullet the coroner digs out of Kempe's brain. For a start, there was no exit wound. My SIGs are powerful guns. If they'd shot Kempe in the head, the bullets would have gone clean through his forehead and out the back of his head. I'm going to credit you with having brains, even if your partner wears enough cologne for there to be a vapor trail following him. As I have said repeatedly, I didn't kill Kempe. I was there in connection with a missing persons case I'm working on." Roche knows he needs to talk his way out of the arrest before the cops look far enough into Kempe's life to learn that he and Savannah had ambushed him at work. There was also the question of what else they might find in Kempe's home that would link him to the attempts on Savannah's life. "Ask yourself this, Detective, why am I talking to you without a lawyer? You're an experienced cop. I bet you can count on one hand the number of times a homicide suspect has volunteered to talk to you without a lawyer present."

"You say experienced and I hear old. Do you think you're going to talk your way out of this by insulting me?"

"Not at all. By my reckoning you're younger than I am and I don't think of myself as old, but yes, I've been round the block enough times to have gained experience. I was crediting you the same."

Ubuane lets a half-smile hit her mouth before her lips tighten. "You're quite the smooth operator. You're slick. Slippery. I bet that you're planning to talk your way out of here and you're so cocky, you're going to do it yourself without any damned lawyer getting involved. What connection does Kempe have to your case? Go on, tell me, what does a forty-one-year-old corporate director from Denver have to do with the disappearance of a kid from Houston?"

"With regards to you calling me a smooth operator, my partner, Leigh, says much the same thing about me on a regular basis."

Roche has only mentioned Leigh to buy himself some time. What he says next is the tricky part of his lie. He needs to have a plausible reason for entering Kempe's house with two guns on his person. His case needs to be serious enough for such a move to be warranted, yet not so serious it would be a police matter.

Roche has an idea. It's one that might just fly. Might just get past the jaded cynicism radiating across the desk. Ubuane wears a wedding ring and in different circumstances could easily fit the role of doting mother.

"Kempe is the kid's father. You'll have heard variations of the story a million times. A business trip. A lonely hotel room. Solace in liquid form. A stranger in the bar. Fumbling, sweating, three grunts and then an arched back. Nine months later the population goes up by one. Fast forward eleven years and the kid overhears his mother telling a new boyfriend about his parentage. Next day the kid's disappeared and the mother is figuring that he's gone to look up his daddy."

"Why didn't she go to the police? Call Kempe herself?"

"Kempe denied all knowledge of the affair. Said there was no way the kid was his. She didn't want to go to the cops because her ex, who's a real scumbag by the way, is a cop in the missing persons department. So she hired me. Hence me sneaking about Kempe's house looking for the kid."

"Why the guns? Why did you feel the need to break into the house? Explain those points for me if you can."

"Only an idiot goes into someone's house without having a way to defend themselves, and for the record, I didn't break in. There was an open skylight I climbed through."

"Why not just walk up the drive and knock on his door? Why risk a home invasion instead of having a door slammed shut on you?"

"In the second Gulf War, the US used a tactic known as shock and awe. It was about pummeling the enemy into submission with massive bombardments from many different directions. My tactics were along the same lines. Kempe had already denied any responsibility for the kid. If I'd gone politely to his door, he'd have laughed me off and left me no further forward. I needed to rattle Kempe from the start. To knock him off his game and put enough fear into him so he'd talk." Roche gives a shrug. "Okay, I'll admit that I was prepared to beat up on Kempe if necessary, but the missing kid is eleven and I'm an ends-justify-the-means kinda guy. I've a kid of my own, so as well as being a private investigator, I have a parent's perspective."

A look slithers from Ubuane to Herron. The young detective shakes his arm, exposing an expensive watch from his sleeve, and opens the file in front of him. "No traces of gunshot residue were found on your hands or your clothes. As you pointed out, no missing rounds could be found in your guns or their magazines." Herron pauses to flick an imaginary piece of fluff from his suit. "What you said about there being no exit wound also tallies with our thinking. The problem is, for all the evidence seems to be acquitting you, your presence at a homicide scene is just far too coincidental for any of us to believe. Your story about a missing kid is a good one, it's plausible. Were Francis Kempe's body not still warm, we might buy it. We have teams speaking to the neighbors. We're hoping someone saw you entering the Kempe property because we don't think you were alone. We think you were part of a hit team. That it was your buddy who shot Kempe and you weren't quick enough to get away, so you played the cards you were dealt, and now you're feeding us a whole load of crap and telling us it's pâté de foie gras. In short, this interview is over for now, but you can rest assured that when we've dug into things a little deeper, it will resume. Big time."

# CHAPTER FORTY-FOUR

Roche doesn't miss the fact that Herron's file is thicker and Ubuane's slouch is deeper. She looks as if she is carrying the weight of the whole world on her shoulders and someone has just added the moon to her burden.

Ubuane dumps herself into a seat and fixes him with a stare that would intimidate a piranha. "Let's cut to the chase, shall we, Roche?" She doesn't wait for an answer, and Roche doesn't interrupt her. "Your story about a missing kid whose father is the victim is the biggest load of hokum since someone sold the Brooklyn Bridge. Are you going to tell us the truth or persist with the lie? You haven't even named the client or the missing kid. That tells me you're being a smart liar and saying the least amount so there's less to trip you up with. So come on, Roche, why don't you save us all some time and tell us why you were really there or at least give us proof of your story? Who's your client? What's the missing kid called?"

"Client confidentiality forbids me from sharing certain information, so I'm afraid broad strokes is all you are going to get from me." Roche is curious about their opening salvo. He is expecting a neighbor to have seen him and Savannah together at Kempe's place. Ubuane and Herron might be holding that back to catch him with it in a moment, but he's very much of the opinion that they would have started with that nugget if they had it.

"You're a private eye, not a lawyer. Client confidentiality isn't something you can hide behind."

"And yet it's what I guarantee my clients."

"So you're going to take the fall in a homicide case to protect your client's identity? Wow, you're real committed, aren't you?"

"I didn't kill Kempe. You said as much yourself earlier. You have nothing but circumstantial evidence; otherwise you'd have charged me. You know full well that if I had a lawyer sitting beside me, they'd be arranging for me to be released."

Herron speaks for the first time. His voice low and bored. "Don't get cute, Roche. It's not a becoming look for someone in your position. You might be interested in what Kempe's neighbors had to say."

"Don't tell me. He was a pillar of the community. They can't believe anyone would kill him. He was always the first to contribute to whatever was looking for contributions. Stuff like that?"

"Yeah, there was all that as well. But that's not the interesting part. The real interesting part of what the neighbors had to say centers on what happened when they heard sirens. That's a good neighborhood, one whose citizens all stand up for their civic duty. They don't hear sirens and carry on with their day, they go to the window. To see what's happening, to see if they can help in any way. Want to guess what they saw?"

"Cop cars. Cops leading me away in handcuffs. A man who was wearing a striped T-shirt, a Lone Ranger mask and carrying a bag marked 'swag.' Perhaps they saw something else, but if they did, I don't know what it is."

Roche leans back in his chair and waits for one of the detectives to mention Savannah. There's no point hoping they don't know about her. That a neighbor didn't see them. The evidence of their knowledge shines in their eyes. For all Ubuane looks exhausted and beaten down, her eyes are as sharp and alert as her mind. Her body language is a smoke screen designed to blind him to the fact she's smart enough to outwit him.

"They saw a woman leave Kempe's place. A young woman. Blonde hair, average looks, but the guy who reported seeing her…"

A look of distaste scours Herron's face. "Well, let's just say that he commented on the size of her chest."

Roche keeps his face as blank as he can. The description of Savannah is accurate, if perverted. Guys will be guys, but some guys haven't the sense to keep their baser observations to themselves.

"We think this mystery woman is the killer." Ubuane picks up from Herron, her gaze probing his depths for untruths. Roche isn't worried about being spotted in a lie. He'd learned to tell successful lies to cops before he left his teens.

"It makes sense, but are you putting me in cahoots with her?"

"You tell us?"

"Okay, first off, as has already been repeated, you've admitted that you have no evidence of me killing Kempe. This woman would appear to have gotten away from the crime scene. If I were working with her, I'd be gone too. That makes sense, right? Also, if I were working with her, why would I stay when I had a chance to escape? You know what I did. I disarmed myself and waited for the cops. Those are the actions of an innocent man. Not a killer, nor of someone working with a killer."

Ubuane's mouth opens and closes again as she chooses not to say what's on her mind. Herron isn't quite so subtle. He reaches for his file, opens it and rifles through it. Unless the cops have already spoken to Kempe's colleagues, Roche isn't worried. The way they'd burst into the office under the guise of horny lovers looking for a quiet space wouldn't highlight in anyone's testimony, unless descriptions of him and Savannah were given and it's too soon for that to have happened yet. "You said earlier about your case. You're trying to hide behind client confidentiality, which isn't a privilege you have. That tells us you're lying. That you're somehow mixed up in all of this or are covering up a different reason for you being there. For the time being, we'll park that. Did you see any sign of this woman when you were in Kempe's house? Did you encounter her at all? Have any kind of standoff?"

"If I met an assassin in a house where they were executing a target, do you really think I'd be here and talking to you? Truth is, I'd be in a morgue drawer next to Kempe."

"Or she would. You forget, we've looked at your record. Your guns are SIG Sauer P220s, .45s. They are serious pistols. You said so yourself. They aren't what your average homeowner would buy for protection, and you have two of them. I'd warrant that you're also a fine shot. This woman may well be an assassin, but I'd say you'd be a fair match for her."

Roche allows a tired smile into his voice. "So, you've now gotten to the point where you've moved from the circumstantial to the hypothetical. Not a good look. Talking straight, you're in a forest and barking up one of the thousands of wrong trees. One or both of you has to admit it, you've got nothing on me. It's time you released me to go about my day. The sooner I find that missing kid, the sooner his mother will know he's safe."

"You're still sticking with that story?"

"My mom used to club my ear when I told lies, so now I tell the truth."

Ubuane heaves herself to her feet. "Okay, you're outta here, but you've not to leave the city in case we need to speak to you again."

"Fair enough." Roche has no intention of obeying Ubuane's instruction, but he's prepared to agree to whatever she says to secure his release.

# CHAPTER FORTY-FIVE

Roche rotates his arms windmill-style to try and invigorate his exhausted body. He needs to connect with Savannah again, but he also needs to speak to Xandra to find out what she's learned from Kempe's digital devices.

He tosses a mental coin for who to contact first. His professionalism tells him he ought to contact his principal first, but the nagging doubts he's had about her have blossomed during the thinking time he had between the interviews with Ubuane and her well-clad sidekick.

A part of Roche thinks he should cut Savannah loose. She won't know about his release. That gives him a window of opportunity to act without scrutiny. This appeals to him. He's used to acting alone. To walking in the shadows of morality with only his wits and willingness to inflict violence on aggressors to protect him.

The problem with cutting his principal loose is that she's headstrong. She'll do something stupid and possibly get herself killed. The biggest fear he's had since sending her away is that whoever killed Kempe was lying in wait. From the comments made by Herron and Ubuane, he knows she got away from the house. However, that doesn't mean Kempe's killer didn't follow her.

This means he's going to have to reconnect with her. With luck she'll be in an out-of-the-way motel like he instructed. A few hours' rest to recharge his batteries at the motel is all he wants right now.

He thumbs his cell and, after checking for any hidden apps the police may have put onto his phone, he calls Xandra. She doesn't answer, which isn't a good sign. A light sleeper, it's rare for her not to pick up. This is a setback he can do without.

His next move is to bring up the number for Savannah. In case the police are monitoring him. Metaphorically getting him to lead them to Savannah. He walks along the street until he finds a payphone in working order.

Savannah answers on the third ring, her voice groggy from sleep. That doesn't worry him. She's alive so that has to be good thing. "Are you out? I didn't expect to hear from you before noon."

"I'm out. They didn't have any evidence, so they had to release me." Roche looks along the deserted street and thinks about how he can get her location without asking. He doubts either of their phones will be bugged, but the rapidity of Kempe's killing has taught him the person behind the hits has resources, a hitman in town and utter ruthlessness. The fewer chances he and Savannah take the better.

"Do you want me to come get you?"

"Not exactly. I'll come to you. Travel at least two blocks from where you are and find a bar or diner that's still open. From there call a cab and have them bring me from the place we got new clothes to where you are." Roche lets out a long sigh at what he has to say next. "Give me an hour to get there before the cab arrives."

"You mean the…" Savannah's voice trails off as she realizes he's not giving any locations. He appreciates that she's smart enough to read between the lines, but the counterpoint to this is the way she's gone from frightened lamb to streetwise panther. For Roche it's yet another black mark in the mistrust column.

"Yeah. There."

Roche sets off walking. His cell phone is returned to factory settings and dumped in the first trash can he passes. The Nordstrom where they'd bought the new outfits is a mile away as the crow flies, but there's no way he's going to travel in a straight line. There's a chance that either Kempe's killer or the cops will be tailing him.

A low-rent shopping mall squats on the other side of the road, so he crosses to it and wanders into its depths. As bad ideas go, this is up there with putting your head in a lion's mouth, or French kissing a rattlesnake. The alleyways of a shopping mall may be bright and cheery during trading hours, but when the sun goes down, they become feeding grounds for street gangs. Their meals those stupid enough to enter the shopping mall at night.

Roche has a gun in each pocket and enough skills to deal with any aggressors who may belch forward from the darkness. He just can't be bothered. He's tired, hungry and he's pissed at the way Savannah is holding out on him. He has far better things to deal with than any attack from muggers.

The shopping mall closes around him like a shroud. It would set most people on edge, but other than staying alert, Roche welcomes the feeling of envelopment. He needs to hide himself away. To lose any tail he may have. A sprawling mall with multiple entrances and exits is the perfect place to do such a thing.

As he walks, the only sound is the rustle of his clothing. Roche takes it as a good sign. It means there's no one else around. He's walking with his head high. Making it clear to any observers that he's not a drunk person. His back is straight and while his hands are in his pockets, each is wrapped around a SIG. The expression on his face is one of grim determination, but even if he wasn't feeling grim and determined, he'd wear that face anyway. Muggers like easy targets. They prey on the weak and the defenseless. Roche is neither and he's making damn sure any muggers in the mall know it. Sometimes the best defense against attack is to make potential attackers fear you so much they daren't challenge you.

Off to the right, Roche sees four human shapes skulking in the doorway of a pawn shop. None of them are large and he sends a hard stare their way. He passes them and arrives in a central area. Once upon a time it would be decorative and welcoming. Now it looks jaded by the mall's downturn and the dim light. A column supporting the atrium's glass roof is adorned with a plan of the mall. It shows the various entrances and exits. Roche selects one that's at ten o'clock from his entry at six and strides towards it.

A scuff behind him sends prickles onto the back of his neck. Rather than show fear by running, he keeps his stride even and draws one hand from his pocket. Illuminated as he is by the moonlight streaming in through the glass ceiling, the SIG he's holding will be unmistakable.

There are no more scuffs, and although he passes a second knot of human shapes, they stick to the shadows and wait for a target they're confident of attacking.

Upon leaving the mall, Roche keeps on going, down one side street after another, until he finds a bushy park he can use to further conceal his presence. He veers off the path as he passes a large bush two steps after turning a corner. The bush's branches part easily as he inserts himself into its womb and waits five minutes. Not once since leaving the police station has he looked back to try and spot a tail. He knows that to do so would trigger a response from those trailing him. They'd be made. Their cover blown. Therefore, they'd have to react. Either to capture or harm him depending upon their reason for trailing him.

Far better to play the fool's role and then set yourself up for a spot of reconnaissance. Then if you spot a tail it's a case of deciding whether to elude or confront it.

No one comes. Not in the first minute, nor the next nine.

Roche levers the branches apart and rejoins the sidewalk. Ahead of him, a club is emptying out its clientele. Lovers and drunks hang off each other. A fight breaks out and a distended circle forms as clubbers observe the spectacle. Off to one side an overly amorous couple are pawing at each other as if in the privacy of a bedroom.

The clubbers are around half Roche's age, but the fact there's a couple of hundred of them is a good thing. He weeds his way in among the crowd and uses them to shield his movements in case his tail is better than expected.

By the time Roche arrives at his destination, he's as sure as he can be that he's shaken off any potential tail.

A cab pulls up and drops a window. "You Roche?"

"That's me." Roche climbs in and tries not to take deep breaths. There's a pine scent in the car that is obviously intended to mask the less-pleasant aromas left by customers, but it's strong enough bring a tear to a glass eye.

"Thought so. Can't be many people round here who look like a badly weathered gargoyle."

Roche lets the insult wash past him in a wave of apathy. So what if Savannah has had a joke at his expense? He's got bigger problems.

# CHAPTER FORTY-SIX

Savannah watches as Roche rolls over and picks up the burner cell beside the bed. Once they'd reconnected he'd gotten a new cell from his Bag of Plenty and fired off a series of messages.

"About time."

Roche's face is hard as he listens to the caller. Try as she might, Savannah can't eavesdrop, can't hear a word that's being spoken to Roche.

She guesses that it's the person he sent the cloned information from Kempe's devices to. It's critical to her that she knows what's going on, but Roche has already asked too many awkward questions and she's fully aware the more she pushes Roche, the more he'll resist and be suspicious.

"Yeah, well, if you'd had the last couple of days I have, you would be impatient and pissed too." A pause as Roche listens, his face inscrutable. "Fair enough. I owe you an apology. Will a meal at Gallo Rosso with the wine of your choice suffice?" Another pause. "Just think of their lemon posset."

Roche rises to his feet and pads across to the bathroom. Savannah is aghast at the thought of him taking a call while at the toilet until she realizes that's not Roche's intent. He's not going to the bathroom. He's using the bathroom to stop her listening in on his call.

He'd questioned her agenda yesterday. Probed at the story she'd told him. It had been a warning that he had doubts about her, but to actively make sure she is excluded from information he's getting, that shows his mistrust of her has grown to a point where he's openly criticizing her.

With the bathroom door closed, Roche's voice is no more than a vague murmur. Savannah's instinct is to call Roche on his actions as soon as he emerges, but she knows she'll get no truck from him. She's astute enough to realize that it's her mistakes that have tipped him off as to her duplicity, and that any confrontation will only compound previous errors. She's going to have to be more subtle. To have him thinking of her as a victim again.

Rather than be caught loitering outside the bathroom door, Savannah moves to the other side of the ratty motel room and perches herself on the chair.

Two minutes later Roche emerges, his face dripping water he makes no attempt to dry off.

"Well? What's next?"

He hesitates. For all his face gives nothing away, she can tell he's thinking what to say to her. How much to say.

"We wait and use the time we're waiting to prepare for the next step."

"And what is the next step?"

"Once I have a name and a location for the leak in the Witness Protection Program, I go and bring them to justice."

"Don't you mean we bring them to justice?"

"Absolutely not. When we leave here, you're going to go on a road trip. I'll hire you a car and then you drive as far as you can each day and stay in motels. You use cash, not cards, and you don't contact anyone at all. When the Leaker is brought to justice, I'll call you and then you'll be able to return to your former life."

"You mean home? Back to Houston?"

"No. You'll never be able to go back to Houston. You were in witness protection for a reason. Plugging the leak in the program won't end the threat from the people who want you dead."

Savannah lets her face drop. She's known all along that she'll never be able to return to her former life. What she needs to do now is make sure Roche doesn't send her away on that road trip.

"That plan sucks." She waves her hand towards Roche's Bag of Plenty. "Think about what would have happened if the cops had found that bag on you at Kempe's house. Me being there to take it with me when I left saved you having to answer a lot of awkward questions. Whether you like it or not, I'm useful to you and there's no way I'm going to risk a road trip. As you've already proven several times, I'm safer when you're around, so I'm sticking with you."

"The plan doesn't suck. It makes sense." There's a resigned tone to Roche's voice that tells Savannah he's prepared to grant her wish that she remains with him. That any arguments he's offering are for appearance's sake. "You will be safe on the road. You'll be at risk if you come with me. The guy who's been leaking must be behind Kempe's murder. He'll be extra vigilant and taking him down will not be easy. If I'm lucky, I'll get concrete proof of his involvement that can be handed to a detective I trust. I don't expect to get lucky though. I figure I'm going to have to take risks. To infiltrate either his home or his workplace. He's going to be ready for me, and we know from what happened to Kempe how he solves problems. No way am I going to waltz up to him with you in tow."

"Don't worry, I'll hang back, but let me put you straight on the road trip. It. Isn't. Happening. Period. If you want to send me away, you'll have to box me up and stick a stamp on the box."

"Don't put ideas in my head. Your life is precious to me. If you die, I won't get paid."

"So, now we've established I'm staying close to you for my own safety. What's the plan?"

"We wait to see what my contact can learn from Kempe's computers and then we make a plan. I'm going to grab a shower, something to eat and then I plan to get some sleep. I suggest you do the same. As soon as we have a lead, we'll be moving."

"Sounds good to me." A thought enters Savannah's head. "How do we know that I wasn't followed from Kempe's place? Or you from the police station?"

"We're still alive. I took counter-surveillance measures after leaving the police station. If you'd been followed from Kempe's place, you'd never have made it to this motel."

"Are you always so reassuring?"

"Only when my principal refuses to follow the instructions designed to keep them alive."

# CHAPTER FORTY-SEVEN

The diner is bustling, which is always a good sign when choosing somewhere to eat. It's a dime-a-dozen replica of diners the country over, but that's what Roche likes about it. The fact it's busy means the food will be good.

A server comes over, her hair in a messy bun and a coffee pot in her hand. "Morning. What can I get ya?"

"Ham, eggs, hash browns and toast twice over, please." Roche looks across at Savannah. "What do you want?"

"A bowl of the Berry Berry Muesli, please, but just the one portion, thanks." When the server scuffs off in the direction of the counter, she shakes her head at Roche. "Do you really need two portions?"

"I didn't eat much yesterday and I don't know when I'll next eat. Didn't you learn when you were in the army you should eat, sleep and crap whenever you get the chance?"

"I was never in the army. And eeeuuwww. Do you have to talk about such things at the breakfast table?"

Roche doesn't answer her. Instead, he focuses on the way she reacted to his question. The denial was instant, but there was a flash of something approaching satisfaction in her eyes. Like she was happy with the way she'd anticipated his question and batted it away for a home run. That in itself is telling. No way will she have prepared for such a question if there wasn't a lie in her answer.

What he can't work out is why she's hidden this information from him. And why she is so insistent on tagging along.

"Have you heard from your friend yet?"

Roche gives Savannah a hard stare. "Have you seen me take any calls? Have you seen me checking my phone? No, you haven't. I ask you, how the hell will I have heard anything?"

"There's no need to be an ass. It was an innocent question."

"It was a stupid question, and I have better uses for my brain than answering stupid questions."

Savannah sinks back into her seat. Her mouth a sullen line. Roche is content to let her sulk. He knows why she asked the question. She was diverting his thoughts away from her army past. He realized long ago that Savannah was a lot smarter than she was projecting, and the more he's learning about her, the less he trusts her.

He plays things out in his mind. Savannah is playing way more of a victim than she is. She can shoot. She was relatively calm under fire. She's never had the kind of total meltdown an ordinary rich girl would in the face of what she's been through.

By the same token, she seems content to follow his lead. She's not setting any courses of action, merely seeking his advice. Her insistence on sticking around could be a genuine fear, or some other motive. The fact she wants to know who and where the leak is coming from is understandable, but to want to help take him down speaks of another agenda.

The more he chews on the problem, along with his two bumper portions of breakfast, the less progress he makes. Events have all been too random for Savannah to have any kind of agenda. She was placed into witness protection and that's not something that can be engineered. No matter how he tries to find a motive for her wanting to take down the Leaker, he keeps coming back to the idea that it's her internal fury at being targeted that's making her want to take down her aggressor. She's also a good person at heart. She'd done the right thing by standing up and being counted when it came to testifying. Her morality had been first class in that instance, and he can't help but think it's that same moral code coupled with a desire to exact a personal revenge that's fueling her now.

"Sorry, if I was an ass. And for asking if you were in the army. You have skills I didn't expect you to have and that threw me off." Roche doesn't mean the apology he's giving. For him it's a way to defuse the animosity radiating from her and hopefully to drop her guard against him. If he's right about her, it may help. And if he's wrong, it's sure to.

"Wow, an apology from Mister Kyle Roche. What next, will there be snow in hell?"

Roche lets the sarcasm slide. He's been insulted before and by people who were far better at it.

A buzzing in his pocket makes him stiffen. Only Savannah and Xandra have the number for his current cell and he's sitting with Savannah.

Xandra's message is short and to the point. He guesses she's still smarting from earlier.

*Location is Boise, Idaho. Cannot be more specific without days of work and giving no guarantees. Proceed or stop?*

Roche messages back asking her to stop. He's got a general location. Now all he has to do is zoom in on it and he's already got a plan about how to do that.

# CHAPTER FORTY-EIGHT

Roche bulldozes his way past a stern receptionist and strides down the hallway to where the meeting room of TG Digital is located. He's back in Dallas, as the best person to pinpoint the exact location and identity of the Leaker is Tomas Gilmoure, the guy who made the operating system for the Witness Protection Program.

The door opens with a refrained squeak and reveals a typical meeting room. There are corporate posters on the wall, a large glass table around which are ten chairs. Off to one side a smaller table is laden with refreshments. Roche helps himself to a banana and uses it as a pointer. His first target is a tall thin guy with a complicated beard and a bemused expression.

"You, Tumbleweed. You get to lead the procession. Take everyone out except your boss and then forget you ever saw us. Can you do that?"

"I don't think so, buddy. We're discussing the algorithmic complications of marrying new database connectivity between existing and futuristic operating systems on a bi-partisanal level. Have you any idea how technical that is and how long it took us to get all of these people in the same room?"

"Do I look like I understood a word of what you've just said? Like I give even the tiniest hoot? I'll say it again, in case you're hard of thinking. Get everyone out except your boss."

Behind Tumbleweed everyone has turned in their chairs, but none of them have risen to their feet. It is a nice piece of corporate solidarity, but Roche isn't impressed.

"It's okay, we'll adjourn for now and pick this up later." Gilmoure has risen to his feet and is gesturing for his staff to do the same. "Go on, guys, head back to your desks for now. If someone could say to Marcia she'll need to free up the rest of my day, that'd be a great help."

Tumbleweed glowers at Roche as he leads the procession out of the meeting room. Roche can tell the younger man wants to barge him with his shoulder, but now Gilmoure has spoken he doesn't dare in case it gets him into trouble with his boss.

Savannah steps into the room after the last of Gilmoure's staff has left and takes up position beside Roche.

"Why are you here? What do you want from me this time?"

"Information. It makes the world go round and round and round. I've been on the trail of the people who were targeting my principal and I've come to something of a roadblock. You're the best man to remove that roadblock."

"Then call me, make an appointment or send me an email. There's no need for you to disrupt my working day."

"Oh, but there is. You see, there was an attempted hit on my principal. Other hits could be happening as we speak. Innocents dying. Slaughtered because scumbags want them dead for their having the temerity to stand up and be counted. To do the honorable thing. The victims of the people I'm hunting are folks whose lives have been upended because they chose to do the right thing. They didn't bow to threats or intimidation. Every day that passes could see another of these fantastic citizens killed. I need you to understand that. To understand that when I request your help, you drop everything to give it."

Roche feels Savannah's hand on his arm as she steps forward and gestures to the laptop in front of Gilmoure. "Look me up. My real name is Savannah Nicholl. If you look in the database, you'll find me in there. Except my name will be listed as Erica Dobbs. You'll see I was relocated to Pagosa Springs in Colorado ten days ago. Two nights ago, Roche saved me from certain death at the hands of two armed intruders. Since then we've been hunted all across Colorado. That will never stop. Witnesses like me will be killed. Our deaths bought and paid for by the people we've testified against. You can say whatever the blazes you like, but if you don't help us, more people will die and their blood will be on your hands."

Gilmoure's arms stretch out and there's a whispered rattle as his fingers caress the laptop. "Yep, you're in there. Okay, okay, I'll help. But seriously, there's no need for you to come down on me so heavily. He did that plenty when he came two days ago. What exactly have you got and what do you want from me?"

"We've got a location for the person who hired the intermediary, who in turn organized the hits. He's in Boise, Idaho, but that's all we have. What we want from you is a deep dive into the people working the Witness Protection Program in Boise."

"Those are US Marshals. Cops, in other words."

"They are. And the fact one of them is selling protected witnesses out makes their betrayal far worse, don't you agree?"

Gilmoure doesn't answer, but the expression on his face says everything. Again, his hands reach for the laptop. Roche supposes that for Gilmoure, the digital world makes more sense than the real one. It'll be his comfort zone, his happy place.

"You know, after you ambushed me the other night. You got me to thinking. They weren't pleasant thoughts. I wrote an algo because I wanted to check some stuff out. More as a belt and brace's piece of security, and, I'm not going to lie here, to protect TG Digital in case any blame came bouncing back down the line."

"What did you find?"

"Actually, I passed the task on to one of my team. I'll go fetch them."

# CHAPTER FORTY-NINE

Much to Savannah's private amusement, when Gilmoure returns he's got Tumbleweed with him. "This is Chris. He's been running the checks for me." Gilmoure gestures at Roche and Savannah. "These are governmental specialists who have been tasked with checking the security values of the WP interface. They're not tech-heads like us, so keep your conversation kindergarten friendly."

"I will if he will."

Roche fixes Chris with a hard stare. "I don't care whether you tell us of your own free will or if I have to beat each syllable out of you. Start talking."

Savannah punches Roche's shoulder. "Ignore him. He's a real grouch when he's not had sex for twenty years."

Gilmoure's eyes shine as he nods at his employee. "Go on, Chris."

Chris opens his laptop after sidling a glance at his boss. It's obvious he's equal parts irritated and intimidated by Roche. "I ran the tests as requested and I found there are certain trends in the data. Each client has regular checks on them entered into the system. The numbers tend to stack up into certain parameters according to time frame. As you'd expect there is an increase in the numbers the longer someone is in the WP program. Certain clients have spikes at certain times. I guess that some of them are more nervous than others. There are also periodical reviews of cases at times and these can create spikes, but these seem to happen from different areas of the country."

"That's all good, Tum... er, Chris. Now, what we want to know is if you can check a specific client and a location for people looking at that client. The client's name is Erica Dobbs. Are you able to do that?"

Chris's expression suggests that he'd be able to do what's being requested of him while juggling rattlesnakes. His fingers dance across the keys as he raises an eyebrow at Roche. "Gonna give me the location you want cross-referenced? And maybe a time frame?"

"Boise, Idaho. As long as there are files."

A rattle of keys, then Chris removes his hands from the laptop and drums his fingers on the table.

"Four people from the US Marshals in Boise accessed her file in the last two weeks. They were in the James A. McClure Federal Building and Courthouse. There's nothing listed before that."

"There won't be. She's a new client, although the fact they checked before she was actually in the program would suggest the marshals knew before the trial that she'd be entering WITSEC."

"A new client who's in the room. You guys aren't attached to the government. You've shown no badges nor any ID of any kind. What's going on, Tomas?"

"I'll catch you up later, Chris. For now, do what these people ask without question. Trust me, they're on the side of the good guys."

"Coulda fooled me."

Savannah digs her nails into Roche's shoulder to keep him from reacting to Chris's slur. She decides a spot of honesty will make things move quicker. "I *am* a client. Clients are being killed, and Roche here has traced the leak in the system back to Boise. What we need from you is everything you can give us on those four people. Names, addresses, service records. Anything you can give us might help. At the risk of being melodramatic, lives could be at stake."

"What about ghost accounts? Dummy ones? Do you want those as well?"

"Ghost accounts?"

"They're ones created for training purposes. There are also dummy accounts. The system has the option for people with certain clearance levels to create new user accounts for those who've recently been onboarded."

Roche's hands clench into fists. "What the hell does onboarded mean?"

"New employees." Savannah answers to let Chris carry on with his task.

"Then why the hell didn't he say that?"

"Okay." Chris has ignored them, which considering how grouchy Roche is today, is probably the safest course of action he could have taken. "I've sent the details of the four marshals to our printer. There's one dummy account, and no ghost accounts have been accessed from that location. I've logged every contact of the client to the office, and on days where there was a contact on the client file, I've taken a full list of the users who'd been active in that office on that day."

"Thank you." Savannah is quick to make sure she answers before Roche can. Whatever has gotten into him today, he's in the foulest of moods. Something he seems intent on taking out on Chris. "If there's anything else, can we call you?"

"You can call me anytime." Chris nods towards Roche. "Him, never."

Savannah doesn't have to ask Roche what their next move is. It's obvious: go to Boise to flush out the Leaker.

# CHAPTER FIFTY

Roche twists the key in the ignition of the latest hire car and scowls at the world in general. After all the cross-country flying today his body doesn't know if it's Tuesday or Thanksgiving.

They'd started out in Denver, flown to Texas and are now in Idaho. It's 10:00 p.m. local time and the weather is as horrible as he feels.

By using Savannah as a shield, he's pored over the printouts to do the cross-referencing Chris had set up. He's certain the computer whizz could probably have done the task in seconds digitally, but didn't out of spite.

It was painstaking work, but now he's got it done he recognizes what doing it the old-fashioned way has shown him. One of the four who'd accessed Savannah's file was ruled out, as they'd accessed it once for a mere six seconds and then never again. No new accounts were created for people who'd joined the Marshals Service, and there were no ghost accounts that had accessed the file.

This left him with three users as his suspects. Three US marshals. Three people who had sworn allegiance to the country. Three people who were trusted to protect witnesses brave enough to testify even though their lives were at threat.

His instinct is to capture all three of them and then persuade them to talk by whatever means necessary. Deep inside himself he knows that's the wrong thing to do, as it means two innocents will also suffer.

The rain buffets the rental car in crashing torrents. Each driven sideways by a wind strong enough to make walking against it nigh on impossible. The car's wipers slough the water off the windshield to the best of their ability, but the task they're being asked to do is akin to draining the Mississippi with an eggcup.

"Find a very cheap motel on the north side of town and set the GPS for it, will you, Savannah?"

"Why the north side of town? And why a very cheap motel? What's wrong with getting somewhere half decent?"

"Because I expect the Leaker to be taking precautions against us coming for him. There will be too many motels in Boise for him to check them all. In his shoes I'd check the ones near the airport and of a certain standard. Only an idiot would drive across a strange city during a storm like this one, so we're going to be idiots by choice. The McClure Federal Building is on the east side of town so that's also out. Therefore, it's a coin flip whether we go north or west. North is up. Psychologically it feels better to be going up, so north we go."

Roche doesn't look at Savannah to see what she's made of his thinking process. His entire focus is on the taillights of the car in front. He can feel the hunch in his shoulders as he strives to drive safely, to not rear-end the car in front, or veer across the slick asphalt. The road markings are invisible under the volume of water plummeting onto them. All he has by way of a navigational aid is the smear of the lights ahead.

"You need to hold left." From the corner of his eye he sees Savannah pointing at the GPS mounted in the center of the dashboard. "There's a turn coming up."

"Thanks. Keep those instructions coming. The way this rain is coming down, I daren't take my eyes off the road."

"You said on the plane that you've whittled the list down to three. How are you going to find out which is the Leaker? Turn coming up."

"I'm not. But I know the right things to look for and who to get to look for them."

"And who might this person be? And what are the questions?"

"Nobody you know and that's my business. You're my principal, not a partner, not a protégé or any other kind of trainee. Your role in all of this is to not get killed to death. So long as that happens, you have no need to know how I identify the Leaker."

"You really are a grouch, aren't you? Stay on this road for two miles."

"You might think that. Those who know the real me might be surprised how tolerant I've been of you. Now hush up unless you're giving directions. I need to concentrate on not crashing."

*

An hour later they're holed up in a motel room that Roche paid cash for. It's so down-at-heel its metaphorical toes would point upwards, but when they draw the bed covers back to inspect the cleanliness, they're surprised to see the sheets are clean, if washed out to the point of grayness.

"I can't speak for you, but I'll be sleeping fully dressed tonight."

Roche gives a nod and doesn't bother pointing out that he always sleeps with his clothes on when on a case. He might be caught napping, but there's no way he won't be ready for action the second he awakens. "See if you can order us some food from a takeout place. Pizza or something like that. Get me a large portion of something with plenty of meat. If they want a card payment, tell them you'll pay double in cash as you've lost your card."

"Pig."

"Pig's acceptable. So is cow, lamb, and chicken."

"Not funny. Those are all animals. Living creatures bred just to satisfy your carnivorous tastes."

"Human beings have incisors for tearing meat. We're genetically constructed to eat both plants and animals. I get your points on the slaughter of animals for food, but you can't deny that without humans eating meat many of those animals would never be bred. Surely it's better to have a life that ends at the abattoir than no life at all?" Roche keeps his tone even to remove any aggression from his statement.

"You're a pig. How you can glory in eating food with a face is beyond me."

Roche doesn't answer. He's had debates with vegetarians and vegans in the past and while he's never let it get heated, he knows they're as unlikely to change their opinion as he is his.

Their debate is interrupted by a double beep from Roche's pocket. He fishes the cell out and reads the message from Xandra twice.

"Well, what does it say? Who's our chief suspect?"

"It says that my friend is still digging and that to get a definite fix on the person we're after is going to take time. My friend says that it's going to be morning before they can give definite results."

"You're very careful not to say whether your friend is male or female, aren't you? Are they nonbinary?"

"Not at all. They just like their privacy and don't want me blabbing about them, as what they're doing is illegal. Very illegal. Surely you can understand the concept of privacy after what you've been through since I rang your doorbell?"

"Of course I can." Savannah leans back, her mouth drawn into a sullen pout.

While Savannah uses a burner cell to locate a takeout place, Roche replies to Xandra and adds a further request to his earlier one. He wants a deep dive into Savannah's life rather than the cursory checks Xandra had initially done. Specifically, he wants to know if she's ever had any military training. His next task is to message his cop buddy, Zimm. He wants to know everything there is to know about the incident that Savannah is alleged to have witnessed.

# CHAPTER FIFTY-ONE

Roche orders a plate of scrambled eggs with toast, and Savannah settles for just toast and orange juice. The late-night pizza has left him still full, but he's eating anyway as there's no knowing when he'll next get the chance.

The diner is nowhere near as busy as the one they'd used in Denver, but it's clean and the coffee is a million times better than the packeted offering in the motel.

A pair of construction workers joke their way into the diner. Each bouncing good-natured jibes at the other. Across the room a man in a worsted suit seems to be steeling himself for the day ahead, his eyes bloodshot hollows and cheeks strewn with spiderwebs of burst capillaries that both speak of alcoholism.

The waiting for Xandra to supply him with information is always something Roche hates. He knows that she'll be doing her best for him, but inactivity never sits well with him. A trait Leigh is often wont to point out. Or use as a stick to beat him with. Leigh enjoys sitting back and watching the day go by, whereas Roche likes to help the day on its way.

Xandra's message comes in as Roche is cramming the last slice of toast into his mouth. As always it's to the point with no unnecessary wording.

*Hal Fielding: 42, Married. One son, 7. Lives Winstead Park. No hidden accounts. Credit card debts of $4,562.55.*

*$67,500 left on mortgage. Excellent service record with 2 commendations. No sign of hidden online presence.*

*Marsha Johnson: 54, Married, four kids 18–23. All in college. Lives West Valley. No hidden accounts. Debts of $302. Mortgage paid in full. Husband tax accountant? Strong service record. Sporadic incognito browsing has taken place on home computer.*

*Bryan Ogden: 36, married. 2 daughters, 6 months & 2. Lives southeast Boise. No hidden accounts. Debts of $585.23. $97,300 on mortgage. Excellent service record with 1 commendation. Regular incognito browsing. Generally late nights/early mornings.*

*Background details on separate sheets for each.*

*All three on shift today.*

*Savannah Nicoll: Low on my priority list. More to follow.*

"We've got some results back. Base details on all three marshals."

"And?" Savannah's eyes shine as she asks the question. "Who is the Leaker? Where do they live? Can we go and get them?"

"We don't have enough proof yet. For all we've got some pointers, there's no way of proving anything yet." Roche pulls a grimace. "You know, unless I or my friend can get some solid proof, I'm thinking of handing everything over to the cops. I know a guy back in Houston who can make sure it gets acted upon. I'm sure your mother has some connections she can lean on as well."

"You're joking." The shine has gone and been replaced with astonishment. "You've come this far and you're giving up. I thought you wanted to make sure the person leaking names got what was coming to them. That they pay for the lives they've taken."

"I do, but I'm a realist. I know when to keep going and when to give up. Don't get me wrong, I'm still all in, but without solid proof there's no way I'm going to take any risks. The Leaker is a person who organizes killings for money. They're real dangerous and, against my better judgment, I've got my principal in tow."

"You said you're still all in. That's good enough for me. So who's your top suspect of the three?"

"Let me think for a moment. Since I got the message, you've been yapping away like an overexcited puppy."

Roche examines all three in his mind. Hal Fielding seems the least likely on first impression. Nothing hidden about him, normal debt levels and a great service record. Next he probes at Marsha Johnson. The fact she has minimal debts, no mortgage and four kids in college ought to be a red flag, but her husband being a tax accountant could explain a lot of that away. Tax accountants make good money and, as a family, the good work Marsha does as a marshal will offset the tax evasions advised by Mr. Johnson.

This leaves Bryan Ogden as a suspect. The late-night use of incognito browsing is a red flag if ever he's seen one. Except for the fact that there are two young kids in the house. Roche can read the subtext. It isn't hard to imagine an exhausted Mrs. Ogden being too tired to excite her husband every night, Ogden then feeling justified to watch a bit of porn when the rest of the house is asleep. The debt levels are what anyone would expect for a couple of their ages with a young family.

Although, if Roche was the Leaker, he'd make damn sure not to show signs of having plenty of money. He'd maintain a mortgage, a lease on a car and have regular amounts on a credit card.

The more Roche thinks about the three suspects, the more he gets a picture of who they are. How their lives are lived. He knows his thinking is merely hypothetical, but he's also confident he's right. One of the big things about his work is that it brings him into contact with people on a regular basis. Not your everyday "good morning. How are you?" contact, but an intimate look into their lives as he delves deep so he can fix a problem. His isn't a job like a kitchen fitter or car salesman who see people excited about positive change. His work involves him prying out secrets and looking at the parts of lives that are kept hidden from the world.

"If I had to point a finger at one of the three, I'd point it at Bryan Ogden. He's got two young kids, a near-six-figure mortgage and a habit of incognito browsing. All the same, he's forty percent compared to thirty each for the other two."

"So what do you do next? Stake him out? Take him into the woods and play with some ropes again?"

"Maybe for the staking out, but certainly not for the other option. Can you imagine the trouble if I did that and it turns out it isn't Ogden who is the leak? No, we're going to have to be much more subtle."

"How?"

"We have an address for each of them. Starting with Ogden, I say we do some covert digging on them. We know they're all on shift today, so we're clear to do a little snooping before anything else. Specifically, I'm talking about speaking to their neighbors, seeing what their peer groups say about them. That kind of thing."

"Won't that alert them to the fact we're hunting them?"

"Nope. We use the cover story that we're from the government and that we're looking to make a splash feature honoring some of our stand-up workers. We'll say we're making sure there's no dirt on our chosen people, but they must keep our questioning secret as it's to be a surprise."

Savannah's lips purse until she nods. "That sounds plausible. I take it that we look into Ogden first?"

"Yep." Roche waves a napkin where he's noted down Ogden's address. "Just let me go to the bathroom first and then we'll head over there."

When Roche returns from the men's room, there's no sign of Savannah. His first thought is that the Leaker has taken her, but there aren't any signs of her having been extracted by force and the napkin with Ogden's address is as missing as Savannah.

# CHAPTER FIFTY-TWO

Roche strides onto the street and looks both ways for signs of Savannah. There aren't any. She's neither left nor right. There's no sign of anyone being hustled against their will, nor of being subversive and sneaking away. He puts a call into her cell and gets its messaging service.

He marches back into the diner and attracts the attention of the elderly waitress who'd taken their order. "The woman I was with, did you see her leave?"

"Nope." The old woman fixes him with a stare. "Whassa problem? She off the clock now?"

"I'm a private eye. She was a client of mine. Not the other way round." Roche knows he's wasting time, but he doesn't like the waitress's insinuation about his and Savannah's relationship.

"You could be Captain Marvel for all I could care. I still didn't see her leave."

Roche ignores her and turns to a couple of teens. Before he even opens his mouth he's on the move. Both teens have cells in their hands, and he long ago learned that unless something happens on a cell's screen, a teenager won't notice it.

Another call to Savannah goes straight to message.

A frazzled-looking woman is also discounted as a potential witness. So is an old man with rheumy eyes.

Roche spies a young man with cropped hair and that haunted look of someone who doesn't fit in and hasn't yet found their niche in life. He's sitting alone and there's no cell to be seen. "Excuse me." Roche points at the table he and Savannah had occupied. "Did you see the woman who was sitting there with me?"

"Your daughter? Yeah, I saw her. What about it?"

"Did you see her leave?" Roche doesn't correct the man's assumption as to how he and Savannah are connected. It's a kinder guess than the waitress's.

"Yeah. She just upped and left soon as you went to the mensroom. Thought maybe you'd been fighting."

"She just got up and left. Nobody came and spoke to her? Nobody forced her to go with them?"

"Nope. You walked one way. Soon as you were outta sight, she went the other."

"Thanks."

Roche drops a few dollars on his table to pay for their breakfasts and walks outside. So far as he can work out, Savannah has fallen for his trap. Ogden isn't his prime suspect. He's a red herring that he's dangled in front of her to see how she'd react, and, lo and behold, she goes missing as soon as he gives her the chance.

In case he's wrong, he positions himself outside the diner and spends a few minutes watching the day go by as he thinks this latest development through. He's also giving Savannah the benefit of the doubt. For all he knows she may have decided to go to the store next door for something.

Ten minutes pass as he waits. For all Savannah has run off on him, he knows time is on his side. He has the keys to the rental car in his pocket, so either she'll have had to walk to wherever she's going or hail a cab. If, as he thinks, she's planning to hunt down the Leaker herself, she'll need to hire herself a car and to get herself a weapon. It's possible she'll try to use a knife against the Leaker, but common sense tells him she'd feel a lot more comfortable with a gun.

Idaho is a friendly state when it comes to gun purchasing. No state permit is needed. A license is required for concealed carry, but as Roche thinks Savannah is planning to shoot the Leaker, he doesn't expect her to worry about committing a far lesser crime.

The question that's plaguing Roche more than any other is whether he should move to stop Savannah. There's little doubt in his mind the Leaker deserves to be punished for his selling out of those in the Witness Protection Program, but is death a fitting punishment? Does he not deserve a fair trial in case any of Roche's evidence is wrong?

There's also the question as to whether Savannah should be allowed to be judge and jury and executioner. If she kills the Leaker, she'll have to live with her actions and face the consequences that come with the taking of a life. Roche can recall the face of every person he's killed.

Another thing to consider is the odds of Savannah being successful in an attempt to kill the Leaker. As Roche sees it, her odds are evens at best. There's every chance she'll be the one who dies and it's this fact that fuels his decision. He has to stop her, as if she gets herself killed he'll lose out on his payday and will have to deal with the knowledge that he's failed a client.

Most of all, though, Roche's thoughts are centered on the change in Savannah. If his suspicions are proven correct, the terrified shrew he'd rescued from Wingnut and his buddy has been replaced with a determined young woman who seems intent on exacting a biblical revenge.

He recalls the conversation they'd had after he'd released Wingnut. Savannah had been amazed he'd let Wingnut live. She hadn't actually advocated killing the man, but it was clear that's what she expected him to do. Had she been disappointed that he hadn't killed Wingnut? Or is she just determined to behead the snake herself and ensure this nightmare ends once and for all?

Roche uses his cell to search for a gun store and then points the rental car in its direction. As a final check, he tries calling Savannah a last time. As with every other attempt he's made since she disappeared, the cell goes straight to its messaging service.

# CHAPTER FIFTY-THREE

Savannah rushes across the motel room and heads straight for Roche's Bag of Plenty. Where once it had contained guns and plenty of ammo, now it's bereft of any weaponry. The guns had been left in a Denver drain as there was no way they'd be able to carry them on a flight. She hauls out a bulletproof vest and stuffs it into her own bag. Next she eyes the collection of spare cell phones. As a means of getting online to run searches they're a brilliant asset, but if Roche has them in his bag he's sure to have his IT-savvy friend tracking them, and the last thing she wants is for Roche to know where she is.

There's another device, similar to the one Roche used to clone Kempe's digital hardware, and what she imagines are other tools of Roche's dubious trade. She recognizes a tracking device, a variety of bugs and an acoustic listening device that has a fold-out antenna dish.

Savannah ignores all of these, but helps herself to two of the cash bricks secreted in a side pocket. She's going to need some funds and when you're up to no good, cash is always best.

As Savannah stuffs the wads of notes into her own bag, she notices the tremble in her hands. Her pulse is racing. Her heart thumps inside her chest. Today might well be the day she's been working towards for two years. The day she finally gets to avenge her brother.

It feels wrong to Savannah that she's stealing from Roche. As much as he's an annoying jerk, he's saved her life, and without him, she'd never have gotten anywhere close to finding the Leaker. For the man she's planning to kill in cold blood, there's nothing but an ugly hatred.

Excitement and blood course through her veins as adrenaline mixes in and prepares her for the challenge ahead. She knows what she must do next. What preparations she has to make.

As a bluff, a red herring, she taps out a message to Roche then writes the number of his current cell onto a piece of paper that gets secreted into her pocket. Keeping his number is a get-out-of-jail card. Her safety net.

She walks out of the motel without so much as a hint of guilt at the way she's shafted Roche. Better for him to be jettisoned before she shoots the Leaker and ends the life of the man who's ruined hers. Better for there to be a degree of separation that will furnish Roche with the luxury of honest deniability.

As she climbs into the waiting cab, Savannah leans back in her seat and exhales a long slow breath.

"Where to now?" The cabbie is unshaven and looks as if he's carried every imaginable kind of fare. His world-weary shoulders slump as he awaits her answer.

"Take me to someplace I can hire a car for myself."

The cab sets off moving, and Savannah touches the pocket where she keeps her new ID. As Erica Dobbs she will hire a car and buy a gun. As Savannah Nicoll she will kill the US marshal who's been leaking the details of those in the Witness Protection Program. Once he's dead, she'll move on and assume a whole new identity. Family money has been siphoned off from her trust fund and used to buy cryptocurrency. It was then moved around between so many places it would be impossible to trace. That was her fund for starting over as Erica Dobbs. It is still available for whoever she becomes when she begins building herself a new life.

# CHAPTER FIFTY-FOUR

Roche purses his lips as he checks the Bag of Plenty. Savannah has done pretty much what she'd outlined in the text message she'd sent him. At least she had the good grace not to take all of the cash and has apologized for what she has taken.

He doesn't buy that she's had a change of heart and has gone on the run to hide out in a motel until the Leaker has been apprehended. She's been too insistent, too often, on joining him in the hunt for the Leaker for her to give up now. There's also no reason why she couldn't have waited until he emerged from the diner's bathroom and let him know her plans in person. He sees the message for the smoke screen it is.

A rapid count of the cells in his Bag of Plenty shows that she's not helped herself to another cell. That's a shame as Xandra could have easily tracked her if she had. Another sure sign of the subterfuge at play is the fact that on her bed Savannah has left the cell she was using.

The missing bulletproof vest makes logical sense in regards to her claim to be afraid for her life. However, coupled with the other details he's noticed, her having it suggests to him that she's intent on targeting the Leaker herself.

He takes a look at his watch and does the math. She's maybe twenty minutes ahead of him. It will take her at least that long to go somewhere and hire a car. Then, like him, she'll have to find somewhere to buy a gun. Maybe a half hour each. That puts them more or less in the same position in terms of how soon they can get to their destination. In most cities he knows someone who can get him a gun quick, but he's never had cause to visit Idaho before so he lacks that contact. Thankfully, Idaho's gun laws work in his favor.

What he now has to work out is if she's bought his lie about Bryan Ogden being their chief suspect, or if she's going to target one of the other two. He also has to factor in the fact he's withheld information from her. She hasn't got the addresses for Hal Fielding or Marsha Johnson, or at least she hasn't gotten them from him. However, he doesn't dare believe that she hasn't got her own, albeit lesser, version of Xandra to help her track people down.

He filters all the known details through his brain as he lets the GPS direct him to the nearest gun store. By the time he arrives he's made a decision and knows what his next move must be.

# CHAPTER FIFTY-FIVE

The Glocks he bought at the gun store don't feel as comfortable against his body as his trusty SIGs do, but he's used enough Glocks over the years to be confident they won't let him down.

He's parked the rental car on a side street a quarter mile away and walked the difference. It's an inconvenience he could have done without, but there's no way he wants to make it obvious to Savannah that he's here. He's replaced his jacket at a thrift store and bought a cheap hat. It won't fool Savannah at anything less than fifty yards, but if she sees him in the distance, she won't be convinced it's him.

Bryan Ogden's home on Victory Avenue stands proud and straight. It's a single-story house with dormer windows. Colorful window boxes adorn each opening, although he can see the flowers have taken a beating from last night's rainstorm.

The entire street screams young families. Kids play in front yards under the watchful eyes of parents and grandparents. Multicolored plastic toys and climbing frames litter the yards, along with bikes and scooters that have been abandoned where their riders disembarked.

This is a wholesome neighborhood, one that would make a great cover for someone as nefarious as the Leaker. Yet, Roche has convinced himself Ogden isn't the Leaker. His record is too strong. The fact he's existing from paycheck to paycheck doesn't gel. The Leaker is sure to be making good money. Real good. It's one thing to hide your surplus cash and not live above your means, but nobody with young children could live the life of a near pauper without dipping into a fund that's bound to hold many hundreds of thousands as a minimum.

That fact, along with another key point, are why he's discounted Ogden from his thoughts.

Roche knows he's jaded and cynical. That he's been chewed up and spat out by life so often it's a miracle he can still have hopes for the future. He's also aware that he's not always been this way. That his natural optimism has been eroded away by the passage of time and the kicks in the teeth life has delivered him at regular intervals. Ogden is still young enough to have the zeal of youth. He'll still believe in ideals, that Uncle Sam's name on his paycheck means he's part of something good, and that the system can change to make the world a better place. As such he's unlikely to line his pockets by selling out not just the potential victims, but also the Witness Protection Program and the US Marshals Service.

Older people who've had years of fruitless collisions with the system, who've been beaten down and spat on by bureaucracy until their spirit is broken, they're the ones who betray. Who start thinking about their pensionable years, what they'd like to do during them and how much it'll cost. They're susceptible to greed, to upending ideals in search of the perfect life for them and their loved ones.

Most telling of all is the fact that Ogden has looked at Savannah's file more than thrice as often as either of his colleagues. While an initial indicator of guilt, it's too obvious for Roche's taste. Nobody who is leaking details is going to leave such an obvious trail to their own door. They'd get everything they need, write it down and then take it from there. They wouldn't keep going back to the source material. It could be the Leaker has learned his colleagues' passwords and login details. That he's used them to run his searches so his own tracks are covered. So far as Roche is concerned, his best guess is that Ogden has been tasked with a routine case review as part of whatever protocols the US Marshals have in place for those brought into the Witness Protection Program.

It has to be Marsha Johnson or Hal Fielding who is the Leaker. If Roche had a 401K, he'd bet that on it.

On his way here, Roche has made sure he's got an idea of the routes to and from Ogden's home so he can best anticipate Savannah's arrival. There's only one route in: from Victory Avenue. The backyard is hemmed in on all sides by neighbors. There's not even a lane wide enough to walk down separating the yards. The rear fences and walls serve two houses the same as the side ones do.

This rules out a rear approach as they did at Kempe's place. In a homey neighborhood like this, there's no way Savannah will want to risk crossing another property to access the Ogden house.

Therefore, she'll have to get to the house from the front. This makes scoping things out easier in terms of anticipating her moves, but also harder, as setting up a covert surveillance in an area where there is a strong neighborly spirit is never easy. Under the cover of darkness it's possible to set up hidden cameras; under a bright morning sun with people around, any attempt will see the cops called within minutes. Parents and grandparents watching over small kids notice things like strangers sitting in cars for extended periods. Doubly so when they're males of a certain age. A cover story about waiting for a breakdown truck will be accepted, but clocks will be checked and when the breakdown truck doesn't arrive, suspicions will be verified.

Roche lengthens his stride and passes by Ogden's house, his mind gnawing at the obstinate problem of how to ensure Savannah doesn't get to Ogden. Of how he can protect an innocent man and his family from someone who seemed hell-bent on revenge.

That's the biggest issue on his mind. Why Savannah wants to kill the Leaker. Yes, the Leaker has sold her down the river. He's traded her life for an unknown sum. But she's still alive; he, Roche, has made sure of that and he can't see why she's taking the risk of going after the Leaker herself. The prudent thing to do is to follow his advice and stay back while he brings the Leaker to justice, yet she seems hell-bent on taking the Leaker down herself. That doesn't add up on any level.

Roche carries on walking until he's got back to his car, climbs in and with his head against the rest closes his eyes to do some serious thinking. He's sure he told Savannah that all three suspects were at work, so he doubts she's going to make any moves during the day. If anyone sees him, they'll assume he's napping.

He fires up the engine of the rental car and sets the GPS for Marsha Johnson's address. Now he's got his thoughts straight, he can go back to his plan of speaking to the neighbors of both Hal Fielding and Martha Johnson in the hope he gets a solid clue as to which of them is the Leaker.

# CHAPTER FIFTY-SIX

Savannah parks on Victory Avenue and walks towards the Ogden house with a spring in her step. Off to one side a toddler wails and stamps its feet in front of a parent who's paying no heed to their tantrum.

A dog is barking excited woofs, and every few houses there's a waft of home cooking on the breeze.

Savannah's focus never wavers. She's got her eyes on the Ogden house, taking in every possible detail. The flower boxes, the garage door that's open to reveal one parked car and an empty space for another. The sides of the garage are an unfussy clutter of repair tools, ladders and kids' toys.

It's a normal space. Everyday, benign, and yet the person who parks in the empty space has by rote tried to kill her.

That's immaterial to her. The normality of her surroundings means nothing. Ogden must pay the ultimate price and she has a plan to make it happen. Sure, it's going to be a shame for his kids, but they're young enough they'll soon adapt to a life without a father they won't remember. Then they'll adapt to the new man or men in her mother's life until she installs a new father for them.

Her planned method of taking out Ogden isn't the way she's imagined doing things, but she's more confident in her new plan than the original ones. It's going to be rough on the wife, but Savannah tries to rationalize that as the consequences of marrying the kind of man her husband is.

She walks up the drive with purpose, as much to make herself seem normal as to comply with her burning desire to get on with the task at hand.

Rather than go to the front door, she skirts the garage and heads into the backyard. Front doors are often locked, whereas rear ones get left open for access to laundry lines, play areas and the yards themselves.

The Ogdens' yard is empty save a neat lawn and a vegetable patch. Savannah removes a gun from her purse. It's a Beretta she paid cash for and fits her hand better than the Glocks she'd had in Pagosa Springs.

Savannah takes a deep breath and reaches for the door handle. Her strung-out nerves might be screaming for action, but every part of her knows that what she's about to do is wrong on every imaginable level.

The door opens without so much as a whisper. From inside, sounds of a kids' TV show bounce around with animated jollity, although there's a snuffling wail underpinning them. Scents of home baking compete with fabric softener for supremacy. It's like the Ogdens are the poster family for the American dream. The interior of the house is a comfortable space filled with baby and toddler accessories, and there's a homey feel to its disorganized state.

Step by step Savannah moves forward, her eyes examining everything in front of her over the sights of the Beretta. The snuffling wail is a beacon that Savannah is getting her heading from. Any person who lives the life the Ogdens do is unlikely to leave a wailing baby unattended. Find the kid, find the mother. Summon the father. Kill the father.

Savannah steps from a hallway into a lounge. A toddler is focused on the TV while Ogden's wife is nursing a baby. The woman is thin with only a hint of a curve to her body. Spindly arms cradle the baby as she works her maternal magic to soothe it to sleep.

Two steps are all it takes for Savannah to get close enough to position the Beretta against the wife's head. "Make no mistake, it's a gun I have to the back of your skull. Don't move and no harm will come to you." Savannah had wanted to add the line "or to your children," but that's a step further than she can manage. To use threats against another woman is one thing. To threaten children is something she can't do, regardless of how much she may have steeled herself for this moment.

Mrs. Ogden stiffens, her entire body tensing. The baby senses it and begins wailing again. This time with purpose. Somehow the kid knows something is wrong and is telling the world the only way it knows how.

Worst of all for Savannah is the toddler's reaction. She turns, sees the gun she's got pointed at her mother's head and makes one using her fingers. "Bang. Bang."

"Frankie, come here, honey." Mrs. Ogden doesn't move any other part of her body than the hand she extends to the kid. When she gets close enough, she wraps Frankie into her body in a way that shields her from Savannah's sight. "What do you want from us?"

"I want you to call your husband. Get him to come home."

"Please don't hurt us." Mrs. Ogden's voice wavers as she speaks, but even though Savannah can't see her face, there's no hiding the effort she's making to appear calm. "What do you want Bryan for?"

"That's my business."

To put more pressure on the wife, Savannah drags the barrel of the Beretta upwards from the base of Mrs. Ogden's skull, the front sights gouging a track into the skin covering her head. When it pops free she bumps it down with enough force to ably make her point. "I don't think you're in any position to be setting terms, do you? Right now your options are kinda limited. You can do as I say or not do as I say. Doing as I say means you survive without another scratch."

In her inner ear, Savannah can hear Roche delivering this speech. It's not one she's rehearsed in any way and she can hear his logic in what she's saying. Strange how much he's influenced her in such a short time.

"But you're probably wondering what will happen if you don't comply with me. You'll be wondering if I'll just slink away, head back to wherever I've come from. You'll be terrified I kill you. That's got to scare anyone. Most of all, though, you'll be wanting to know what happens to your kids if I do blow your brains across the room. Will I go on to kill them? Will I take them with me? Or will I just leave them in here to sit with your corpse?"

"No. Please. Don't harm my girls. They're too precious. Don't harm them. Don't steal their mother from them." Any trace of calmness has vanished from the woman's voice. It now crackles and wobbles.

"I've already decided what I will do with them if you make me kill you. Decided long before I stepped on your property." Savannah did make that decision. It was a no-brainer. The kids are innocent. They're going to lose their father because of her. To also take their mother away is a step too far. "What you've got to do is decide whether you do the right thing and protect them, or whether you make me follow my decision through."

Savannah is glad she can't see the woman's face. Glad that she can't be seen by her lest she give her a clue about how big a bluff her threats are.

A sob is followed by a long breath that's dragged into Mrs. Ogden's lungs through her nose. "My cell is in the kitchen. I'll need that to call Bryan. But please, please promise me you won't hurt him."

Savannah's answer to the entreaty is another pistol bump on the back of Mrs. Ogden's head. "Using slow steady movements, stand up and go get your cell. Needless to say, my gun is going to be aimed at you the whole time."

Mrs. Ogden rises with such slowness, Savannah feels confident that she's not going to make a run for it, or try to disarm her. She's got the baby in her arms and little Frankie grabbing hold of her pants leg. No mother would risk a silly move in such circumstances. All the same, Savannah stays five feet away from her. Close enough to react if she tries to run, and far enough away to have time to prepare for any attempt to snatch the gun from her.

No attempts to do either are made or even hinted at.

The cell is retrieved from a kitchen worktop, and Mrs. Ogden turns to look at Savannah for the first time. Savannah can see the fear in the woman's face. It's etched into every pore, it's fueling the salty rivers running down her cheeks and it radiates from her eyes like the beam from a lighthouse. Her hands tremble and it's all she can do to pick up the cell.

Savannah tries to keep her face impassive. Hard. To use it to further intimidate Ogden's wife. If the woman makes any kind of plea now, Savannah knows she'll crumble.

"Take a couple breaths before calling him. Tell him the baby is ill or something like that. Tell him he needs to get home right away. Don't stray from that. Don't answer any of his questions. Say what you have to say and then hang up on him. If he calls back, don't answer."

Mrs. Ogden nods, the action flicking droplets from her cheeks. She juggles the baby to her left arm and uses a juddering finger to operate her cell. "Bryan? It's me. The baby isn't well and I can't find the car keys to take her to the ER. You have to come home. Right now!" She hangs up the call and looks at Savannah. "Now what?"

"Now we wait."

The cell rings and is shown to Savannah. There's a picture of a man holding the two kids and the word "Hubster" in a white font. Upon seeing Ogden's face, it's all Savannah can do not to take aim at the face smiling out of the phone and shoot his picture.

Instead, she gives a side nod. "We'll wait in there. Maybe the TV will stop the kid acting up."

Their return to the lounge is uneventful, but as they enter the room and Mrs. Ogden takes her seat again, movement at the corner of her eye catches Savannah's attention. It's a car going by. The same color and make as the one Roche hired upon their arrival in Boise. If it's him, his arriving is a complication she could do without; but if he interferes with her plan, there's enough bullets in her gun to solve any problem he creates.

The car keeps on going without any hint of slowing down or pulling over, and Savannah releases the breath she didn't realize she'd been holding.

# CHAPTER FIFTY-SEVEN

Roche snarls at himself in the rearview mirror once he's driven past Ogden's house. He wants to get on scoping the houses of the other two marshals. He wants to put a call into Xandra to find out what she'd learned and apply a gentle hurrying force to her efforts, but what he's seen in the Ogden house has him doubting whether that's a wise course of action.

The sun glinting from a corner of the window had meant the figures in the house were nothing more than silhouettes, but he'd swear one has the same body shape as Savannah. The shape's arm had been extended towards a thinner, less curvaceous human shape. A flat object had protruded from the hand, extending the arm to an unnatural length.

Roche has nothing but doubts. It was a fleeting glance between watching the road and looking at the house as a whole. There could be a simple explanation for the shapes. It could have been a friend passing over a remote control or a million other everyday scenarios. These are all likely, probable even.

What Roche doesn't get is the nagging doubt at the back of his mind. It's corrosive in the way it's eating at his confidence. He's set up Ogden as a suspect and laid him out in front of Savannah as bait. If anything happens to Ogden or his family, their blood will stain his, and only his, hands.

In his mind he can easily see a way for Savannah to flush Ogden into a trap. A gun pointed at one of the kids' heads would make the wife summon Ogden. After that it's bang bang, out the back door and off across the horizon before the cops are called.

The idea innocents may die because of his desire to reveal Savannah's true intent is abhorrent. He knows he can't allow it to happen, but by the same token, he's also conscious of the fact that if his uneasy feeling is wrong then his breaking into the house is sure to have an adverse effect on the case. Ogden's wife will tell her husband about him. In turn, Ogden will either call it in or mention it to his colleagues. One of whom is the Leaker. When the Leaker hears of a mistaken home invasion at a colleague's house, they're sure to recognize that a net is closing around them and react accordingly. That reaction will be a disappearing act. They'll vanish. Who better than someone who works in the Witness Protection Program to create a new life for themselves?

The whole destiny of the case rests on the decision he's facing right now. If Savannah hadn't left her cell at the motel, he'd be able to get Xandra to use it to locate her. Yet Savannah has thought of that. Which means she wants to be off the grid from him. That she knows he'll stop her doing whatever it is she plans to do.

Not one of these trains of thoughts gives him any respite from the doubts and fears he's experiencing. He has to act, has to try and prevent a calamitous situation getting any worse.

He spies a payphone and pulls over. A Google search gets him the number for the US Marshals office. He gets rerouted through three departments, but he eventually gets patched through to the witness protection team.

"Hi, Deputy Johnson out of Oklahoma here. I need to speak to one of your guys, a Bryan Ogden, regarding a consult."

The voice at the end of the phone is feminine, friendly and polite.

"I'm sorry, Deputy. He's not at his desk just now. He's due back in a while, though, if that helps."

"Can you patch me through to his cell? It's imperative I speak with him as soon as possible."

"So sorry, but no can do. As I understand it, it's a personal matter he's dealing with. Can I take a message?"

Roche doesn't answer the woman and replaces the phone in its cradle. The personal matter could well be a trip to the dentist, but that happening right when he suspects Savannah may have used Ogden's wife to summon him is a coincidence he can't believe has happened. He knows he no longer has a choice. He *must* get into the house and stop Savannah before Ogden returns home.

# CHAPTER FIFTY-EIGHT

Roche's instincts are to rush to Ogden's house, storm his way in and make sure the man's wife and kids are safe from Savannah. He knows better though. So far he still has the advantage over Savannah in that she can't know for certain that he's onto her.

As compelling as the urge to rush is, he makes sure he doesn't do anything rash. If Savannah has forced Ogden's wife to summon her husband, then there's at least a half hour's travel time across the city, unless he travels with lights and sirens. That won't happen because if the rush was that great, he'd have sent other cops, ambulances or fire engines to the house, knowing they could get there far quicker than he could.

This gives Roche a window of opportunity he intends to climb through. Not knowing how long it is since the call was made, he halves the travel time and figures on his window being fifteen minutes wide. That tallies with his look past the house and the time spent calling Ogden's office.

Another thing wrong with storming into the house is that it may well be a case of mistaken identity, and his charging about with guns in his hand will only end up with petrified citizens and a US marshal intent on finding out who'd terrified his wife and kids.

Roche walks back along Victory Avenue, its trees offering hiding places, but that's not the game he's playing. When you skulk behind trees and peer out, you draw twice the attention to yourself than you do when walking normally.

He gets within a half block and eases his pace. If Savannah is watching for the arrival of Ogden, she's sure to see him walking along the sidewalk. There's nothing he can do about that except duck into a neighbor's yard and hop over a fence or wall.

While that may work in a lot of circumstances, the houses of Victory Avenue aren't the closed-in homes of those who are trying to keep the world out. They're welcoming places with low walls and clear lines of sight. Maybe if this was the dead of the night he could crawl his way closer without being spotted, but it isn't, and he doesn't have time to wait for darkness.

With every step he takes, he's trying to work out what's going on in the house. Second-guessing himself as to whether Savannah has slaughtered Ogden's family, or if she's keeping them alive to use as leverage should she need it. In practical terms, it makes more sense to keep the family alive, but that doesn't mean it's what Savannah has or will do. Nothing about her desire for vengeance is making sense. A part of him is even wondering if he and his actions bear any responsibility. Since meeting Savannah he's killed a man, encouraged her to shoot at a moving car and tortured a man with enough brutality to break his spirit and force him to talk. None of that can have sat well atop the fragile state of mind of someone who's been uprooted from their life and forced to start anew simply because they did the right and honorable thing. Has his showing a different world to Savannah changed her outlook? Has he created the monster she appears to be becoming?

More information on Savannah and her background would be good and he throws a hypothetical curse at Xandra and Zimm for not yet getting the information he's requested from them.

Roche passes the neighbor's house and draws level with the edge of the Ogden property. He knows what he needs to do now. How best to get into the house. The question is, will he find a bloodbath in there, or a hostage situation?

As he steps off the sidewalk and arrows for the corner of the house, he feels a vibration in his pocket. How typical that Xandra's or Zimm's reply comes at a time when he can't stop to read it.

# CHAPTER FIFTY-NINE

Savannah casts her eyes around the room and tries not to let the surreal situation freak her out. She's in the home of strangers. In front of her a child is watching a kids' show while a housewife cradles her whimpering baby.

Toys are scattered around and there's a crib in one corner. The air is heady with the smell of baby powder and home-cooked food. Yet here she is, gun in hand, waiting for the man of the house to return home so she can gun him down. The wife and kids are sure to be traumatized. Certainly the wife, although it's to be hoped she can execute Ogden without the wife seeing it happen. She's conscious she needs to avoid little Frankie seeing it. The poor kid will have nightmares for years and she doesn't want to be the cause of that.

Savannah tries to push the name out of her mind. The toddler isn't Frankie, she's a little kid. Not a named person, just a bystander whose name is irrelevant.

The mother's face creases into a frown, and she lifts the baby up in front of her face and sniffs. The creases deepen as she straightens her arms. It's something that all parents do to check if their kid needs changing, but it's not something Savannah has ever really understood. Who in their right mind does a sniff test to see if a baby has crapped itself?

The mother's head turns Savannah's way. "Excuse me. I'm going to need to change little Lucy."

"Then change her. Just don't do anything stupid."

In one respect, Savannah is glad the mother has consulted her before changing the baby, but the way the wife named the kid grates on Savannah. No longer will she be leaving two unknown kids without a father. She'll be doing it to Frankie and Lucy.

Even as Savannah does it, she knows she's overcompensating for the situation, but her hand still moves round from her back until the muzzle of the Beretta is a foot away from the back of Frankie's head.

"P-p-please. There's no need for that." The mother's wobbling voice causes Frankie to look her way for a moment before the TV recaptures her interest. A finger extends from the mother's hand and points across the room to the lower part of a cabinet that has shooting trophies on display. "I'm going to need the changing mat, wipes and a clean diaper."

The shooting trophies unnerve Savannah. The fact they exist shows that Ogden is a good shot. The quantity of them proves he's an excellent one. Whatever happens, she cannot afford to give him a chance to draw his weapon.

"Get them." Savannah moves the Beretta to within four inches of Frankie's skull. "But don't do anything stupid."

"I w-w-won't, I p-p-promise."

Even as the mother walks across the room to get what she needs, Savannah can feel her own self-loathing increase tenfold. She has to force herself to relax a little. To not grip the gun in her hand so tightly. It's taking every shred of self-control she possesses to keep this up. To not turn and flee the house. When she'd decided on this course of action, she'd realized it would take a huge emotional toll on her, but she'd never expected that she'd have to endure anything like this. That she'd end up as a home invader with a mother and two kids held at gunpoint.

Savannah watches as the mother changes Lucy—no, not Lucy. The baby. Always the baby—with skill and dexterity despite the baby's attempts to wriggle from her grasp. The stench is overpowering as it beats up the home-baking scent from earlier.

With the baby again dressed, the mother sidles her way onto the couch beside the kid and cradles the baby in front of her.

Savannah changes her position in the room. No longer does she want to be between the mother and the door. Instead, she wants to be able to cover the mother, but also see out of the front window. She has to have advance warning of Ogden's arrival.

The rear corner of the room is cast in shadow and it's perfect. She takes up station and tries to ignore the snuffling wails of the baby.

"Lucy's hungry. I'm going to feed her."

"Okay."

Savannah's first thought is that the mother is doing this to personalize herself and the kids. The second is that the mother is using the kids' welfare as a smoke screen to attempt to try and fight back, but the baby snuffling against the mother's chest as she unbuttons her blouse erodes her suspicions.

The normality and domesticity of the whole situation become too much for Savannah. She just wants to run. To leave.

Except she can't. Not until Ogden is dead.

# CHAPTER SIXTY

Roche sidles along the clapboard of Ogden's house and ducks below a window. He doesn't know if Savannah is in the house or whether she's seen his approach. He's got to the side of the house by approaching at a perfect forty-five degrees to minimize the chances of being seen from a window facing either front or side. Every move he's making is based on the assumption that Savannah is inside the house and will be hostile towards him.

Down beneath the window he pads his way towards the back of the house, gun in hand. If Savannah's in there she'll be desperate, strung out and jumpy. It's probable she'll be holding the wife hostage at gunpoint, which means she'll be waiting gun in hand. Stealth is his only ally.

There's a passage between the garage and the house he uses to make his way to the backyard. He suspects that's how Savannah has gotten inside, and he knows from experience that while a front facing door may be locked at all times, rear ones are rarely locked during the day.

As he's slinking around the corner, he hears the screech of tires followed by the sound of an engine being pushed to its limits.

There's only one conclusion he can draw from such a noise and it fills him with dread. Ogden's arrival is imminent.

Roche steps forward and rests his free hand on the handle of the rear door. If the screech of tires has been heard by Savannah, she'll be even more keyed up. Her finger that fraction tighter on the trigger.

The door opens without a sound, or at least, not one that can be heard over the approaching engine.

There's a shorter squeal from the protesting tires and then the sound of a car door being slammed.

Roche enters a kitchen, and over the sights of his gun, he moves forward towards a door that leads to the rest of the house.

As much as he wants to rush, he daren't open the door without announcing his presence, or taking sensible precautions. Savannah will be prepared for someone rushing into the room. She'll be poised to shoot first and ask questions later. Or perhaps never.

He throws the door open after ducking against the kitchen cabinets beside it.

A pair of shots slam through the opening and into one of the wall cabinets. They are followed by two more, which are fired in a different direction.

Roche swirls into the doorway, the sights of his Glock searching out targets.

# CHAPTER SIXTY-ONE

Savannah is reeling from the sight of Roche standing in the kitchen doorway with his gun aimed at her. All the same, she doesn't let it alter her plan. She's confident she has the upper hand. "Ogden. I have a gun to your wife's head. If you don't step into the room with your gun held by the barrel, I will kill her." Even as Savannah speaks she can hear the stress in her voice.

"Don't shoot." Savannah sees a gun appear butt first in the doorway to the hall. "Ellie, are you okay? Are the girls?"

"Yes. We are… so far."

The fear in Ellie's voice tears at Savannah's heart. She now knows the entire family unit by name. That isn't part of the plan and never was.

"Moving real slow, Ogden, put your empty hand on your head and your gun down on the floor."

"Don't do it. She made me call you here for a reason and the only reason I can think of is that she wants to kill you."

This is the last thing Savannah wanted or expected. The wife to have the courage to call her bluff. To force her to make a decision. She tightens her grip on the gun and works out the angles. The second the gun fires, all hell will break loose. Ogden will reverse the gun in his hand and shoot at her. Roche might too. It's too much to hope that he'll turn his gun on Ogden to protect her if she kills an innocent.

So far, money has seemed a powerful motivator for Roche, but when it comes to the cold-blooded murder of an innocent woman, his morals are sure to kick in and turn all thoughts of a financial payday from his mind.

"Please. I'll put down my gun. If you want to kill me, you can kill me, but I need to know my wife and girls are safe." Savannah feels things are turning her way and it's all she can do not to smile in triumph.

"That's not going to happen. Nobody in this room is going to be killed." Roche steps in front of Savannah. "Ogden isn't the Leaker. I said he was because I didn't trust you. I was trying to get proof of how you have your own agenda, but I never dreamed you'd go this far. I swear to you, Savannah, if you shoot Ogden, you're killing an innocent man."

Savannah tries to ignore the gun Roche holds two feet from her head, but it's harder now she's less confident in Ogden's guilt.

Ogden halts mid-bending over and twists to look their way. "I know you, you're in the program. Erica Dobbs, isn't it? Or should I call you by your real name: Savannah? And who or what is this Leaker you're referring to?"

"He's someone who's selling out protected witnesses. As you've recognized, she was one such protected witness. I've been paid by her family to find and protect her."

"And you told her I was the person leaking? Jeez. This mess is all your fault. So help me, if anything happens to any of my family, I'll make sure you pay."

"Shut up. Shut up. Shut up." Savannah fires an angry look Roche's way, but doesn't let her gun move from Ellie's head. "Roche, you're a liar. He *is* the Leaker and he's going to die for what he's done."

"No, he's not. Nobody is going to die. Ogden is *not* the Leaker. He's innocent. As innocent as his baby girl."

Damn, Roche. Why does he have to bring the kids into this?

"What's your plan, Savannah? Is it to turn your gun on him the second he's defenseless? To swoop it up and put two bullets in him as soon as his gun hits the floor? What then? What do you think will happen? Here's a clue. As soon as I see your gun begin to move, I'll shoot you. Not a fatal wound, but one that will feel that way."

Savannah can see Roche lowering his aim.

"I don't care whether your mom pays me or not. I'll shoot you, right through your gut. There's a mess of intestines and smaller organs in there. Speak to any old soldier and they'll tell you they can remember the screams of those who got themselves shot in the gut. That's what'll happen to you and then there'll be a trial. You'll have three eye witnesses and forensics against you. You'll do time. Hard time. And don't for one second think I won't shoot you. The most important thing in my world right now isn't money, it's making sure you don't harm an innocent woman or her husband."

"Say you're telling me the truth. What happens next? Do we all go our separate ways?"

"I'll let you go. I won't do anything to stop you. I just want my wife and daughters to be safe. I want to survive this with all my family intact."

"We all want to survive this. Do the right thing and leave now before you make a mistake you'll remember until you're lying on your deathbed."

Ogden's voice is calm but strong as he speaks. "Listen to me a moment, please. I'm still going to put my gun down. I'm doing it as a show of good faith. I'm not the person who has been leaking details of people in the program. I've heard whispered rumors of it, but I swear on the lives of my three girls I'm not the person you're looking for."

"You'll come after me. You'll hunt me down for this, won't you?" Savannah can feel her grip on the Beretta tightening and relaxes it a fraction lest Roche follow through on his threat. "As soon as I'm out the door, you'll be picking up your gun and coming after me. I'll be lucky to make it to the end of the street before you have a gun aimed my way."

"I promise I won't. If you let me and my family live, I swear I won't chase after you." Ogden lets the gun drop the final three inches to the floor and eases himself slowly to a standing position.

"Whether you're lying or telling the truth, you need to take a step away from this." Savannah can see Roche has extended a finger towards Ogden, but his eyes have never left her. "This is far bigger than you can imagine. You know she *was* a protected witness. Three days ago she was in the program. Three nights ago two heavily armed gunmen tried to kill her. Two days ago we found the person who hired those killers murdered in his home. Then we learned the Leaker works out of your office. You might not be the Leaker yourself, but you know the person who is. You work with them. Sure, you may score yourself another commendation if you try following this all the way through. But if I was you, I'd be more focused on not getting tarred with someone else's brush. You said you'd heard rumors. Those rumors are true. I'm a private eye and I've been running this case back upstream to the source. I don't take kindly to someone selling others out, and I take even less kindly to gunmen trying to kill me. I'll be handing over the Leaker to the local cops or the feds when I have the proof they'll need to convict him."

Savannah can see Ogden's eyes widen as he absorbs all of Roche's damning words. She can tell he's out of his depth, and will remain that way until he has time to get his head around things. Using careful movements, she removes the gun from Ellie's head and points it to the floor before reversing her grip on it and tucking it into her waistband.

She heads for the door aware that Roche is covering her in case she makes any attempt to shoot Ogden.

Savannah has no intention of shooting anyone. All she wants to do is get away from this house. She pauses at the back door, turns her head and raises her voice. "I'm sorry."

# CHAPTER SIXTY-TWO

Roche takes a pull on his soda. It's sweet and cool, but that doesn't mean it rinses the taste of betrayal from his mouth. By the time he'd laid a final warning onto Ogden, gotten his cell number and made his way out of the Ogden house, Savannah was already halfway along the street in her rental car.

His primary thought was to let her go. Ogden will be sure to put a BOLO on her. She'll surely be picked up in a few days' time, unless she's a lot better at hiding than he expects.

Savannah has betrayed his trust. She's used him from the get-go. He can see it all now he's had word from Zimm and Xandra. He pushes thoughts of Savannah's duplicity from his mind. After this mistake she'll have to retreat, reassess and then start over. She doesn't know the addresses of the other two suspects. Doesn't know which of them is the Leaker and, now she's in the wind, she can't use him to lead him to the Leaker.

Roche knows who the Leaker is and that means he now has a target. A proper target with no hint of ambiguity. No room for error and no chance he's mistaken.

In a lot of ways he should turn this over to the cops. Zimm would snaffle it up like a dog eating its dinner, but that's not how he wants this to play out. The evidence provided by Xandra is concrete, but is totally inadmissible due to the manner in which she obtained it. Any cops presented with this evidence would have to start over, to mount their own investigation. To repeat the steps Xandra has taken. This route has room for error, for people less capable than Xandra to screw things up. There will be a constant danger the target gets tipped off in some way. Should that happen, the target would take to the wind and never be heard of again. US marshals who work in the Witness Protection Program are trained in creating new identities and lives for people, and the Leaker is sure to have their exit strategy already covered and in place.

Roche dumps the soda can in a trash can and climbs back into the rental car. Hal Fielding will still be at work, so it's a good time to check out his home. Perhaps there'll be an opportunity to sneak in and lie in wait. He doesn't expect there will be any evidence of the leaking in Fielding's home, but that's not his plan. Instead of getting physical evidence, he's going to extract a confession from Fielding.

There are many ways to inflict unbearable agony on someone without leaving significant signs of harm. A recording can be doctored to omit agonized screams. That's what he's going to do to Fielding. Force him to confess and then hand him over to the local feds trussed up like an oven-ready turkey.

If Fielding tries to resist or fight back in any way, Roche is comfortable with the idea that he may have to kill the man.

Traffic is light as he makes his way across town to Winstead Park. His information is as up to date as it can be. As well as digging into Fielding's finances, Xandra explored his personal life. Fielding's wife left him a month ago and moved back to her parent's home with their son. The separation had gotten ugly on social media, with the blame for the wife leaving the marital home laid squarely on Fielding's dalliance with their son's babysitter.

Roche cannot understand why people would air their personal misfortune in such a public manner, but he's long ago given up trying to understand social media platforms and the public's love of them.

*

When Roche pulls up outside Fielding's house he can't help but compare it to Bryan Ogden's place. Ogden lives on a street that has a sense of community to it. A street where there will be backyard barbecues with all the neighbors in attendance, lifts to Little League or other events will be done on a rotating basis with all families taking their turn, and there will be the peace of mind that comes with knowing those who live around you will look out for you.

Fielding, on the other hand, lives in a place that's more like a prison than a home. His garden is walled to waist height, with the top of the wall extended five feet upwards with timber panels. A wrought-iron gate blocks the drive, and there are a pair of Alsatians pacing back and forth across the short grass.

The house itself stands tall and dominant, like a drill sergeant about to inspect his latest recruits. Two stories of red brick, uniform windows and a steep roof.

In addition to the canine security, Roche spots sensors atop the fence panels and, considering everything else he's seen, he expects there will be security cameras hidden around the property.

Where once upon a time security cameras were useless if the property they guarded was empty, Roche knows technological advances have made it possible for the cameras to be linked to Fielding's cell phone.

Roche drives on a half mile, finds a parking lot and bends his mind to the many problems involved in breaching Fielding's security without being detected.

# CHAPTER SIXTY-THREE

The bug Savannah has planted on Roche's rental car does its job with aplomb. Unknown to him, Roche isn't the only one with a few tricks up their sleeve. A part of Savannah regrets not shooting Roche in the leg to take him out of the equation, but deep inside she knows she needs him to lead her to the Leaker.

As much as she despises Roche, she also respects him, and the fact that he's saved her life and is largely an innocent are the reasons she didn't follow through on that idea.

The house Roche slows beside is in the right district of Boise to belong to Hal Fielding. It could be that he's aware of the tracker and is playing her, but she'd planted the device while he was in the shower and for all he'll be suspicious of her, she's never allowed him to know that she's as well-prepared and equipped as he is. She's also taken the precaution of hanging back and following the tracker, rather than risk getting spotted by Roche.

The blip on her cell screen shows Roche's vehicle moving at a greater speed, so she figures he's driving off. Whether he's going to check out the other suspect or has a different purpose is unknown to her, but when she sees the blip remain stationary a half mile away, she can't stop a smug smile creeping onto her face. The place where Roche has stopped shows as the parking lot at the front of a strip mall.

Whatever his reason for heading to the strip mall might be, Savannah isn't worried about it. He's led her to Fielding's house and, from there, it's now up to her to take matters into her own hands.

She drives to the place where Roche had all but stopped and takes a look for herself. The smugness she felt moments ago is blown away by the vista in front of her eyes. In combat terms, Fielding's home is surrounded by a killing ground. Flat grass with no cover. The access limited to walls to be climbed over or a gate to be breached. A glance at the corner of the walls shows cables running back and forth, and she doubts they'll be for lighting. They'll be attached to cameras, or motion sensors, or some other type of security devices. The dogs on patrol are an added complication, although she figures a piece of meat stuffed with something like sleeping pills will solve that issue. The counterpoint to drugging the dogs is that unless she gets the dosage just right, them being dead to the world when Fielding arrives will be a huge warning to him.

The problems in breaching the house force Savannah to consider other options. Following on from the Kempe situation, Fielding is sure to have upped his game in terms of the precautions he takes with his own security.

Savannah runs through options in her mind. She could lie in wait for him to leave the house and then block his exit route and shoot him through his windshield. This idea is dismissed as soon as she has it. All Fielding would have to do is duck down so he was below the windshield and then drive back into his fortress. Alternatively, he could power forward and ram into her car. Savannah might be confident in her shooting skills, but she doesn't want to get into a straight gunfight as it could go either way for her.

Her next idea is to stake the place out and follow Fielding until she has an opportunity to get close to him. This idea also gets nixed. Fielding will be sure to spot her long before she gets close to him. A disguise might help a little, but he'll be on high alert and is sure to be paying extra attention to anyone who even looks remotely like her. Likewise, he'll be on the lookout for anyone wearing a hooded sweatshirt or tightly pulled down cap to try and obscure their face. Even if she can get close enough to kill him, the chances are it will have to happen in a public place and then she'll be taking a far greater risk than she's comfortable with. No matter how desperately she wants to kill Fielding, she's not prepared to spend her life in prison for doing so.

The same principles apply to trailing Fielding until she can draw up alongside his car and then shoot him through the window. She'd either end up in a gunfight or a prison cell.

With Roche out of the way, she parks around the corner and takes a walk until she's at the rear entrance to Fielding's place. It's little more than a door-sized gate. Unlike the front gate, it's timber rather than wrought iron, but the timber is stout and new.

Savannah knows it's a risk, but she needs more information. Her hands grasp the top of the gate and using the combined power of her arms and a starting jump, she hauls herself upwards until she can take a look into the backyard.

The two dogs hear her toes scrabbling for purchase and come towards the rear gate with subterranean woofs and saliva spilling from slavering mouths.

Savannah waits until the last moment before dropping back to the ground, her eyes absorbing every possible detail. It's another expanse of uneventful grass without a shred of cover. There are no plants, no bushes or flowers, just billiard-table-flat lawn.

But as hard as it may be to get inside Fielding's house this way, it's still the best option available to her.

# CHAPTER SIXTY-FOUR

Roche stands by the front gates of Fielding's house and peers inside. The dogs are barking up a storm and running towards the rear of the property. He can't see a rear gate but there's got to be something going on behind the house. It's possible the dogs are reacting to a bird or a wild animal that's gotten in, but he doesn't think so. The barks from the dogs aren't warning ones, and nor are they ones of welcome. They're angry and hostile barks designed to intimidate an enemy.

It could be a handyman or just someone passing the rear of the property. Whatever it is, he's confident it can't be Savannah. He's never shared Fielding's address, and since he left the Ogden property, he's weaved all across town and made sure that he wasn't being tailed.

He waits. It's all he can do. Rather than risk the dogs barking up a storm when they spot him, he shifts his position so he's leaning against the wall. In a street like Victory Avenue where the Ogdens live, it wouldn't be possible to loiter the way he is, but Fielding lives in an area where the houses seem fashioned for privacy rather than community.

The barking subsides and he starts to inch back towards the gateway. The dogs appear in the distance, and he bends down to their level.

"Good dogs. Good boy. Good girl." Roche can't tell the dogs' gender at this distance, but he's using the soft tones of a dog lover.

"Come on. Come and say hello." Roche reaches into the bag that holds the shopping he got at the strip mall and takes out one of the balls of meat he's created.

As the dogs come charging his way, he tosses the meatball between the gate's railings and lets it land in front of the two Alsatians.

The larger one on the right that he can now see is a bitch reaches the meatball first and disappears the treat in a single mouthful. He aims a second meatball so the other, smaller dog can get to it first. It too snaffles the meatball in one go.

Roche waits ten minutes for the sleeping tablets inside the meatballs to kick in. The dogs are more docile, but they're still more than alert enough to rip his throat out should he try opening or crossing the gates.

Five minutes after the second dose, the smaller dog lies down as if settling for sleep; but although it's showing signs of drowsiness, the head is never rested as it watches him waiting for a third treat.

With the third round of meatballs delivered, Roche starts to see real results. Both dogs are now lying on the drive and fighting to keep their heads off their paws.

The larger bitch is the last to fully succumb and, when she does, her body rolls with her lolling head until she's lying flat on her side.

Still Roche doesn't take any chances. He's given the dogs the minimum doses possible to get them to sleep, in the hope they'll awaken by the time Fielding returns home and not trigger his suspicions. He reaches an arm through the railings and gives a low whistle. Neither dog stirs. He bumps his keys against the metal of the gates and gets the same lack of response. Now it's a simple case of picking the gate's lock.

As he straightens to a standing position he hears a noise behind him. It's the scuff of a shoe, and as his head turns he gets a fleeting glance of Savannah's face and the butt of the pistol she's arcing towards his temple. His arm shoots up to block the blow, but he's a day late and a dollar short.

The collision between gun and temple takes no prisoners, and Roche's last thought as he slumps to the ground is Savannah is going to kill him.

# CHAPTER SIXTY-FIVE

Roche comes back to consciousness with the same torpidity as continental drift. He opens his eyes and sees nothing except the same blackness that was present when they were closed. He's lying on his left side and both his temples are throbbing like a trapped fingernail. Both his head and his feet are pressed against something hard and unyielding. He can hear traffic sounds, and wherever he is smells of chemical cleaners.

As a way to determine his location, he tries reaching in front of him only to find his hands are bound together. A touch to his face identifies the bindings as duct tape. He extends his arms out from his body until his knuckles collide with something furry and firm and flat. He traces along the material and lifts his hands up to confirm his suspicions.

He's in the trunk of a car. The uneven floor digging into his side and the flat, furry and firm surface of the back of the rear seats tell him this much. As frustrating as it is to be trapped like this, he'd not expected to ever wake up again, so he counts being in the trunk as a bonus. Not that it's a bonus he wants to collect too often.

As a modicum of clear thought comes back to him, he recalls the knife he keeps in his left boot. A scrubbing of his legs on the trunk's floor informs him the knife is where it should be. The scrubbing makes him aware his legs are also bound. Now the trick is to get the knife from his boots into his hands. Because he's lying with his bound feet on top of the knife, the first thing he has to do is rotate himself so his fingers can draw the knife from its sheath.

He uses his arms to gauge the height of the trunk. The last thing he wants to do is get halfway rolled over and find his shoulders or knees are jamming him against the trunk's lid.

Roche's elbow finds the trunk lid sooner than he'd hoped but later than he'd feared. It will be tight, but not impossible. He starts the roll by lying his arms as near over his hips as the bindings allow and corkscrews his back until momentum and gravity start to assist. Inch by precarious inch his body rolls. He can feel the trunk lid brush his shoulders and then his knees as he flops onto his back.

Now he's got this far, he shuffles himself as far towards the rear seats as he can.

Roche wriggles and squirms his body every which way he can to better improve his chances of rolling onto his other side. When he can get no farther forward he reaches for the rear of the trunk, his fingers looking for something to give him a handhold. He doesn't find one, so he leaves his arms extended that way and sweeps his knees in the same direction.

To complete the move, Roche has to convulse his body like a striking snake, but he manages to roll onto his right side, even if the effort costs him an already woolly head bouncing off the unforgiving side of the trunk.

The aggressive thumping of a stereo playing dance music passes outside the trunk but he pays it no heed.

Roche tucks his knees to his chest and sends his hands arrowing downwards towards the knife. Towards the first steps to freedom.

He gets his fingertips to the knife with far more ease than he dared hope. Or he would if the knife's entire hilt wasn't encased in the duct tape wrapping his lower legs and ankles together.

Damn that Savannah. So help him, if he catches up with her the first thing he is going to do is hand her over to the feds for what she did to the Ogdens.

Roche brings his arms up to his face, and using the tip of his nose as a sensor, he gently slides the duct tape back and forth until he's identified where the end of the tape is. He finds the end and grunts at Savannah's mistake. Instead of making sure the end was underneath his hands, where he couldn't get it near his mouth, she's left it at the sides of his hands where he can use his teeth to unpeel it.

Five, ten, fifteen times he grates his bottom teeth over the corner of the tape. On the sixteenth attempt he feels the teeth dig in instead of sliding over. He raises a corner and, while it feels large in his mouth, he's sure it'll be no bigger than a half inch. His next gouge extends the peeled section by half as much again.

Roche feeds the loose end of the tape into his mouth and clamps it between gritted teeth. He pulls his hands away from his face, doing all he can to rotate his wrists to aid the unpeeling. When he has gone as far as he can go, he releases the end of the tape and bites anew on the now two-inch strip.

It takes him five minutes to release his hands and he considers it time well spent. With his hands now usable, he finds the end of the tape binding his legs and unwinds enough of it to free his knife.

# CHAPTER SIXTY-SIX

Savannah trots her way back to Fielding's house at a steady pace. She could go faster, but as she's planning to lie in wait for Fielding she's taking care to make sure she's not doused in perspiration. Fielding getting a noseful of her sweat may well tip him off to her presence and she wants to make sure the advantage is all hers.

As she approaches the gate she sees the two Alsatians are still dozing like a grandfather on Thanksgiving. The lock in the middle of the gate is large and she figures it's beyond her meager picking skills.

Before she tries getting through or over the gate, she tosses a pebble at each of their flanks. Neither stirs, although she can't help feeling a pang of guilt for tossing stones, however small, at an animal.

Savannah takes a surreptitious look along the street. There's not a person to be seen, nobody is driving past, walking their dog or washing a car. A look at the houses sees nobody watching her from a window.

Before setting out on her mission, Savannah had bought a set of lock picks and taught herself how to use them. It's not a skill she's proficient at, but she inserts a pick into the lock and curses as she fumbles to pick it. The lock is resolute in the face of her attempts, and she daren't spend too long with the task in case a neighbor passes by, so she decides to climb over instead.

The gate isn't designed to be used as a climbing frame. It's nothing more than a series of vertical railings interspersed with two rows of horizontal ones at waist level. For someone as limber as

Savannah, getting up so that her feet are on the waist-high railing isn't hard. It's getting over the top that is the problem.

The top of the gate is curved to form an arch shape, and although she's able to reach the top railing, there's nothing for her to plant her feet on so she can scale her way over the gate.

To give herself a fighting chance, she shimmies across from the gatepost until her arms are at full stretch but still have a firm grip of the top rail. In one swift movement she both jumps as high as she can and hoists herself upwards.

Savannah's arms strain to pull her body over the gate. She's got her elbows level with the curving top rail, but a series of fleur-de-lis ornaments prevent her from lodging them atop the rail and then levering herself upwards.

As her shoulders are now at the same height as her hands, Savannah shoots her left leg out from her right, thrusting both sideways and upwards.

Her toes miss catching over the top rail by two inches. A second attempt sees them get within one inch. Savannah grits her teeth into a snarl either of the Alsatians would be proud of and summons every last morsel of her strength for a final try, before she has to drop down and rest before starting over.

"Come on, Sav, you can do it."

Whether its desperation or the words of self-encouragement that work doesn't matter to Savannah. All that matters is that she's got a foot hooked over the top rail and braced against a fleur-de-lis. Her body is twisted at an awkward angle, and she can feel the muscles of her arms burning in protest at her unusual demands of them.

Fraction by torturous fraction, Savannah manages to lift herself upwards until she can hook an elbow over one of the fleur-de-lis. Her next move is to lift herself and brace her other elbow against a fleur-de-lis and free the other arm.

Every movement is a delicate mixture of maintaining balance and drawing upon reserves of strength and grit. Savannah frees the hooked elbow, and by using the fleur-de-lis as backstops manages to walk her upper body towards the foot she has braced.

Two minutes after first clambering onto the gate, Savannah has her feet resting on the top rail. The smart thing to do would be to lower herself down in a more graceful fashion than the way she'd scaled the gate, but she doesn't have the will or strength to do that. She's also spent way more time getting past the gate than she'd intended, so she opts for the quick method and leaps towards the lawn beside the drive.

Savannah's knees are bent to absorb the impact, and she makes sure she tumbles into a roll to break the fall.

She's in, or at least into the yard. Now it's a case of getting into the house and finding a good spot to lie in wait for Fielding's return.

# CHAPTER SIXTY-SEVEN

Now he's free from his bindings, Roche turns to the hardest part of his escape act: getting free of the trunk. He pats his pockets looking for his cell. It's gone from the shirt pocket he keeps it in, and he can find no sign of it by rubbing the floor of the trunk. Likewise, his gun has been removed from its holster. All he has is the knife and his wits.

In theory, he could use the knife to cut his way into the rear of the car, but that would be a long and arduous task, as the seats are sure to have metal springs inside plus a plastic rear edge.

When he explores the trunk lid looking for the opening mechanism, he finds that it's all sealed in by a covering panel. His fingertips trace its surface until he finds one of the plastic buttons that cover a fixing.

A gentle probing twist of his knife pops the button. In the darkness he can't see the head of the fixing, but by tracing it with the tip of his knife, he determines that it has a sunken hexagonal hole for an Allen wrench to slot into.

Roche pushes the point of his knife into the indented socket and tries to give it a turn. The knife doesn't want to rotate. This is a good sign; it means that enough of the knife's tip is getting a decent hold for him to exert enough pressure to remove the fixing.

Sweat beads spring up all over his body as he pushes the knife into the socket to stop it twisting out as he puts the necessary muscle required into unscrewing the fixing. The beads of sweat don't even get noticed as the screw begins to turn.

It takes Roche ten minutes to remove all three of the fixings from the base of the trunk lid. He places one hand on the base of the covering and pulls. The covering creases towards him far enough for him to slip his other hand beneath it and up towards the point where the lock mechanism will be housed.

Roches's fingers find the space where the lock is and feels around it. There's an electric motor and sensor, no doubt for the blipper on the keys. Short of having some electronic gadgetry, there isn't much he can do to make that work, but the trunk has an old-fashioned lock as backup. There's a rod traveling down from the keyhole to the lock mechanism.

Straining fingers wrap themselves around the rod in its narrow home and grip tight. Roche jerks up and then down without success. He tries again and hears the most wonderful metallic pop he's ever heard.

He lifts the lid of the trunk and breathes in clean fresh air. A woman unloading a shopping cart into an SUV turns his way, her face a mixture of shock and fear.

Roche levers himself from the trunk and sends a rueful glance in the woman's direction. "That's the last time I go on a bachelor party with those guys."

Her response is to give him the kind of look that's normally reserved for rioting hordes.

She can go hang. He has other things on his mind. Most important of all is working out where he is.

He looks around and sees a strip mall across the road. He's in the parking lot of a supermarket, and the car he's been imprisoned in is his rental SUV. The car keys rest on the back seat beside his Bag of Plenty. He tries the door and finds it unlocked. The trunk had been locked, but he figures the way he'd popped the lock must have triggered some form of safety mechanism that unlocked all doors. The fact Savannah left the keys spoke to an inherent decency at odds with her behavior at Ogden's place.

A more detailed look around tells him the supermarket is across the street from the strip mall he'd visited earlier. This is good news. It means he knows where he is. How to get back to Fielding's house.

Despite this tiny piece of good fortune, Roche knows he needs to arm himself again and to do that he's going to need money and ID. Or at least, to legally obtain a weapon, that's what he needs.

He casts his eyes into the back of the rental car. Savannah has made another mistake. Instead of stealing his Bag of Plenty, she's left it for him.

It takes him less than three seconds to get the Bag of Plenty opened up. As he expected, Savannah has been in the bag again and his guns are gone, but she's dropped his cell and wallet into the bag, which means he has ID. Savannah has left the bricks of cash, although it hadn't escaped him that she'd taken two when she ditched him earlier in the day.

Roche stretches out his aching limbs and wills his brain to work at its usual capacity. He needs to get a gun and then get back to Fielding's house before Savannah kills him. Her motive, if there is one beyond righteous anger at being targeted, is something he can puzzle over later.

# CHAPTER SIXTY-EIGHT

Savannah works her way around the house looking for an entry point. It's a complete waste of time. There are no open windows. The doors are all locked and there are no fake rocks playing home to a spare key. In a lot of ways the house seems impregnable.

It isn't, of course. There are always ways in. She could smash a window at the rear and set up her ambush at a point where she would be able to take down Fielding long before he realizes she's broken a window. As tempting as the idea might be, she knows real life isn't like the movies. A movie star might be able to smash a window and have the fake glass all fall to the ground, leaving no shards to shred them as they climbed through.

Back when she was ten, Mother had replaced all the windows of their home. She'd watched the carpenters as they'd worked to remove all the old glass before cutting out the frames. Not once had the glass broken neatly. Every time a pane was smashed there were jagged shards left protruding from every surface. Another reason for her reticence to break a window are the two Alsatians. Sooner or later they'll wake up and resume their patrolling of the grounds. The last thing she wants is for either of the dogs to cut their paws or their noses if they go snuffling at the foreign objects in their domain.

If the level of security Fielding is displaying for his grounds is carried into his home, she's sure he'll have a good quality lock on his doors. All the same, at least here she can't be seen as she works at picking the lock.

Other than breaking a window, she has no other option.

Savannah inserts her picks into the lock of the rear door. It's a typical mortise lock and from what she can tell it has five tumblers. Five separate parts to locate and activate before the door will allow her into the house.

She wipes her forehead against the top of her arm and focuses every part of her brain onto the messages being transferred along the lock picks and onto her fingers.

One by one she shifts the well-oiled mechanisms inside the lock until she hears a defined click.

Step one was always gain entry. Step two is where things will get tricky. Fielding won't be easy to ambush.

Savannah pushes the door wide open and prepares to sprint towards the back gate if she hears the sound of an alarm.

There's no alarm so she slips into the house and closes the door behind her. She estimates it's unlikely Fielding will come this way, as the other door is much closer to the drive, so she grabs a broom and jams one end of it against a wall and the other on the handle side of the door. No matter how many keys Fielding has in his pocket, he won't be able to open this door until the broom is removed.

Next she starts a full and proper search of the house. She's looking for weapons caches, and any hint of Fielding's trade in delivering protected witnesses to waiting assassins.

Room by room she checks the house. She looks in closets, drawers and teases paintings off walls in her search.

Nowhere does she find what she's looking for. The house is devoid of feminine touches, there are no soft furnishings and none of the things she expected to find in the home of a kid. It's as she's going through the closet spaces that she makes a discovery. It's more what she doesn't find than what she does. There are no clothes or toys in the kid's bedroom. No female clothes or cosmetics in the master bedroom. The empty closets and drawers speak of divorce rather than vacation.

With the house not yielding any notable result beyond a password-protected laptop, Savannah moves her search for weapons to the garage.

The garage has been converted into a carpenter's workshop. There are various woodworking machines, each with a skirt of shavings or sawdust around it, and an assembly bench that bears a half-assembled chair, and a wall board from which woodworking tools hang. The scent of pine might hang in the air, but none of these items hold Savannah's attention for more than a fraction of a second. Not with the other thing she's seen.

Affixed to one wall is what she suspects is a gun cabinet. It's metal, four feet tall, three wide and around nine inches deep. Its door is guarded by an electronic keypad, and there are traces of what looks to be a felt seal poking out from the sides of the door. The seal makes sense. Fielding will want his guns to be kept dust free, and Savannah is prepared to bet her inheritance that, at the very least, the guns inside the cabinet are draped in a dustsheet.

Savannah bends forward and peers at the keypad. She's looking for signs of wear on the keys in the hope of getting a clue as to the code, but none are worn more than any other.

Rather than waste time trying random sequences, Savannah doesn't worry herself too much about the gun cabinet. She knows where it is and that knowledge will protect her. If things don't go to plan with Fielding, she knows where he'll try to make for, and now she has this knowledge, she'll be able to position herself to always be between him and the gun cabinet.

It takes her but a few seconds to find a vantage point where she'll be able to shoot Fielding as soon as he enters the door and yet still keep herself between him and his gun cabinet. She's even afforded a view of the drive so she'll have fair warning of Fielding's arrival.

# CHAPTER SIXTY-NINE

Roche squints at the sun's brightness as he walks across to the strip mall. Both temples throb and his thought processes are slower than he'd like them to be. Worst of all is the stiffness he feels from his time spent in the trunk.

He checks his watch and is relieved to see that it's not yet late enough in the day for Fielding to have finished his shift, but there's a fair chance he'll soon be on his way home. As much as his aching muscles allow, he hustles as fast as he can towards the gun store. In an ideal world he'd check out the other stores, but with the ticking clock against him, he doesn't have that luxury.

The guy behind the counter is a wrinkled specimen with gray hairs sprouting from several parts of his chin. They remind Roche of the trees that remain standing after a hurricane has passed by.

Roche doesn't waste any time browsing. He just walks straight up to the old guy who is leafing through a manufacturer's catalogue. "Hi. I'm after a pair of SIGs, preferably 228s or 226s if you don't have 228s. I also want holsters for them, four spare magazines and a pump-action shotgun, 12 gauge."

"You fixin' to go to war, sonny?" The old guy speaks from the side of his mouth, his lips drawn into a sideways teardrop.

Roche is prepared for such a reaction and has concocted a lie. "No way, sir. My wife threw my guns out in an argument. Right into the back of the garbage truck they went. They were all gobbled up before I could get the guys to stop."

"Sure as hell seems like you's goin' to war."

"No, sir. Just making sure I can keep my family safe." Roche is careful not to show any impatience in his body language. "There have been some break-ins on our street, and one woman was held at gunpoint while her house was robbed. I don't want that happening to me or any of my family."

"I hear you, sonny, I hear you." A gnarled hand gestures at a gun safe. "You want somewhere to keep 'em safe from your wife? It's got one of those keypads you can set a code for."

"No, thanks. I've got one and I've already changed the code."

"Fair enough." The old guy shuffles off at a pace a tortoise would be ashamed of. "Got both SIGs; you wanted 228s, right? How does a Remington 870 sound for the shotgun?"

"The 228s, please. Yeah, the Remington sounds good. What's it hold?"

"Six, plus one up the spout if'n you're dumb enough to leave it around like that."

"I'll take it. I'll need a box of cartridges and a couple boxes of nine mil rounds for the SIGs."

The old guy unlocks a display cabinet and takes a shotgun out; he lays it on the counter and adds the two SIGs and the requested ammo along with holsters for the SIGs. "How you payin', card?"

"Cash." Roche pulls out one of the bundles of notes from his Bag of Plenty and looks at the old guy, who's eyeing the sheaf of cash as if it's the most important thing in the world. "How much?"

"With the tax added, four and a half K."

"That's quite a bit more than I paid for the first guns." Roche knows he's being gouged and can't stop himself resisting, although he recognizes that he should never have brought out the wad of notes before asking how much. He's also aware that if he shows too much knowledge of the real price the guns should be the old guy will be more likely to question his motives. "I figured it'd be around four."

"How long since you last bought you'self a gun? Inflation hits everything, even the right to bear arms."

"Okay, okay. My bad."

On a normal day Roche would have haggled with the guy, but his need to get back to Fielding's place before the marshal returns from his day's work is more pressing than saving a couple of hundred bucks.

Five minutes after leaving the gun store, Roche is in his car and heading back towards Fielding's house. Whether he'll run into Savannah at the house again, or Fielding, is unknown to him, but he knows that's where his best chance of catching up with them both lies.

# CHAPTER SEVENTY

Roche pulls a pair of binoculars from his Bag of Plenty and focuses them on the Fielding house. He's parked on a side street a quarter mile from the house and has a vantage point where he can see the house's frontage. He's working on the principle that Fielding will finish work at either five or six and then head straight home. It might be that Fielding stops off for some groceries or maybe an after-work beer or two, but some time in the next few hours, the US marshal will return home.

At least that's the theory. If Ogden has blown the whistle, there's a good chance Fielding has either gone to ground or vanished to start over somewhere else. There's no knowing if this is the case, but time will tell.

Roche puts a call into Xandra.

"What do you want me to do now?" Her voice is weary and flat.

"Is that any way to greet a close friend? The greatest admirer of your digital skills alive today?"

"Cut the bull, Roche. I've had eight hours' sleep in the last seventy-two, and you're responsible for that. Tell me what you want, let me get it and then some shut-eye."

"I want to know more about Hal Fielding. Specifically his movements. Trace his cell and let me know where he is, what car he drives and if there's a panic in the US Marshals office."

"At least one of those requests is worthy of my talents." Roche smiles to himself at Xandra's grouching. She knows her value and hates running what she calls kindergarten searches. What she likes to do is get into the places where getting caught means serious jail time, not run searches any kid with basic hacking skills could do. "Did you list them in order of importance?"

"Sure did."

"I though as much."

There's a pause but Roche has relied on Xandra often enough to know she'll have fallen silent as she concentrates on something on the screen in front of her.

"Aaaaaand, I'm in. Let me see now. Fielding is on the move and is traveling towards his home address. He's maybe ten minutes or so away, depending on traffic."

"You're a marvel. What car does he have?"

"Your flattery would be a lot more effective if you didn't make it so obvious you're just keeping me sweet. He drives a black BMW X1. It's two years old and was bought new."

Roche jots down the license plate and checks his watch. He's going to be on full alert from now on.

"What kind of panic are you talking about in the Marshals office?"

"Things got somewhat fracacious with one of the other marshals. Savannah was involved and so was the marshal's family. Guns were drawn and aimed. If he's called it in, there will be all manner of emails and calls flying in and out of the office."

"You and your made-up words. What the hell kind of word is fracacious? Tell you what, don't bother giving me an answer. As for the flap, I can't see anything of note but I'll keep an eye on things for you."

"Thanks." Roche narrows his eyes as a black BMW passes by. As soon as he realizes that it's a lower, sleeker model than an X1, he relaxes, but only a fraction. "If Fielding is indeed heading home, it suggests to me the other marshal has kept his mouth shut, but how long that lasts very much depends on how frightened we left him."

"Ah yes, you always did have a way of leaving a lasting impression on people. Once or twice over the years those impressions have even been positive."

"And you say I'm a charmer. Keep me posted if you see anything."

Roche cuts the call and lifts the binoculars back to his eyes. If his directional sense is correct, Fielding will drive past him on his way home. On the other hand, there's a chance he'll come the opposite way if he makes any stops on his way home.

As he's about to lower the binoculars, he hears an insistent tapping at his window. It's enough to make him start and set his heart racing. He turns to see who's tapping, one hand already reaching for a SIG.

Roche pauses the hand before it gets to the weapon. The tapper of his window is a little old lady. She's dressed in velour and has a pair of glasses hanging from a neck chain. Beneath her white hair her face is scrunched in anger.

"What the dickens do you think you're doing, mister? Are you one of those perverts we hear about on the news?" Her mouth puckers into a horrified sneer as she folds an arm over her chest. "That's what you are, aren't you? A pervert."

"I'm none of those things, ma'am. You have entirely the wrong idea. Let me show you my ID. I'm a private eye and I'm currently on a surveillance detail."

The old woman's eyes squint at his license as she fumbles her glasses into place. "Pah. That's a fake if ever I saw one. You're a liar, mister, and I'm not falling for it. I'll get your license plate and call the cops. Maybe you'll want to explain yourself to them."

Roche doesn't like where this is going. The feisty old woman is being a good citizen. She's calling out a potential predator with no thought for her own safety. She ought to be commended for her actions. So far as he's concerned, she's ruining everything. He does the only thing he can do and plucks the glasses from her face, flicks their chain over her head and drives off backwards as fast as the rental will go. Once he's traveled fifty yards, he makes a show of dropping the glasses out of the window, making sure they land on the soft grass instead of the hard road.

He swings the car around and drives until he's two streets over and once again in sight of what he expects to be Fielding's route home.

# CHAPTER SEVENTY-ONE

The more time passes, the more Savannah's nerves jangle in anticipation. Very soon she's going to either get her chance to kill Fielding, or she's going to die. If Ogden has called their earlier visit in, Fielding will return home armed to the teeth and accompanied by a SWAT team.

Whatever happens, things will be settled tonight, for good, or bad.

Fielding has to die. Of that there is no ambiguity in her mind. Not for her, not when it comes to Fielding. Because he's the man she blames for Richard's death.

Richard was the best brother a girl could ever wish for. Her protector, her guide through life and a wonderful sounding board for her thoughts and ideas. It was Richard who'd smuggled her past their parents when she got drunk at thirteen, who'd helped her with her homework and acted as a buffer zone between her and her mother.

Richard's strong moral compass was his greatest asset and his biggest flaw. He witnessed a kidnapping taking place and called the police. He'd given evidence in court that had led to three members of a Houston street gang receiving stiff prison sentences. Threats had been made against Richard's life and, to protect him, the police had placed him in the Witness Protection Program. His car allegedly plunging into the San Jacinto River had been nothing more than a smoke screen to alleviate the threat to him. The whole thing faked in an attempt to fool those who wanted him dead. It hadn't worked.

One month after their tearful parting, a somber US marshal and a police commissioner arrived at the family home. Richard had been killed. Shot in his bed. Nothing was taken from his home, there had been no burglary and there were no signs of a forced entry. The marshal and the commissioner had confessed Richard's homicide had all the hallmarks of a professional hit.

The more she thought about the way Richard had died, the more she realized the Witness Protection Program was compromised. No matter how many times she analyzed how, she couldn't shake the surety that somewhere, in some office, one of the US marshals involved in the program was leaking the details or arranging the hits. As unlikely as that idea seemed, her theories have borne fruit and led her to Fielding. The idea that there may be more than one Leaker is one she's never countenanced. One is too many. Too improbable. For there to be more than one is unthinkable. As she's always seen it, if Richard was killed because of the Leaker, he wouldn't be the only one. There would be others scattered around the USA in random supposedly safe locations.

When the grief had abated enough for anger to overtake it, Savannah had concocted a plan. Her mom had refused it at first, scared of losing her too, but Savannah told her that she'd follow her plan with or without her mother's support. It took weeks of persuasion to bring her mother round, but in the end she relented and agreed to do her part.

Savannah feels shame the Perez guy had to die for her plan to work, but she used the links his family had to a crime gang to salve her conscience. A bigger shame is the way she'd fitted up an innocent man for Perez's homicide. Albie might have been an ass, but he didn't deserve to be set up for a homicide he didn't commit. That gnaws at her gut. Twisting knots of contempt and self-loathing.

She'd wanted to select her victim from the gang Richard testified against, but had decided against it. Two witnesses from the same family providing evidence against the same gang for separate crimes years apart wasn't a coincidence she felt would be believed, so she chose a different victim and aimed her vengeance at the unscrupulous jerk who'd made it possible for Richard to be executed.

Once she'd followed her brother's path into the Witness Protection Program, the rest had fallen into place. Mother had approached Roche, and Savannah had played the helpless victim. Except she's made mistakes. Roche seems to be on to her. He's picked up that she's not what she's presenting herself as. He's challenged her on it. Sure, she'd paid a buddy in the army to delete her name from the records and gotten a friend at a Houston publisher to falsify her employment for the same period. She'd endured a year of army training and had then bought herself out when she'd learned the skills to avenge Richard.

Roche has been her ticket to finding the Leaker, to identifying Fielding as the person who's commissioned the hits, but now he's served his purpose she's ditched Roche and gone her own way. She's made sure Roche won't be around when she kills the Leaker; otherwise she would have to kill him to preserve her own innocence, and as annoying as Roche may be, he's saved her life and she doesn't want to kill him, but she knows she would if she had to.

The longer she waits, the longer it takes for time to pass. Seconds seem like hours and the ticking of the clock on the mantelpiece is a form of auditory Chinese water torture.

From her vantage point she sees the two Alsatians begin to stir. First it's a claw that paws at the air, and then slowly their massive heads are prized off the ground. They look around as if bewildered and struggle themselves into a more alert lying position. One adopting the same stance as the Sphinx, the other watching the gates with its head twisted.

The dogs recovering from whatever drug Roche has spiked them with is a good thing, as them being their normal selves is one less thing to potentially tip Fielding off about her presence. It also means that once she's dealt with Fielding, she's going to have to lure the dogs into the house and somehow trap them in a room so that she can get away without them chewing on her.

Savannah spies a car through the gates. It's a black SUV traveling at crawling pace and looking as if it's about to turn in. She grips the Beretta that little bit tighter and tries to regulate both her breathing and the shakes that have developed in her hands.

The slow-moving SUV has set her teeth on edge. It could be Fielding or some other law-enforcement agent scoping the place out before the SWAT team do their thing. There could, of course, be a much more innocent explanation for the vehicle's sedentary pace. An elderly driver, a cautious mom or just someone reprograming their GPS without first pulling over.

Whatever the reason, Savannah's heart is now beating that bit faster, her mouth is drier and every one of her senses is enhanced. The tick of the clock is louder, the floor she's kneeling on harder, the gate clearer in her vision and the scent of Fielding's home more distinct.

At the gate a car pulls up and stops with its nose in front of the gates. A man she doesn't recognize steps out and reaches through the gates to pet the dogs who run towards him. Savannah watches as an arm points beyond the gates and the man's mouth opens. It has to be Fielding: he's wearing a US Marshals uniform.

The dogs obey their master and trot back to a point halfway to the house and sit watching as Fielding opens first one gate and then the other.

Savannah checks the safety is off on her Beretta and takes long slow breaths to prepare herself for the few seconds of intense action she knows are about to come her way. To further calm herself, she imagines the satisfaction that will come with finally being able to avenge the brother she adored.

# CHAPTER SEVENTY-TWO

Roche pulls out from the side street and guns his engine as hard as he can without making it seem obvious he is chasing after Fielding. The black BMW X1 has shot past him at an illegal pace, but considering everything else Fielding has done, speeding has to be his least offensive crime.

As he sets off in pursuit he sees Fielding is out of his car and is opening the gates manually. It's a stroke of luck. The fact Fielding has to physically open the gates himself has removed any advantage the marshal may have had from the head start his speeding has given him.

Roche pulls to a halt by the sidewalk. Fielding casts a look his way, but is focused on climbing back into his car. As Fielding climbs behind the wheel, Roche exits his own car and makes a show of checking his front tire.

Once Fielding is out of sight, Roche slinks his way to the wall and pulls out his two SIGS. The shotgun is strapped to his back ready for use.

Footsteps scrunch the gravel drive. They're the measured scrunches of a human stride rather than the pitter patter of a dog's feet.

As soon as he hears the squeak of the gates being swung to, Roche makes his move; peeling himself from the wall he swirls round until he's facing Fielding. Both of his guns are pointed at the marshal. One in his face to intimidate and the other at his chest to guarantee a hit should Fielding try anything.

"Don't move. Don't even think about reaching for the gun on your belt. And if you try to set your dogs on me, I'll put a bullet into them and then blow your nutsack clean across the lawn. Got me?"

"Yeah, I got you." There's defiance in Fielding's every expression and his body language as he raises his hands and stares at Roche. "No guns, no dogs. Would it be out of order for me to ask who you are and why you're pointing those guns at me?"

"It wouldn't. But in your position, I'd exercise some patience and keep my bazoo shut. I recommend you do just that. If you're as smart as I think you are, you'll soon work out why I'm here."

Fielding's eyes give away his surprise and sudden understanding. There's a fatalism in his expression that makes Roche wonder if he's made a mistake tipping his hand in such a way. He doesn't waste time thinking about it. Fielding would have soon reached the same conclusion.

"Okay, Fielding, I want you to use very slow movements and take off your utility belt and toss it over behind the wall. I see you've got a screen at the back of your car. I want you to put the dogs in. I like dogs and I don't want you forcing me into a position where I have to shoot them."

Fielding does as he's told. His movements are slow and deliberate, but there's no mistaking his anger or the unspoken curse words that litter his face.

With the tasks finished he looks at Roche with a questioning eyebrow raised.

"Now we go to the house for a chat. You're going to tell me all about how you've been selling out the good people put into the Witness Protection Program."

"Like hell I will."

"You will. I'm not going to threaten to hurt you every time you show me any resistance. Life's too short to take the long route. But take it as read that after this little stand, I'll start putting bullets into you every time you don't do as I ask. Don't worry, I won't kill you. The bullets will go into your joints. Ankles, knees, elbows and wrists. Every bullet will rob you of some mobility. Steal a piece of your freedom of movement. Oh, and yeah, they'll hurt like you've never imagined anything hurting. Now start walking towards the house."

"My house keys are in the car. I'll need to get them."

This is a complication Roche could do without. Fielding may have a gun or some other weapon stashed in the car. He could always retrieve the keys himself, but to do that he'll have to holster a gun and he really doesn't want to do that. Fielding is facing a very bleak immediate future. He'll be expecting to die, or at the very least be tortured with crippling shots to his joints. He'll be desperate and desperate men do desperate things. They make desperate moves fueled by utter desperation.

Roche takes a look at Fielding's forearms. He's wearing his watch on his left wrist, which suggests that his right hand is the dominant one.

"Use your right hand to grab hold of the back of your collar and the left to get the keys. I have one gun trained on your knees and the other the base of your spine in case you try to do something stupid. When you have the keys I want you to display them over your shoulder before turning around."

There's a hunch to Fielding's shoulders as he leans into the car. Whether it's caused by the right hand holding his collar or the animosity he's sure to be feeling towards Roche doesn't matter. He once again does as he's told.

Roche trails Fielding to the house and onto the porch. There's rattan furniture and a stout door leading into the house. Roche makes sure he's close enough to react to any desperate move Fielding may try, but not so close he's within reach.

Fielding feeds a key into the lock and twists it. Then he reaches for the handle.

In one swift movement Fielding throws the door open, ducks inside and yells "attack."

Roche hesitates before pulling his trigger. He doesn't want any gunshots heard. Not after the confrontation with the elderly neighbor.

There are furious barks behind him, and he twists to see the dogs running his way as he hears Fielding slamming the door closed.

# CHAPTER SEVENTY-THREE

Savannah fires as soon as Fielding steps through the door. The Beretta bucks in her hand as she sends two pairs of shots at Fielding. Due to Roche's intervention, he's moving far quicker than expected and her first shots are well wide. The second pair are closer, but only one of them is close enough to pluck at the sleeve of Fielding's uniform.

He reacts to her threat with predictable speed. He'd known about Roche, but not her. As such he's moving fast anyway. She'd watched as Roche had captured Fielding and then brought him to the house. Fielding had been hers to kill and, because of Roche's interference, she's missed her chance. There will be another one though. Of that she's sure.

Fielding has seen her and recognized her face. She caught the widening of his eyes and knows it's more than just fear of another threat. Now he's made the connection and been shot at by her, he'll be under no illusion as to her intent.

Rather than try to reach his gun cache in the garage-cum-workshop, Fielding has ducked into what she knows is a formal dining room.

Savannah's instinct is to go after him, but she fights the urge. The dining room has two doors: one to the hall and another that leads to the kitchen. If she follows him in via the hall door, she'll give him the opportunity to swing round behind her and make his way to his gun cabinet.

Instead of setting off in pursuit, she opens the door to the kitchen, steps into the opening and keeps a vigil on both doors.

The door from dining room to kitchen inches open then swings wide as if given a gentle push. Savannah trains her sights two feet from the opening, expecting Fielding to come through at pace.

He doesn't.

Fielding's head pops into and out of the doorway too quick for her to react and send a shot at him. She knows at once that he's taken a look. That he's now aware of her position and that she's got her gun trained his way.

Now he knows where her focus is, she now expects he'll try and flank her by exiting the dining room back into the hall.

There's a simple counter to such a move but the same principles as before count. If she follows him into the dining room he could exit into the hall, skirt round her and get his weapons. He could also have armed himself with a steak knife or some projectiles, such as a heavy plate or a lamp he could crash down on her head.

As most of Savannah's focus is on the hall, it's only the corner of her eye that sees the movement of something coming into the kitchen from the dining room.

Even as she's swinging the gun back, she recognizes the object coming through the doorway. It's a hand and it's holding a small gun.

Savannah just has time to duck as the gun sends three un-aimed shots her way. Two of the shots miss, but the third gouges a furrow in her left arm.

"Damn you, Fielding. You're going to die screaming for that."

"Screw you, bitch."

Fielding dashes into the room and takes a headlong dive behind the central island. Savannah sends a pair of shots his way as he moves across the room, but she's way slow and knows it.

"You're supposed to be dead. I'd set it up at the weekend. That guy outside, is he with you?"

"Hell yeah he is." Savannah is comfortable with the lie. The more Fielding thinks he's outnumbered, the more desperate he'll become and desperate people make mistakes. Right now, she needs Fielding to make a mistake.

"I'm not sure about that, honey. He's a pro. You're not."

"You'll see what a pro I am when I put a bullet in your brain, you festering sack of bull crap."

\*

Roche has five seconds at most to react before the snarling Alsatians are upon him. The door has a Yale key, which means that it will have relocked itself when slammed shut. He takes two steps across the porch, holstering his pistols as he goes, and grabs the nearest rattan chair with one hand while retrieving the shotgun with the other.

Shots can be heard booming inside the house. A pair of double taps fired by someone who knows what they're doing. Roche is prepared to bet all he owns the shooter is Savannah.

If he's quick, he'll be able to get into the house without harming either of the dogs. However, if it becomes a case of him or them, there won't be any hesitation in his actions.

Roche drags the rattan chair sideways and uses it as a barrier to fend off the dogs. The larger one sinks its teeth into the thin straps of the chair and tries to worry it free of his grasp.

When the second one does the same thing, Roche hangs on as tight as he can with one hand while aiming the shotgun at the lock. He makes sure he's not square on to the lock, in case a ricochet comes straight back at him, and pulls the trigger.

At near-point-blank range the lock doesn't stand a chance against the shotgun. It gets blown inside the house, leaving a splintered hole where it belonged.

Roche slips inside the house; he leaves the rattan chair across the opening and slams the door back, driving across the bolt fastened to the top of the door.

\*

Savannah knows Fielding is behind the island but she doesn't know where exactly. She can hear shuffled movements, but whether he's going to pop up over the island or move to the left or right is unknown. All the options are his.

To limit the risk, she moves three paces to the left.

"I count six shots from you, honey. Figuring to myself that you have two, maybe three left. Maybe you want to head off now while you're still alive."

Savannah doesn't like the way Fielding is so clued in. Despite him being the one under threat, he's thinking steps ahead of her and is right about the number of rounds she has left. That doesn't mean she can't react with positivity.

"I've more than one gun, jerkweed." Savannah finishes by putting two shots into the knife block on the island, driving it over the edge and onto Fielding. As soon as the second shot is fired, she slams a new magazine into the Beretta.

"My, my, what a liar you are, Miss Nicoll. If you had more than one gun, you wouldn't have just changed your mag."

Three knives come sailing over the island. They're all tumbling wildly, but Savannah still has to take evasive action so they don't hit her. The knife block comes next and crashes off her already-wounded arm. She can't stop the agonized scream. Nor when she hears Fielding laughing can she stop herself from firing four shots into the gas stove at the other side of the kitchen. If she can hit a pipe and cause a fire or explosion, Fielding will either be killed or forced to show himself.

*

Now free of the threat from the dogs, Roche turns his attention to the threats inside the house.

Fielding will kill him to save himself. That's a given and totally understandable. Savannah is the unknown quantity; she's sure to hate him for interfering with her plan to kill Fielding, but whether she'll turn her gun on him is a mystery to Roche. While waiting for Fielding to return from work, Xandra had delivered her deep-dive report on Savannah and it certainly helped him make sense of things, but right now he needs to know if he has one person trying to kill him or two. Savannah had the chance to kill him earlier and she didn't take it, but since then he's disrupted her plans a second time, and now she has Fielding in her sights, her primal instincts are far more likely to kick in.

There's no doubt in his mind that until he has a lot of evidence otherwise, he has to treat Savannah as if she's as great a threat to his life as Fielding.

After staying alive, preventing Savannah from killing Fielding is his top priority. He cannot allow her to turn murderer. In her head the reasons for killing Fielding may be just, and a lot of people would agree with her, but he's being paid to protect her life and for him that includes keeping her out of prison.

Gunshots echo out from the kitchen, and he hears Savannah and Fielding engage in dialogue. He can't make out what they're saying to each other, but he guesses they aren't discussing weather or politics.

Roche swaps the shotgun for the SIGs. In a close environment, a handgun is far better suited to being switched to a new target in a hurry, and with two foes in different places, a gun in each hand will allow him to cover them both.

Step by silent step Roche creeps towards the rear of the house where he can hear Savannah and Fielding. He's keeping himself close to the walls and as far out of sight as he can from anyone in the kitchen.

He stops when he gets to the kitchen wall. Things have fallen silent in there, and he's waiting to see what happens before stepping into the room and creating a distraction that will hand an advantage to either party.

"So, I know who you are. Who's the guy outside?"

# CHAPTER SEVENTY-FOUR

Roche waits for Savannah's response before acting. How she answers Fielding's question will give him a clue as to how she's currently feeling about him.

"Roche? He's just a private eye who I hired to help me find you."

"You hired him to find me? You were in the program. What reason would you have to find me?"

"Oh purleeese." Savannah's voice is laden with scoff. "You're the Leaker. The man who's been selling out people in witness protection. You're the man who has been making money by organizing the murder of good people. Righteous people. Of course I know what you are. And thanks to Roche, I've been able to find you. You're going to die for what you've done. To me, to my family, and God knows how many other families. Surely you knew that eventually this day would come. That someone would escape the killers sent by you and work their way back to you, the source."

"It's never happened before. Tell me, how did you know there was going to be a hit on you? From what I heard, that Roche guy was there with you when the hit was due to go down. That tells me you knew in advance there was going to be a hit, and unless you planned on having Roche or another bodyguard around all the time, there is no way you could have known about the hit."

"Of course I knew there would be a hit. I made sure of it. You really have no idea how long I've been planning this. I got myself involved in a homicide on purpose. I killed a man and framed a guy who was trying to get into my pants. I made sure the guy who got killed was from a family that could and would seek vengeance upon me. I set the whole thing up so I could come after you. That asshole Roche has been a patsy all along. He's an old guy with an old guy's mentality, but I needed someone with a private eye's tracking skills to find you, so I've had to tolerate him."

"But how did you know I existed to come after me? Why are you even here?"

"Because my brother was in the program and he was murdered. He was an unidentified witness, but somehow the people he was testifying against learned who the star witness was and told other members of their gang. After he'd testified, the threat against him was judged to be so great and vicious the US Marshals even faked a car crash where he plunged into a river and hid him away. The more I tried to dig into how he died, the more I smelled a cover-up. That made me dig even more. Eventually I spoke to a lawyer in the DA's office who said he'd heard rumors that someone was selling out the fine citizens who wound up in the program. That information gave me a target. I didn't know the target's name or where they lived. But I do now and I'm standing in his house and talking to him. I spent a year in the army learning how to handle a gun for this moment. I risked my life acting as bait for your killers so there was a trail to follow."

None of what Savannah is saying is news to Roche. He'd gotten time to read the reports from both Xandra and Zimm. They'd uncovered enough to allow him to join the dots. The brother's crash into the San Jacinto River was a huge red flag to him. Not so much the accident as the response. Someone with the family money of the Parker-Nicoll family wouldn't have taken no for an answer when confronted with the authorities' lackluster efforts to find Richard or his car. They'd have spoken to their high-level connections and demanded action. Even if that had drawn a blank, they'd have paid private salvagers to conduct such searches and would have offered a reward if anyone happened to find anything of Richard or his car.

Roche lives in Houston and he knows enough of the people who'd have been involved in any concerted effort to have heard of such a search around the time of Richard's alleged crash. He'd heard nothing; therefore the search didn't happen, and if the search didn't happen, by turn that brought the crash under suspicion. However, at the time of Richard's disappearance, a mystery witness gave evidence that saw several high-ranking gang members given stiff prison sentences.

Zimm's report on the case that had catapulted Savannah into a new life was less ambiguous than the reports on Richard's crash, until Roche applied the growing suspicions he already had. Then it was a case of trying to find answers for the many questions his mind was throwing up.

Savannah's unwavering insistence to stick by his side regardless of the risk, the training she tried so hard to hide and deny, and the way her personality had changed so dramatically since their first meeting all suggested an ulterior motive. A stronger driving force than a desire to lash out at the person trying to have her killed. In Roche's experience, the only things that could push ordinary people to such lengths was love or money. Savannah's family had plenty of money; therefore love must be her driving force. And that love had turned itself inside out and became hatred. Hatred for the person who'd sold out her brother. This is what Roche believes has transformed Savannah from someone intent on doing only good into someone out for a biblical revenge.

In the kitchen, Fielding and Savannah are still goading each other.

"Bad news. You're not going to kill me today. I'm going to kill you. You have one gun. It doesn't have a lot of bullets left in it and mine does. While you've been telling your oh-so-boring life story, I've reloaded."

To Roche's ears, Savannah's voice is full of cheer. "Hey, scumbag. I can smell gas. How about you? Guessing you're not going to want to fire your gun at me right now."

"Screw you, bitch. You ain't gonna be firing yours neither."

"I'm sorry, Hal, that's the wrong answer. Do you want to go for double jeopardy?"

Roche hears a single shot being fired, but other than a metallic clang, there is no whoosh of igniting gas.

"Yep, you've guessed it. I'm prepared to die today, just so long as I see you die first."

# CHAPTER SEVENTY-FIVE

Savannah is taking a more careful aim at the stove when her sixth sense jangles an alarm. Even as she's turning to meet whatever her subconscious has warned her of, she feels an arm snaking around her throat and the muzzle of a pistol being jammed in her ear.

"Don't move." It's Roche's voice that growls the order. Of course it is. She should have killed him, or at least put a crippling shot into him, instead of leaving him trussed up in the trunk of his car.

"Damn you, Roche. You have no right to interfere like this. You were supposed to lead me here. Nothing more."

"Yeah, so I heard. Heard a whole lot of other stuff too. Real incriminating stuff. Bad news, I'm not your patsy any more. Now, put your gun down."

"No. You won't kill me. You won't risk losing your payday. Before I set this up, I had you thoroughly checked out. You're paying enough alimony to make Bill Gates's eyes water. You need the money this case will make you, and while I know you're capable of murder, I know you also value human life. You should have killed Wingnut, but you didn't, you let him go. You won't kill me, I'm your principal."

Savannah only half believes what she's saying. Roche could go either way, but she's taking heart from the fact he's put a gun to her head rather than a bullet in her back. She can see how control of the situation has escaped her and she needs to wrest it back. If she doesn't kill Fielding now, she's never going to get another chance.

The Beretta transforms from a piece of fashioned metal into a part of her as she takes aim once more. Her entire focus is centered on what she's seeing over the Beretta's sights. The stove becomes crystal clear, and when she's locked onto a metallic part that's sure to spark when shot, she pulls the trigger.

There's no whooshing fireball as gas ignites, and before Savannah can fire a second time, she can feel Roche hauling her backwards away from the kitchen. The last thing she sees in the kitchen is Fielding's hand cresting the island and then she hears three rapid shots. Something punches her hard in the upper thigh and she can feel her entire leg deaden and become useless.

Roche drags her around a corner and twists the Beretta from her grasp. She writhes and squirms against his hold, but he's too strong for her. The kicks she aims with her one good leg all miss, and the elbows she throws at his ribs earn nothing more than a muted grunt.

Savannah doubles her efforts and manages to curl one of Roche's fingers back. She intends to keep bending it until it snaps or he releases her.

In front of her she sees Fielding dash out of the kitchen and head for his workshop. Thanks to fighting her, Roche can't get a shot off. Fielding gets through the door and before the door slams shut, he tosses a lit Zippo back towards the kitchen.

There's a crashing thud against Savannah's temple and then nothing.

# CHAPTER SEVENTY-SIX

The kitchen engulfs itself in a spectacular fireball, but beyond that initial burn there is little short-term risk from the fire. The gas escaping the pipe will burn with ferocity and that in turn will burn down the house. Gas lines into houses have one-way fire valves fitted to them to prevent any potential fires returning to the tank and exploding it, so Roche doesn't have to worry about that. In time, the fire in the kitchen will become deadly, but it won't happen in the next few seconds. Fielding shooting at him will.

Roche doesn't waste too much time worrying about Savannah. He's knocked her out cold and now needs to get on with getting after Fielding. All the same, he takes a moment to drag Savannah away from the kitchen and leave her by the front door.

His primary goal now is to capture Fielding, but he's enough of a realist to know that if he can't make Fielding his captive, he'll have to kill the man.

Roche swaps back to the shotgun and blasts a couple of shots at the door Fielding disappeared through. At this range, the shot spreads enough to not do any major damage to the door, but Roche knew that would be the case. What he's doing is keeping the pressure on Fielding. Making sure that the marshal is in constant fear of him and isn't able to launch a counterattack without taking great risk.

As much as Roche wants to storm through the door and bring Fielding under his control, there are too many unknown elements for such a move. There were other exits from the kitchen, yet

Fielding chose this one. That suggests a specific reason and the only good reason he can think of is that Fielding is going after another weapon. He'd fired three shots at them in the kitchen but none when dashing past them. The moments when he and Savannah were wrestling with each other was the perfect opportunity for Fielding to take them out. He didn't. Roche knows it wouldn't be by choice. Therefore, Fielding is out of ammo.

Now Roche has reached this conclusion, he's caught in a quandary. If he rushes through the door too soon, he might well run into a physical ambush. Too late and Fielding could have reloaded or picked up another gun.

He solves the problem by walking forward and putting shot after shot into the door. The closer he gets, the more damage each blast from the shotgun does to it. The final shot he pumps in blows a ragged hole in the door.

Roche steps to one side, and using one hand he pokes the shotgun's muzzle through the hole and sweeps its trajectory through an arc as if seeking a target. He expects one of two things to happen. Either Fielding will fire at the door and the opening, or he'll lay his hands on the nine inches of barrel that he's pushed through. If Fielding does grab the barrel and haul it through the hole, it won't matter as Roche has made sure he's fired all the shells he'd loaded into the shotgun.

Neither happen in the first three seconds. This informs Roche that Fielding hasn't yet got a loaded gun in his hand, and that he's not waiting to club him the second he goes through the door.

Roche kicks the door open and steps into the room, a SIG in each hand. His eyes are scanning every surface looking for Fielding. He finds him at the other side of the room. He's standing beside a gun cabinet that's open and has a pistol in one hand while the other reaches for a magazine to slide into the weapon. Roche empties the SIG in his left hand at the gun cabinet, forcing Fielding to retreat before he can grab a magazine.

Stride by stride Roche moves forward as Fielding ducks behind one of the woodworking machines bolted to the floor of the room.

"You should have killed that crazy bitch, Roche. Sooner or later she'll get you killed."

"Not me she won't." Roche aims his remaining SIG at the wood planer Fielding cowers behind. "I'll be handing her over to the feds at the same time I hand you over. Now, slowly, very, very slowly, I want you to lay yourself face down where I can see you. Hands on the back of your head. Do that and you'll get to survive this day, and then it'll be up to you as to how talkative you are to prevent yourself from feeling any pain."

"Screw you. We got the death penalty in Idaho. If I talk to you before you turn me in, I'm as good as a dead man. Not... going... to... happen."

Something flies out from behind the planer. It doesn't travel anywhere near where he is so there's no threat, but instinct makes his eyes follow the object's trajectory. His gun does too.

By the time he snaps his focus back to where it should be it's too late. Fielding has slung a pair of chisels his way and is coming at him from a low crouching position. Neither of the chisels strike him blade first, which is a bonus, but his luck runs out there.

The first chisel to connect hits Roche square on the nose. This shouldn't be a problem to Roche, whose nose has been broken many times over the years, but his eyes instantly water. The second chisel handle thuds into his right hand, its uncompromising plastic handle crashing onto the top knuckle of his trigger finger and smashing the joint. He's now blinded and holding a gun whose trigger he can't squeeze.

Roche tosses the pistol behind him and gets ready for the impact of Fielding's desperation-fueled charge.

It's like being hit by a herd of stampeding rhinoceroses. Roche finds himself driven backwards until the base of his spine collides with a hard surface. He's bent backwards over the point of collision until his feet leave the floor. Every fiber of Roche's brain is trying to recall what he's seen in the room. He's not far enough for Fielding to have carried him to the benches ringing the workspace; therefore he must be against a piece of woodworking machinery.

At the exact moment when Roche squirms onto his front and sees he's lying over a table saw, he hears a click followed by a building whine. There's a breath of air as the saw blade begins to rotate and generates a building breeze. Never in Roche's life has something as innocuous as a breeze felt so threatening.

He writhes to escape the spinning blade. A fall face first onto the rough concrete floor seems like a wonderful alternative. It's not going to happen. Fielding has balled his hands into Roche's jacket and is pressing his head towards the whirling teeth of the saw's blade.

# CHAPTER SEVENTY-SEVEN

Roche's face is six inches from the saw, and regardless of how he's trying to resist Fielding's efforts to feed him to the machine, he's slowly being inched towards it.

Five inches.

Roche beats at the hands pushing him forward with no luck. He tries to isolate one of Fielding's fingers but they're tightly wrapped in his jacket.

Four inches.

Unable to change his trajectory, Roche tries to find a way to sabotage the saw. Something metal like a wrench fed into it would be sure to jam the mechanism and stop the blade from spinning, but there's nothing at hand.

Three inches.

In a panic Roches wonders what would happen if he offered up an arm to the saw. Would the saw stop dead when it hit the bones of his forearm? Or would it chew through them like a glutton at an all-you-can-eat buffet?

Two inches.

Roche is screwing up the courage to use his left arm as bait for the saw when he spots a piece of timber at the side of the saw's table, just beyond the guardrail. The timber is fashioned to have a rough handle at one end and the other has a notch cut out of it. It's what carpenters call a push stick. Used for the final few inches of a saw cut to keep fingers from spinning blades, it's about eighteen inches long and the best chance Roche has of escaping from the saw.

Roche's fingers grasp the push stick's handle, the smashed knuckle protesting with all its nerve endings. He doesn't waste any time aiming. He just swings the push stick back towards where he suspects Fielding's face is. Rather than a striking movement he's going for a straight jab. The points either side of the notch are sharp enough to do damage to an eye or to knock the wind out of an Adam's apple.

One inch. The breath of air hitting Roche's cheek is now a roiling torrent at this distance from its source.

The push stick strikes against Fielding's face. Roche doesn't know what part of him he's hit, but he knows it's soft and squishy. He hits it a second time and feels the push on his end. Twice more he strikes until he can roll off the table and land on the floor with a grateful whump.

Roche doesn't have time to gather his wits as one of Fielding's service boots arrows towards his gut.

The kick doubles him over, but he straightens a leg, driving the sole of his foot into Fielding's knee. The blow drawing a yelp from his opponent. Roche goes to repeat the move, but Fielding steps back out of the way.

Being on the ground against a standing opponent is never a good idea, so Roche goes to clamber up. His hands levering against a bench to aid the pace of his ascent.

He sees the wooden hammer Fielding has picked up and swung downwards at his head in time to move his head so the hammer misses his skull.

The hand he's got braced on a workbench isn't so lucky. It is directly under where his head was a fraction of a second ago.

Fielding's hammer doesn't miss his hand. It lands smack in the middle and it's got a lot of force behind it. Roche's hand explodes in agony as he hears the bones smash.

# CHAPTER SEVENTY-EIGHT

Fielding raises the hammer to inflict a second blow. After the impact of the first one, there's no way Roche can allow another blow to land. He swings his right arm in a powerful uppercut, clenching his teeth against the pain of his shattered left hand, and powers his fist into Fielding's groin.

The ruined knuckle of his right hand joins forces with the radiating waves of pain from his broken left. In spite of the pain, his uppercut fulfills its intended purpose and doubles Fielding over, both of his hands going towards his wounded groin.

Roche grabs the front of Fielding's uniform at the neck, and raising a leg to trip the marshal, drags him forward. Doubled over as he is, Fielding cannot fight the momentum and he stumbles forward, catches a foot on Roche's raised leg and sprawls onto the ground, the hammer skittering away in front of him to rest beside the pistol Roche discarded earlier.

As soon as he lands, Fielding begins to lever himself upwards and crawls towards the weapons.

With one hand out of commission and the other damaged, Roche knows the odds aren't in his favor, but he has to stop Fielding before he can reach either weapon, as there's little he can do to compete if Fielding gets them.

Roche chops the back of Fielding's knees, partly to protect his broken knuckle, but mostly because a chop to the tendons can be delivered with far greater accuracy and impact than a punch.

A boot flies backwards and careens off his head, but there's not too much force behind it, so Roche clambers onto Fielding's back and begins raining the hardest punches he can onto the right side of Fielding's head.

After three punches, Roche's knuckle is screaming as loud as his ruined left hand. Fielding has worked out that Roche can't use his left hand and turned his face so that only the back of his head can be hit by Roche's punches.

If Fielding had anything more than a dusting of hair, Roche would grab a handful and repeatedly smash the marshal's head against the floor until the man was unconscious.

A powerful squirm from Fielding sees him rotate himself under Roche. When his hand appears he's holding one of the chisels. As it arrows towards his heart, Roche has just enough time to see that it's at least an inch and a half wide.

The chisel goes right through his shirt, tee and the muscle over his heart before stopping dead. In his hurry to strike a blow, Fielding has made a mistake. The chisel's blade is vertical and it's stopped by at least one rib. Had it been held ninety degrees over, it would have slipped between his ribs and killed him.

With the last of his strength, Roche throws a straight right at Fielding's jaw and knocks him out.

As much as he wants to lie down and nurse his injuries, to allow the waves of nausea passing over him to reach a headland, Roche knows he has to keep moving. That he has to get a confession from Fielding and then get the marshal, Savannah and himself out of the house before the fire in the kitchen spreads any farther.

The first thing Roche does when he regains his feet is retrieve the SIG he'd earlier tossed. It gets slotted into the holster. He'd have to fire it with his middle finger on the trigger, but now Fielding is unconscious there's going to be much less urgency about any shots he needs to make.

He dares to take a look at his left hand and wishes he hadn't. It's a swollen mess that's already starting to discolor. He knows the swelling is his body's way of healing itself, but the knowledge doesn't offer him any comfort.

Roche twists his three working fingers into the collar of Fielding's shirt and hauls the man across the room until he has him where he wants him. A zip tie from a bench is used to secure Fielding's right hand to an immovable part of the planer. Fielding's other hand is fed into the clamping mechanism of a woodworking machine that's backed up against a wall.

Roche uses his knee to hold Fielding's arm in place by bracing it against the man's elbow. With the arm where he wants it, Roche tightens the clamp until Fielding's arm is trapped.

Now that he has Fielding where he wants him, Roche uses his pinkie to prod at Fielding's face until he wakes up.

Fielding's eyes flit back and forth as he realizes how he's been imprisoned.

"I'm not going to talk. Not prepared to give you the satisfaction. Just kill me now and save yourself the trouble of trying to make me talk."

Roche can't help laughing despite the pain he feels. "Save myself the trouble. My god, that's rich. You're the one who's going to be in trouble if you don't talk, not me."

"Screw you."

"Let's just dispense with the insults and move on to story time." Roche points to the door. "Your kitchen is on fire, and I'd rather get this done and by with before we have to worry about smoke inhalation or burning to death."

"You're wasting your time. I'm not going to confess."

"You are. And here's why. You see, many years ago, I used to love going to see my grandma and grandpops. Grandpops was a carpenter all his life. When he retired he kept a workshop in his garage, just like this one. When I got older, he used to let me help him. I liked that, it was good to spend time with my grandpops. Anyway, I know how all these machines work. What their purpose is. You might think that I've trapped your arm in the mortise machine's clamp because it's handy. You'd be wrong, very, very wrong. You're where you are so I can cut a mortise into your wrist if you don't feel talkative. I spent hours in Grandpops' workshop using one of these to cut nice square mortise holes in the furniture he was making. I got to be quite the expert with it." Roche gestures at the mortise machine. "Imagine that. You know how it works; of course you do, it's your machine. Just imagine what it'll be like though. I'll position your wrist right below the chisel. Can you imagine what it'll feel like when I pull the lever that sinks the box chisel into your wrist? Can you imagine what it'll feel like to feel the chisel slicing your flesh as the drill inside spins away, burrowing through bone, cartilage and flesh with equal ease? Just in case you don't know, wrists are a whole mess of bones and cartilage and nerves and veins."

Fielding doesn't speak, but the way his jaw trembles and his eyes are focused on the arched tip of the box chisel display his fears, but he still has a last reserve of bravado. "You won't do it. So many times you could have killed me but didn't. You're bluffing."

Rather than speak, Roche leans across and prods the mortiser's start button with his pinkie. The mortise whirls into life, its drill emitting a high shrieking noise as it spins inside the box chisel. He twists the control wheel to drag the clamp sideways until Fielding's wrist is directly underneath the box chisel.

Roche doesn't look at Fielding as he reaches for the handle that will lower the box chisel and the motor above it down onto Fielding's wrist.

Fielding howls in pain as all four corners of the box chisel make contact with the skin of his wrist. To prove he's not bluffing, Roche adds a slight amount of pressure and allows the tip of the chisel's internal drill to scour at Fielding's flesh.

In a slow movement, Roche returns the lever to its starting position and switches the mortiser off before looking at Fielding.

"I think you can now be reasonably confident I'm not bluffing. The question is, are you feeling brave, or talkative?" Roche retrieves a cell from his pocket and prepares a recording app. "If you tell the full story of what you've been doing to the cell, I'll get you out of here without hurting you any further. Start with your name, rank and then take your confession wherever it goes. We're talking full disclosure. If you don't do that, I'll put that chisel right through your wrist and then start working my way up your arm. You've had a taster, an *amuse-bouche*; don't be a hero and think you can handle the mixed grill, you can't."

Fielding's face is ashen, his eyes darting back and forth between Roche and the chisel. Roche knows what he's thinking. Fielding will be weighing up whether it's better to hold out and die today than face years of trials and appeals before he leaves death row for one final time. It's a coin toss as to what he'll choose. If Roche was in Fielding's shoes, he'd want to hang out in the hope some piece of evidence would be mishandled and thus ensure his freedom, but every man is different and Fielding is sure to know what care will be taken with any evidence against him.

Fielding's head bobs forward once in a sharp movement, so Roche activates the recording app.

"My name is Hal Fielding. I'm a US marshal based out of Boise, Idaho and I'm sorry to say that I have contracted the homicides of twenty-seven people in the Witness Protection Program…"

Roche does his best to listen to the confession without reacting, but it's all he can do not to start the mortiser again to cut a hole in Fielding for every one of his victims.

# CHAPTER SEVENTY-NINE

Savannah comes to in slow increments. At first all she's aware of is the pain in her temple and a serious numbness in her leg. Next she feels a series of hard objects pressing into her back.

She opens her eyes and sees she's been laid on the stairs. That will be Roche's doing as Fielding would have killed her. The air smells of smoke, and over the roar of fire she can hear barking and the shrieking whine of some machinery.

The shrieking whine ends and she puts two and two together. Fielding had been making for his gun cache. Roche is sure to have gone after him. She must too.

Savannah pats herself down and looks for a weapon. There are none to be seen and all of hers have been removed. Whether Roche has them or has stashed them somewhere is unknown. For the time being she's going to have to improvise.

Her bullet-struck leg protests against her requests that it bear her weight, but it holds firm. Blood has made her leg sticky, but from what she can tell it's a flesh wound, and if she wants to kill Fielding then escape with her freedom, she's going to have to tough it out.

Her teeth are gritted as she presses forward. The injured leg drags a little, but other than stiffness and the pain it's causing her, it doesn't prevent her hobbling her way to the workshop.

As she passes the kitchen she retrieves a knife. Against two men with guns it'll probably be useless, but it's still way better than nothing.

The door to the workshop stands open, a pump-action shotgun fed through a hole in the wooden door. She slides the knife into a rear pocket and carefully looks into the room. Fielding is tied to some machines and has his head down. Roche is looking at him, his back to her.

With slow and careful movements, she pulls the shotgun from the door and steps into the room.

Roche's entire focus is on Fielding. No wonder. She can hear the confession tumbling from the marshal's lips. The callous way he's describing his actions is mind-numbing to her. All she can see is the man who arranged her brother's homicide. The man who's caused an unknown amount of good people to be killed. There's also Roche, a man who now knows the full extent of her guilt.

In a series of rapid movements Savannah pumps the shotgun, aims it in the general direction of the two men and pulls the trigger. There should be a thunderous boom. Fielding should be dead or dying. Roche the same.

The shotgun makes a clicking sound.

Savannah tries again. Pump, aim, fire.

Another click.

"If it was out of ammo the first time you tried, it won't have reloaded itself in time for your second attempt." Roche has turned her way. He's holding a pistol, but awkwardly, with his middle finger on the trigger instead of his index finger.

"Bite me." Savannah drops the shotgun, reaches for the knife and sets off for Fielding. If she can't shoot him, she can always slash his throat or stab his black heart.

Roche moves to intercept her, so she takes a wild slash in his direction. As well as killing Fielding, she knows that now Roche has the full picture, he also has to die if she's to have any chance of getting away with this.

The slash misses, but she's put so much into it she can't recall the knife to a defensive position in time to counter Roche's opening move. It's a brutal one. His right-foot stomp on her leg lands right where the bullet hit her. The pain in her leg goes from white hot to volcanic in a single microsecond. The knife is on its way back, but she's tumbling backwards and her attempt to gouge Roche misses by a foot.

"Drop the knife." He brandishes the gun at her, but he's not shot her yet and she doesn't believe he will now.

Savannah hauls herself up. "Leave and I'll let you live. Stay and your death will be your own fault."

A crackling whoosh from the direction of the kitchen is followed by a huge waft of smoke that billows into the workshop.

"Nobody is going to die. You're going to lay down that knife and then all three of us are going to leave here before that fire gets any worse."

Savannah raises herself to a standing position, but she's only bearing weight on one leg. "Fielding is going to die, and you'll have to kill me to stop me."

"Drop the knife. Last warning." Roche raises the pistol and sights it to amplify his threat. "The state will kill Fielding. If you kill him, the state will kill you too."

"Then I'll die a happy woman."

Savannah allows herself to topple forward. With only one working leg she can't get as much spring forward as she'd like, but she believes she'll get close enough to deliver a fatal wound.

Roche's body thumps into hers. She feels the shift in her momentum from forwards to sideways, sees the knife in her hand score a gash in the top of Fielding's bicep instead of across his throat. It's a survivable wound. Eminently so.

Roche's charge crashes her to the floor and then his boot collides with her solar plexus, driving every last shred of breath from her lungs. Even as she's gasping for air, she can feel Roche dragging her arms behind her back and applying zip ties to her wrists.

Savannah's head slumps as she realizes she's lost. She hasn't killed Fielding. Michel Perez's homicide case is sure to be reopened. Idaho and Texas police will battle as to who gets to imprison her. She's going to end up in prison. Potentially even on death row.

# CHAPTER EIGHTY

The smoke coming their way from the kitchen is getting worse, but Roche is already planning his next move when he hears Fielding speak.

"Hey, how's about we talk?"

"We're done talking. You've confessed. That's all we need to discuss."

"You sure? Because if you let me talk for a minute more, I can change your life for the better. I heard what she said before. How alimony payments are keeping you down. That's a problem that can go away."

Roche fixes Fielding with a look and tries to prevent himself lashing out. "What? You're gonna get both my ex-wives killed to ease the financial burden on me?"

"I was thinking of a simpler solution, but that's an option too."

Roche sends a boot at Fielding's knee with enough power to dislodge the kneecap. "That's the mothers of my kids you're talking about. I might not love them any more, but that doesn't mean I want them dead."

"Then how about a straight ten million bucks?" Fielding nods at his shirt pocket. "Get my cell for me and I can transfer that amount to your account in under a minute. Think about it. Ten million dollars, tax-free and untraceable."

"And what do I have to do to earn this ten million dollars?"

"It'll be the easiest money you've ever made. You let me go and leave the cell with my confession on it. You walk one way. I walk the other and we both go about our lives. You know how to get to me and I to you. However, that money transfer will always link us. Think of it as a source of mutually assured destruction. If either of us goes after the other, we're opening up a source of trouble for ourselves."

"You're making an interesting offer."

"Really, Roche. After all your moralizing you're going to take his money? Jeez, I can't believe you. Really can't get my head round where you're at."

Roche drops his eyes to Savannah. "Do you think your mom will pay my bill after I hand you over to the cops? That she'll hand over my bonus for finding Fielding? I'm guessing not."

Savannah's eyes flash angry sparks at him, but he ignores her and turns back to Fielding.

"Say I take your money. What do we do with her?"

"She'll have to die. She knows too much."

"Yeah. I figured that."

Roche reaches forward, plucks Fielding's cell from his pocket and crashes his elbow into the side of the man's jaw.

"No deal. I much prefer the idea of earning my money honestly and not killing people. Even if they do turn out to be double-crossing and homicidal."

While Fielding is recovering from the elbow, Roche releases both of the man's hands and then uses the handcuffs on Fielding's belt to secure his arms behind his back. No way was he taking any of the man's money, but the cell is still recording and Fielding has just tried to bribe him, then suggested they murder Savannah. Every scrap of evidence against him would be very welcome.

It's tempting to steal the cell and have Xandra use her skills to raid Fielding's money, but it wouldn't be right. Besides, regardless of Xandra's love of digital trespassing and shafting travel companies, she's otherwise honest and would never help him to acquire blood money, even if he offered her an equal share.

Roche finds a length of rope that he strings between the bound arms of his captives.

"Here's the deal. I'm going to open up that garage door. Fielding, you make sure them dogs of yours stay back. When we get to the car, order them back in and I'll make damned sure they stay put this time. I'll shoot them if they come for me and, while I think they're innocent, don't for one second think I'll hesitate. Savannah, you try and get at Fielding in any way and I'll put a bullet into your hip. If you're lucky, you spend the rest of your life walking with a cane."

"I can match his offer, Roche. I can give you millions if you let me go."

Roche lifts an eyebrow into a gothic arch as he looks at her. "Really? After the way you've screwed me over from the minute your mother got in touch, you think I'm going to trust you now? I may be dumb to have fallen for your lies, but I'm insulted you think I'm dumb enough to trust you again."

"Worth a try." Savannah accompanies her words with an accepting shrug.

With the dogs loaded into the back of Fielding's car, Roche ties the end of the rope to one of the gates and uses Fielding's cell to put a call into Ogden. After what had happened at his house earlier, it's only fitting he be the one to make the arrest.

# CHAPTER EIGHTY-ONE

"You do know Fielding's confession is useless in a court of law, don't you?" Ogden's face is stern and he's giving Roche the kind of look that can penetrate far deeper than any mining drill.

"Yeah, I know." Roche looks up from the gurney. He's been awake no more than ten minutes after a four-hour surgery to repair his shattered hand. "There's plenty there to get you to open a formal investigation though. You're standing there all tall and foreboding, but there's no guard inside this room. My wrist isn't handcuffed to the bed. That tells me you've reached the right decision and believed my story. I *did* tell you the truth. I'm guessing you've even checked to the point of reviewing the CCTV tapes of my meeting with Mrs. Parker-Nicoll. You'll have checked flight manifests and seen how we traveled back and forth over the country."

Ogden can't help a half-smile decorating the lower portion of his face. "We've checked all that and a lot more. There will be an awful lot of questions for you to answer in the future, Mr. Roche."

"Actually, I don't think there will."

"You gotta be kidding me. There's going to be the mother of all inquiries over this. You'll be questioned by US marshals, all manner of feds and then the DA will want a turn with you."

"I can see why you'd think that, but it won't happen."

Ogden's smile straightens into a hard line. "Go on then, why won't it happen?"

"Because one of your own went rogue. Somewhere, at some level, people in expensive suits are thinking about the optics. Can you see how this will play out in the media? On social media? The Witness Protection Program will be shot within a month. Court cases won't go to trial. Witnesses will be overcome with an even greater reluctance to come forward if word gets out the government can't keep them safe. This will be buried and buried deep. Don't think I haven't noticed the battle fatigues underneath the white coats of the doctors. I'm in a military hospital. And why's that? My guess is to make sure I don't talk to anyone who hasn't been vetted. Fielding and Savannah will be either shipped off to secure psychiatric units, where they'll be fed a cocktail of meds that will keep them so anesthetized they'll never speak sense again, or they'll be disappeared into an unmarked grave."

"What about the likes of me and you, who also know about what Fielding was doing?"

Roche doesn't even have to pause for thought. "You'll be advised to let the matter be handled by the feds. Vague threats and bribes will be made to you. I'm guessing something along the lines of keep your mouth shut and your career could soar. Speak out and you could be jeopardizing everything you've ever worked towards. As for me… Sometime later today, I'm expecting someone in a tailored suit to come in and discuss things with me. Like you, there will be threats made. They'll probably try to send me to prison for some of the things I've done. I'll respond by saying I had a bad feeling about this case from the start, and as such insulated myself by documenting everything that happened in a sworn deposition that I added to twice a day. That deposition is in the hands of a lawyer, and if that lawyer doesn't hear from me every Monday morning, copies of the deposition will be sent to every news outlet in the northern hemisphere."

"You're nobody's fool, Roche. Whether or not that deposition actually exists, they won't dare take the chance it does."

"Exactly. That's why I created it." Roche allows a smile to reach his lips. "It's also why that suit will end up offering me a deal for my continued silence. Obviously all my medical bills will be covered by the government. I'm guessing that when pushed they'll sling a few bucks my way as compensation for my help in solving what could have been a real problem for them."

"Is there anything you haven't thought of?"

"I'm sure there are plenty of things I haven't thought of. Chief of which is what I'm going to say to my Leigh when I'm asked why I haven't been home or called since Sunday morning."

# A LETTER FROM JOHN

I want to say a huge thank you for choosing to read *The Witness*. If you did enjoy it, and want to keep up to date with all my latest releases, just sign up at the following link. Your email address will never be shared and you can unsubscribe at any time.

*www.bookouture.com/john-ryder*

My sincere thanks to everyone who's made it this far. I do hope you've enjoyed the time spent with Roche and Savannah. For me they were a great pair of characters to have in the same room so often. Diverse in their views, upbringing and social status, I had immense fun plotting out the many different ways I could keep them at loggerheads with each other. Savannah's duplicity was the framework I assembled this novel on, but Roche's straight-talking manner was, I felt, the perfect foil as he sees the world for the fascinatingly jumbled-up place that it is. Savannah was correct the Leaker had to be stopped, but vigilantism is never the answer.

Yes, this was a departure from my Grant Fletcher series, but *The Witness* has fulfilled a long-held desire of mine to write a standalone novel. Although, having said that, Roche's gruff voice is constantly in my ear grouching about the fact he has more stories to tell. Typically, he's using words he's invented to convey his message, but I can generally understand the point he's making.

The whole topic of witness protection made for a wonderful playground. It set both Roche and me a real challenge, as if I was

# ACKNOWLEDGMENTS

As always there are so many wonderful people to thank for their help and input. It's only right I mention family and close friends first. Without their support and encouragement I'd still be toying with idea of putting pen to paper. I'm fantastically lucky to have a wide circle of friends within the writing community, all of them are great for bouncing ideas off, checking research details or sharing sources. My Crime and Publishment writing group is the best of a wonderful bunch.

From my publisher, Bookouture, I am lucky to have my writing career in the hands of the best in the business at what they do. My editor, Isobel Akenhead, has a marvelously sharp eye for detail and has always been fantastically supportive of me and my writing, even if she doesn't always agree with Roche's tendency to create his own language. The backroom staff are brilliant at what they do and they deserve huge credit for the amazing covers, fantastic editorial work and the million other ways they make my books better. The marketing team are first class and I consider myself to be incredibly fortunate to have Noelle Holten and Sarah Hardy s publicists.

Finally, I say a massive thank you to all the readers. Whether you read, review or blog, I hope to continue entertaining you with t-paced stories. After all, without readers, I'm nothing more an a typist who's not very good at typing.

to have him find the unfindable, I knew I had to devise a way that would be credible to all my discerning readers.

There are several passages/sentences within *The Witness* where the virtues are extolled about those who have the courage to stand up and be counted when it really matters. To me, every one of the people who have had to enter a Witness Protection Program because their life is at risk after testifying are shining examples of the best of humanity. They knew the risks and they did it regardless. Bravo to them all.

I'm going to hold my hands up and confess the research I did on the Witness Protection Program was minimal. Those of you who know better may recognize there are elements where I got things wrong. I feel no shame in getting these details incorrect as the last thing I wanted to do was expose some of the secret methods involved in the Witness Protection Program.

I love hearing from my readers—you can get in touch on my Facebook page, through Twitter, Goodreads or my website

Thanks,
John

JohnRyderAuthor

@JohnRyder101

johnryderauthor.com

Made in United States
North Haven, CT
04 January 2022

14195994R00173